The *Inheritance* of Being

CORA LOCKHART

Paramour Press

Dedicated to all the victims of the Eugenics Movement:
the living, the dead, the dust and the shadows.

"The realities of life do not allow
themselves to be forgotten."
-Victor Hugo

To Michael —

My most favorite gymnast and my most gorgeous friend!

I love you!

Cora

＊ Can't wait to see your new moves!

NOTE FROM THE AUTHOR

Though this novel is a work of fiction, the Eugenics Movement was not. Many states in the U.S. participated in genetic cleansing, which unknown to many, greatly influenced Nazi Germany. I chose Oregon as the setting for this particular piece not because I wanted to implicate or denigrate it in any way, but rather simply, I chose it for its astounding beauty. What better place for something so unimaginably horrific to happen.

Cape Perpetua, an uninhabited forest on the Oregon Coast, is an actual place—one straight from the pages of a fairytale, but it is not cursed by anything other than unreserved magnificence. There is no orphanage or asylum there and no city of twins; yet, I found the existence of these things easier to consider because somehow they were more plausible than the idea of involuntary sterilization.

The seed for *The Inheritance of Being* was planted a few years ago when I came across photographs of the unclaimed human ashes that lined the shelves of the deteriorating Oregon State Hospital in Salem. It was these forgotten souls that gave my story life but any coincidence ends there. All names, characters, places, incidents and people, living or dead, are either a product of my imagination or if based on history, used fictitiously.

ACKNOWLEDGMENTS

Writing often begins long before the actual recording of words on paper and frequently lingers after a piece is completed. The writing process involves many people who may not even realize they have in some way assisted you. As a child, I sat on my grandfather's lap, listening to his stories—some he learned as a boy and others he crafted just for me. I could have inherited the storyteller gene from him or maybe it was my Irish grandmother who gave it to me. She read Nancy Drew to me every night before bed and at a young age, I became captivated by mystery. So thank you John and Sylvia. One day when I get the courage, I'm going to return for that skeleton key. I hope it's still there.

I'd also like to express my eternal gratitude to James McFarland, the love of my life—of all my lives. Next time I'll wear red.

Many thanks to Daniel Lawless and Linda LaPointe. You both changed my life.

I would like to thank my precious editors, Betsy Bulat Turner and Sarah Rosenberg and also all my friends who persistently asked about this novel and encouraged me to finish it. There are far too many to list but the Greiwes, Amy Snell, the Wismers who have the most amazing B&B and never let me pay for anything when I visit, Ashley Herd, Theresia Moser, the Schatz's, Marsha Parsons who sends me books about the dead, the Watkins, Carla Kerns, Amey Randall, and Paramour Press. A special thanks to the many photojournalists whose haunting asylum images gave a voice not only to my words but to those who were not able to speak for themselves.

Prologue

The woman had ached for a child for so long, and over a period of years, after several unsuccessful attempts, the doctor's wife finally became pregnant. She thought at first it must have been the seasickness returning in the middle of the night when she vomited over the railing of the ship. But, a few days later when she woke to that familiarity of cold crimson wetness beneath her, she realized she had once again hemorrhaged. What her husband could give to her, she could not hold. After three miscarriages she could no longer continue believing it was because of him as she secretly had for the ten years they had tried. He had succeeded in fulfilling his part. It was she who could not. She was the one whose insides were made of egg shells and dust.

The chiromancer in Jackson Square had promised her she would be a mother soon and because she had lost faith in everything else, she clung to this prediction with the ruthless tenacity of a fierce winter storm.

The old creased seer, who spoke with a thick French tongue, had no idea that the woman she read for that day was blessed with the gift and could have easily read for her had she not been so disheartened for so long with her inability to conceive. The doctor's wife was the daughter of Louis Hamon, an Irish clairvoyant who went by the name of Cheiro, famous for his ability to pass between the gate that separated the living from the dead as easily as he crossed the street. People speculated that it was his birth on All Souls Day, a day recognized for celebrating the dead that made this faculty possible.

Madame Brusseau was chewing on a clove the day she saw the walnut-sized seed in the woman's stomach as she cautiously approached her table, which sat in slight defiance in front of the St. Louis Cathedral where it was draped in black point d'Alencon lace—la dentelle des reines. Queen's lace. Sometimes she imagined it laid over the hands of those she read for like fenestrated capillaries that allowed the future to be seen as clearly as peering through an open window.

The two women faced each other in a dense, territorial silence until the clairvoyant gave in and reached across the table for the desperate woman's hand, forcing her to sit. The reader held the pale, small hand in hers with such care that it could have been a priceless piece of fine bone china. She began to study it with her eyes, two glossy black buttons sewn tightly into her puckered face; then she ran her spindly fingers, thin and bent like the roots of an old banyan tree, across the grooves in her palm. The air was thick with the cloying scent of beignets.

"Your heart and head lines merge into one," she finally spoke. "This means that you are focused. You desire only one thing of life and it is something you cannot live without, but..." and after a

2

slight hesitation where she held the clove between her front teeth as if this helped her with divination, "...it is something you do not have."

The doctor's wife nodded slowly in stoic agreement, and the old woman pulled the hand closer to her face. Her lashes fluttered against the palm. A breeze cooled the August air around them, pulling the coven of fallen leaves into a dancing circle near the table and loosening strands of the clairvoyant's long white hair from her chignon. A piece as thick as rope blew across her eye but she was not distracted. She had been a reader since even before she could speak, and she had never seen a life line as wide. Wide and shallow. It seemed to fade into the fat of the palm and she knew the woman had existed only faintly above what was necessary in order to function as a wife, as a human being.

The woman's pale skin was as thin and delicate as a page from an old bible. So thin, it was as if Madame Brousseau was reading the hand of a ghost or a piece of newly sewn lace. Strong but transparent. She could tell by the way her life line deepened just before disappearing into her wrist that the doctor's wife would die horrifically, but she did not tell her this. She could not for her eyes were so filled with desperation, she surely must have already known. The veins of the woman's skin were like *la trace*, the foundation threads that bound the cloth so securely to the lace stitch that only a razor could separate the two. Because her travel lines stopped abruptly, her death would be quick but not effortless and when the palmist recognized this, she spoke again.

"*Un enfant.* There will be...a child."

The doctor's wife upon hearing this glowed like a bride beneath an intricate lace veil. She kept this radiance until she miscarried the final time on the ship, the *Twin Sisters*, where she had made the commitment to travel with her husband for one last voyage to dispense medicine to the sick, mostly Indians of the Pacific Northwest. The vessel was packed with yams from the African coast—a vegetable that the doctor believed would strengthen the heart and immune system of those who had developed typhus. He injected every yam with the medicine, a concoction made from the roots and seeds of the magical Angelica plant.

The woman made this one last trip, not because she believed her husband truly needed her assistance but because she had an ulterior motive. Something that belonged to her and only her. A choice. She would end her pain. She would take her own life. It was the one thing she could cradle in her hands. But when they docked in New Orleans, the fortune teller had changed her plans. Until now, of course, the morning she discovered the blood in her bed and mistook early pregnancy bleeding for a miscarriage.

The iron railing was cold, and she did not grasp it too tightly in the event her hands might adhere to it. The idea of being forced to remain in a place of such debilitating pain tore at her insides.

She stood starboard on the deck of the ship because she knew she would be pulled immediately under the water with no chance of resurfacing. It would be easier on her husband, she felt, if her disappearance remained a mystery. Perhaps he might even believe it was accidental. He deserved this. He was a good man, a patient man, and she felt horrible leaving him with that last lingering image of their child, an amorphous red flower, spread upon the mattress. But, she felt she had no choice.

Even the name of the ship made her long for children and she whispered it in a cold tight Irish breath, one that filled with December air, hurt her chest. *Cupla deirfuracha. Twin Sisters.* She lifted one bare foot onto the stinging bottom rail and pulled herself up. She had not even bothered to change out of her sleeping attire and her long white robe covered only moderately the heart-shaped blood stain that had seeped into her gown, which blew forcefully behind her with the grace of two great wings as she adjusted both feet on the rail. She had always felt so ornamental in life and she smirked at the irony of this when she raised her hands back behind her and leaned into the wind, a Flying Lady on the hood of an expensive car. A Silver Ghost. She had lived life equivalently, a soubriquet, a doctor's wife who could not bear children. A sharp laugh burst from her lungs as she choked back the tears.

The water appeared calm, inviting. It would be as easy and instinctive as falling into a deep sleep, one as endless and bottomless as the sea. Standing there at that precise moment at the prow of the ship, she was in control. With her wings of silk spun behind her, she gave the erroneous appearance that she was somehow victorious. A goddess. The great Nike. There was no way for her to know that she had not miscarried. The seed the palm reader saw growing in the woman's insides had split into two perfect halves: Twin girls grew inside her and the doctor's wife did not realize she would be taking two other lives besides her own when she dove from the ship that morning as Billie Holiday swooned the captain with *I'll Be Seeing You* on the Victrola his father had given him the year he married the sea. He had just given the helm to the young man who had, the entire trip, shown great interest in one day being a captain of his own vessel.

In the single stream of sunlight that pervaded the dark motionless sky, the woman appeared like a sliver of glass that with great determination pierced the black velvet water and disappeared beneath it. That early morning in 1948, the *Twin Sisters* was thrown into the rocks of Cape Perpetua and people assumed it was because of the storm. For many years afterward, yams could still be seen floating in the water, drifting up on shore where some caught in the gorse and grew rampant in the sand. By 1950, the city had become populated with twins, a curse that came to be associated with Una Madigan and her mysterious twin girls.

Part One

The Thief

My mother was just a girl when the *Twins Sisters* slammed into Cape Perpetua's rocky coast. I read this in her journal, which only by coincidence I found at the asylum. A credible story should have few coincidences. It should begin in the middle though I prefer the end, which may or may not have something to due with my declining health. But I'm getting ahead of myself. I do this sometimes. It's part of my condition. There are many parts to my *condition*, though I've forgotten many of them. At fifty-seven, my memories are full of holes, and I can't blame all of this on age. I suffer from a type of memory loss that has left gaps in my mind. An hour. A week. And once, an entire year disappeared from my recollection as if someone had just reached in and took it as easily as pulling a book from a shelf. But the brain is designed to preserve the most painful memories, I believe. There are two that haunt me daily.

One is a sound. There are noises a person can get used to over time: screams, moans, mumbling, buckles tinkling against the iron bed frame, the echo of laughter up and down a disinfected corridor, silver trays chiming against the floor like a church bell and the hum of running water so cold there is no air in the room. But the sound of a crying baby is relentless. I hear it on the bus. I hear it in the elevator of the Guardian where I now live. I even hear it in my sleep.

The other is the memory of my twin sister, Nix, who disappeared over thirty years ago from the asylum where we were institutionalized and with great remorse, I don't know what became of her. My heart grows weaker everyday; time is running out. I must find my sister and beg her to forgive me for stealing her only love. I wish I could say it was unintentional. But there I go jumping ahead again. Let me start once more at the beginning.

My name is Lux Madigan and sometimes I take things that don't belong to me. But even this is not the beginning.

My sister and I were not normal twins. This was easy to see as soon as we were born, a photograph and its negative. I came out first like a blast of angelic light with glowing blond hair and white skin, my eyes so transparently blue they feared I was blind. It was said that I lit the way for Nix who appeared moments later with the same pale skin and light eyes but with a head of hair so thick and black it caused commotion among the staff at St. Jerome's Home for Orphaned Children for months afterward, especially since our mother claimed to have contact with the dead. Because she would not name our father, it was believed that Una Madigan had been impregnated by an inexplicable force, one that due to our bizarre appearances was feared to be malevolent. She was held responsible for the curse of twins that haunted the city of Cape Perpetua in the years to follow. How would people have reacted if they'd known that biologically Nix and I belonged to Father Donovan? There I go again getting ahead of myself.

The day my sister disappeared. Yes. I should start there. October 13th, 1969. Cape Perpetua's Asylum for the Insane. It was a day that for Nix and I marked our beginning but also our end; a birthday that I refused to celebrate again without her. So much time has passed since then, but the events of that day still find me as if they too cling to the same impervious hope that one day my twin will return.

Dust and Shadow

October 1969

"Miss Madigan," Dr. Warner addressed me curtly as he passed in the hall, his words blurred behind short quick steps. His coat, a white wall.

Dr. Warner had always been distant with me, never saying more than necessary, never catching me directly in the eye. He looked not at me but passed me as if he were analyzing something behind me—my shadow or a past that only he could see. He seemed to have a sense of urgency which called him away when it came to me or my sister. Though I never really trusted him, I was always polite to him. I nodded respectfully and then headed downstairs to find my sister.

Nix spent a great deal of time in the library and this would have made me feel better if it had been a room of books, but instead it was a library of dust, a collection of unclaimed cremations stored in tin cans in the basement of the asylum where they were shelved like spices. Instead of rosemary, sage and thyme, however, the canisters were marked with numbers. Even in death, they were the shelved confirmation of a failing mental health system that lingered in humiliation and great disrepair.

The cremains as they were called dated back to the early 1900s, some so old that the copper urns had greened and fused together. Lining the walls were thousands of these cans. They each had identification numbers, scribbled on short strips of masking tape, which had either faded or crumbled like the exfoliation of dead skin. These were people who had died while at the asylum and because no one claimed them, they were initially interred in graves on the surrounding property. When the state needed this land to build onto the state penitentiary just down the street on St. Dismas, *the good thief,* Way, the bodies were exhumed and cremated in the crematorium built at the asylum especially for that purpose. Imagine being able to dispose of people so easily without anyone inquiring. This practice was stopped in 1970, a year after Nix disappeared from the asylum. A law was passed that stated that anyone who died at the asylum had to be taken to a funeral home before any type of burial or cremation could occur. But those that were already there remained in elapsed abandonment in the dim green storage room next to the basement, which housed the mortuary and the crematorium. *Pulvis et umbra sumus.* We are but dust and shadow, Horace, the great Roman poet, wrote, and it filled me with immense sorrow to realize that one day my sister and I would be part of them.

Maybe Nix felt comfortable among these forgotten souls because of her ability to communicate with them. She would remain in the library of dust for hours at a time, so much in fact that Michael pushed a chair inside the makeshift catacomb for her to sit. Though the room was supposed to be off limits to patients, Michael, a psych nurse who was training to become a doctor, was very fond of Nix and because of this, she was permitted access to places others weren't, like the Cremains Room. He had even given her a key. She showed it to me in secret, and I remember finding the old tarnished pass key appropriate for such a room—one that had no bones but many skeletons.

Nix often told me things I shouldn't have known. For one, Michael didn't always follow regulations. He shared cigarettes with patients, he didn't accurately chart medications, and he liked beautiful young women with eyes of untamable volatility, particularly those who were not afraid of a dark linen closet. He got away with these things because Michael's father, Dr. Warner, was the superintendent at Cape Perpetua's Asylum. He'd been with the hospital for over twenty years as both attending physician and psychiatrist. I attributed his indifference toward me and my sister to the responsibility he must have felt as a man who'd taken a vow to preserve lives yet failed to do so with our mother.

I'd always sensed a sort of furtiveness in Dr. Warner's polished pewter gaze if only in the fleeting moments I managed to capture it. I believe he really despised me and my sister. Maybe he held us responsible in some way because our mother, Una Madigan, had taken her own life. But, what I really think is that knowing he failed to save her greatly dented his ego.

I tapped lightly on the door. "Nix? You in there?" I could hear fervent whisperings, the kind audible from just outside a confessional. I couldn't make out what was being said but this was not unusual. Our entire lives had been a whisper.

When I opened the door, the room became silenced and I was confronted with the scent of lilacs. Michael kept my sister well stocked with lilac soap. It was one of two things she would not share with me. The lingering aroma of flowers in the room was slightly tainted with the scent of nonexistence, a thick moldy odor suggestive of the interior of an old suitcase or more accurately, a freshly unearthed coffin.

Nix was sitting on the chair with her back against the wall, her knees up, her arms around them. She was wearing a state-issued dress and a blue wool cardigan that had been eaten in places by moths. The asylum was overrun with these creatures. They were considered pests, but I always found great beauty in things that continually searched for light.

Instinctively, Nix adjusted her sleeves. Even when it was warm, my sister covered her arms to hide the marks she'd made when she was upset—something that began about the same time Father Donovan starting calling her into his quarters for late night talks. Her waist length inky hair surrounded her like a shadow. A radiant smile emanated from both her mouth and her eyes. Winks of blue glitter sparkled on her skin.

"Lux. Hi," she said. "How did you find me?" She stood and embraced me as if she had not seen me for days though we shared a room.

"It wasn't hard since you always seem to be here," I told her. "It's rather morbid, don't you think? Why do you spend so much time down here? It's cold. Damp. It's not good for you. Come on. Let's go outside and get some fresh air before they call for lunch."

She nodded obsequiously and we went upstairs. The door to the courtyard was not the gate to freedom as doors that are always locked seemed to allude. It made a loud buzzing noise when opened to alert the staff to those coming and going even though the immediate area beyond was surrounded by a high fence that was topped with razor wire, coiled along the edge like an infinitely sharp Slinky. William Blake, the poet, distrusted fences because he was never quite certain of their intention. Were they meant to keep people from getting out or others from coming in?

We hurried outside and sat at a table that had a rusty Folger's can in the middle of it. The staff used these cans for ashtrays during cigarette breaks. Nix and Michael shared cigarettes out here in the middle of the night. They had no idea that I'd followed them on more than one occasion. Maybe Michael didn't care that it wasn't the cigarette Nix was interested in but the match. The flame that quelled her inner pain.

The coffee can was filled with sand and cigarette ashes, and I remember Nix staring pensively into its contents. "Abigail's dead," she spoke as if she were reading ingredients listed on the side of the can. It took me a minute or so to understand that she must have been referring to the coffee heiress who was murdered only months before. I'd heard on the news that it was some type of cult murder, but I didn't get all the details because Imogene-the-TV-Queen kept switching the station to *Here's Lucy*. Imogene was a hebephrenic; she had the laughing disease so she didn't really need comedy to express her laughter, but she would become verbally aggressive when she didn't get her way. Nix never watched TV or listened to the radio so I'm not sure how she knew about Abigail Folger. Unless...well let's just say my sister had a certain bond with the dead. Or at least that's what she claimed. She told me once that one of the urns in the Cremains Room was empty and she mentioned this again to me as we sat at the table that day. I asked her how she knew this since the cans were all sealed, some merged together like conjoined twins as if they'd intentionally been welded that way.

"Because she told me."

"Who told you, Nix?"

"I don't know. The woman with the locket...," she trailed off, smiling, her eyes focusing suddenly on the door. And Michael. "...and the baby," she spoke with soft reticence.

Nix had always heard and saw things that I didn't. She took medication for these hallucinations, but sometimes the determined ones still found her. I asked her once if she ever saw our mother, but she said it didn't work that way and that for whatever reason our mother had chosen not to return. I couldn't help but wonder if this was because she couldn't bear the thought of being at the asylum again.

Out the door, Michael came into view with a cake. He was singing *Happy Birthday* but because the buzzer was so loud, the first part of his song was cut off so all we heard was "to you," and I knew the *YOU* was Nix. It had always been her. Michael resented me for what I'd done, my trickery, but he was forced to play along otherwise I'd tell my sister about us.

"Happy Birthday," he said looking exclusively at her. He set the cake on the table. A round white cake, a little lopsided and embellished with large blue flowers. Blue was Nix's favorite color. The cake had a single candle glowing from its center. I should have remembered then that one birthday at the asylum, even if it was for two people, merited one candle. I'm sure it was because supplies were rationed, but it still bothered me because I knew in my heart that the candle was not for me.

Michael reached for the camera around his neck, and Nix and I moved closer together. He snapped a picture that I was sure excluded me. If it didn't, I'm sure I was at least out of focus and off to the side, an art show study of aperture. We had very few art books in the asylum's book library. Most of our collection was donated; helping to organize them permitted me some unsupervised freedom, though that is not the reason I volunteered. Organizing things was something I did without really knowing I was doing it.

"Lux, why didn't you remind me about our birthday?" my sister asked.

After six years at the asylum, the days had blended into one another. I hadn't known myself that it was our birthday until I overheard one of the women in the kitchen talking about the cake. Nix glowed brighter than the candles when I told her that it was because I wanted to surprise her. "Happy Birthday," I said, then furtively handed her the sparkly brooch that one of the nurses, the older one with the limp, had yet to notice missing from her purse. Nix loved anything that sparkled.

She held the pin carefully in her palm, rocking it back and forth as it caught in the illumination of the candle's light. "It's beautiful. Are those real sapphires?" she asked.

"Sshh…" I nodded even though I knew it was ridiculous to assume the brooch was anything but cheap costume jewelry. There was a time that I was captivated by Nix's naïveté, but since she'd begun spending so much time with Michael, I'd found it more and more irritating.

"I'll keep it always," Nix promised. "Forever."

I felt Michael looking awkwardly in my direction. He still didn't like me even after what had happened between us. The secret we shared. Any story of value always has a secret. When I thought of ours, a warm vibration stirred inside me.

The asylum frowned on gift giving, but by the way Michael was looking at Nix's smile, I knew she would be allowed to keep the brooch—at least until its rightful owner discovered it missing and reclaimed it. I felt horrible lying about the brooch. The thing about my sister was that she was always truthful with me, and this is why it was difficult for me not to believe her when she talked about the dead that visited her daily. I knew she would keep the pin until she no longer could.

Dr. Warner who was carefully watching our small celebration from another table said these *visitors* were a part of Nix's psychosis, something that was bequeathed to her by our mother Una who also had delusions. Nix was given Thorazine just as our mother was to help suppress the hallucinations and voices that called to her from another realm. I'd noticed that on the occasion when Una Madigan's name was mentioned, an empty sheen took over Dr. Warner's shifting gray eyes. His bottom lip quivered and his breath became deeper, slower, as if he'd lost his air and was desperately searching every sac in the bottom of his lungs to find it. Then he would leave abruptly after glancing at the watch fastened to his wrist by a simple brown leather band. It lent him a sense of immediacy—not necessarily intended for others as much as for himself. In hindsight, I believe *he* was the person he was trying to allude.

He must have once been a striking man, Dr. Warner, for I remember this handsomeness clinging to him. It did not want to leave, manifesting itself in his olive complexion, his perfectly arched brows, dark and thick and spun with the same silver threads as his hair. His square black glasses did not distract from his gray eyes, which appeared at times metallic. That afternoon, twitching and moving in his chair uncomfortably as he watched how Michael and Nix interacted, he must have known that his son was in love with one of the afflicted—a woman whose inheritance made the free will allotted by God impossible; for how can one have any control over their choices when they are led solely by their inborn traits?

Michael pulled the camera up to his face again and said, "Close your eyes and make a wish." I only partially closed my eyes so that I could see the way he looked at my sister. Though we are twins, she was by far the most beautiful, and I feel she must have known this, which was one of the reasons she continually hurt herself. She did not want this responsibility. This burden of beauty. There was no doubt what Father Donovan had seen in her. A beauty that even reputations of evil could not dispel. True beauty should only be measured with closed eyes. I believed Gretchen, the blind girl on our floor, had an inconceivable advantage in this way.

Nix closed her eyes tightly and pursed her plump lips in determined preparation, no doubt believing that wishes made in such circumstance might actually come true. I imagined Michael would have given anything at that moment to kiss her or to be a part of her wish. This made me both happy and jealous. So happy I wanted to give her my wish, so jealous I became angry—an anger I hid beneath a tight smile. I let Nix blow out the candle, my eyes ricocheting from the cake to the Pentax camera that Michael had removed from his neck and set on the table as he whispered something in my sister's ear—words I would never know but would continue to think about long after she vanished from my life. The bell sounded and everyone went inside to prepare for lunch. Everyone but me. I lingered behind to talk to Dr. Warner, but I don't remember why.

It was then that I could hear the prison's loudspeaker as it echoed across the empty field that was once replete with the bones of the forgotten—most now on the shelf in the library of dust. There was a large span of property between the asylum and the prison but only a thin line between the institutionalized and the imprisoned. Both were criminals in the eyes of the world, but it was intent that separated them—a darkness that Victor Hugo believed society had created. *Les Miserables* has always been one of my favorite books. I'm drawn to the story not only because it is about a system corrupted by the very people enforcing it, but because Jean Valjean was a thief whose heart was good even though his hands were not. A repentant thief like St. Dismas. I kept a worn copy of Hugo's novel tucked into a slice in my mattress. It was my special hiding place, one that even my sister didn't know about.

After lunch that day, Nix and I went to our room for our daily nap as all patients are required to do. The patients on other floors were more difficult to convince so they were often forced to sleep with injections and pills. They were crammed in large rooms, their beds lined up like tombstones against the wall. We were fortunate because we were a part of the most lenient ward in the building, though we hadn't always been.

The walls of our room were decorated in magazine clippings depicting women in fashionable clothes and images of places we'd never see. Nix's artwork was taped around a yellowed world map that was there upon our arrival. It was so old that it was becoming part of the chipped wall, a new country fading into the plaster yearly; it was a painful way to mark our time there. In fact, it was more traumatizing to see places on the map diminish before our eyes than to know we would never be able to visit them in person. When Ireland began to pale, my sister and I cried for days. It was like losing a piece of who we were, and we had already lost so many pieces, that sometimes, I didn't know how we would be able to continue.

There were few pleasures at the asylum, but Nix and I both found joy in books. I helped organize the small collection in our community library, which really only consisted of a few shelves tucked into an alcove of the room that housed the television and tables where many patients sat and played cards. Our room was littered with stacks of books on the floor, the nightstand and even the chair. I would organize them daily, sometimes by author, sometimes by title. Other times by color. Organizing was and is another part of who I am, who I became at the asylum. I read fiction primarily. Nix preferred poetry. The Bronte sisters, Blake, Plath, Sexton. It is my opinion that she was drawn to these writers because of their immense darkness, their complacency with death, which is one of the reasons she also was fond of Latin—a dead language that somehow gave her comfort. I found comfort in it also; the Latin dictionary that Sister Madeline had given me at the orphanage was always within my reach. Nix and I had both been given one, but she often had a difficult time with writing and she immersed herself in painting and music. Even though the piano in the community room was missing keys and out of tune, it always sounded so beautiful when Nix played.

Sometimes in the middle of the night, I'd wake to hear her humming the song our mother used to play for us on that same piano. Other times, I'd find her sitting trancelike, staring intently out the window where wire was intricately woven between the glass panes. She seemed to be hypnotized by the fountain in front of the building and on occasion I'd have to shake her to pull her from this fugue. Many of her paintings were of the fountain's angels. They were often abstract but never completely unrecognizable as I believed angels would be should they exist.

Next to the radiator in our room was an old wooden desk, its surface cracked from the dry heat. It was kept stocked with paper and pens because Nix occasionally wrote Michael love letters. Or tried to. Once, she left an unfinished letter on the desk. At first I thought that it was written in a foreign language and that is why I couldn't read it. I knew it wasn't Latin and believed it to be some secret code I couldn't decipher; she had always written strangely. It was something Father Donovan said was malicious, an evil that was born into her like the way she liked fire. This reputation for fire had followed her to the asylum. Whenever one of the staff found matches in our room, she lost her paper and pen rights for a week. It's how I made sure Nix wasn't in the room the night I tricked Michael. I planted matches under her pillow, and she was taken to therapy when the nurse found them. But I couldn't feel guilty about this at the time. Once at the orphanage, Nix caught the sheets on fire and blamed me for it. Sister Madeline paddled me and I was forced to stay in the confessional until I admitted to it. Father Donovan sat on the other side of the dark screen that divided the little box where all sins were magically purged. I recognized the heaviness of his breath. He was an odd man, short and round man with the tiniest eyes I've ever seen, reptilious, with no apparent lashes and a tongue thick with soured wine. How many orphans, I wondered, would leave the orphanage with the faith they were instructed to possess by the man in the magic box?

Since she started taking Thorazine, faith was something Nix had little of anymore, though I agreed with Nietzsche that a walk through a lunatic asylum renders faith almost laughable. People subjected to neuroleptics like Thorazine become zombies. Nix was no exception, even though at first she was only administered a very low dose. Dr. Warner thought it helped repress her hallucinations, but according to my sister the dead still came to her only they did so in a dream-like state that made her believe she was hallucinating. It didn't take her long to realize that any mention of her visitors would subject her to increased dosages of Thorazine, and this is why she so seldom spoke of them.

My medication, Librium, was much less severe. It was supposed to help me to stop counting and also limit my desire to take things that didn't belong to me, behavior that became more apparent each day at the asylum. Nix was different though. She always had been. For as long as I could remember she claimed to see the spirits of those who had passed on. This coupled with the cuts and burns on her arms earned her the title of schizophrenic. Orphan and Schizophrenic. Two labels that somehow become so deeply embedded into your existence that trying to remove them was like trying to wash off your skin. Dr. Warner frequently used the words Dissociative Identity Disorder or Multiple Personality Disorder, both euphemisms for schizophrenia. I asked him if he had any gentler words for *orphan* but he just looked at me with those empty steel eyes. I knew then how he felt about us. Even so, I didn't believe we truly belonged at the asylum; we were only there because of the inheritance. What our mother had given us.

I tried desperately to keep my faith in God even after what Father Donovan had done and even though Nix had long since let hers go. The only hint of it hung just above her iron bed: A simple wooden cross that she'd embellished with a silvery blue glitter, which occasionally snowed down on her stained pillow case. I'd seen traces of it in her hair where it caught the morning light like drops of dew. This is also how I came to know when she'd borrowed one of my sweaters or when she'd been with Michael.

There were a few other signs that my sister had given up on God. She no longer kept her Bible nearby, and I noticed that the rosary she once draped over her lamp had been tucked in her nightstand drawer. She started hiding it when Michael began visiting late at night when he thought I was asleep. On those nights, I could hear the rustling of the sheets on my sister's bed, but I kept my eyes closed. The rusty springs sounded like an old iron swing—the kind we used to have in the playground behind the chapel. The movement was so strong at times, it shook my bed. It was during one of those visits a few weeks before our birthday that the idea came to me. A way to make Michael love me like he loved Nix.

Peggy, one of the day nurses woke us from our nap when she came for Nix.

"Nixie. Dr. Warner wants to see you right away."

Nix sat up and rubbed her eyes. "What time is it?"

"It's almost three."

"In the morning?"

"No, honey. Three in the afternoon." Peggy had an accent that made most people giggle. She was a tall thin woman from Texas but when she said it, it sounded like *tick-sis*. Peggy won a beauty pageant when she was nineteen. She told me this often as if she was the one who needed to be reminded of it. *Well almost,* she always added. *Runner up.* I liked Peggy. She was painfully honest. Other than Nix, I didn't have any friends. Peggy would have made a good one, I believed, if circumstances were different.

"Now hurry up," she said to Nix. "You know how impatient that man can be. By the way, Happy Birthday. To both of you lovely ladies."

"You remembered."

"How could I forget my favorite residents?" She said it like we were vacationing at a resort for the summer. "Here." She laid the examination gown on the bed and Nix's eyes filled with tears.

"Now don't go *gettin'* all upset," Peggy told her. "The doctor just wants to make sure you're being good to yourself." She pushed up one of Nix's sweater sleeves and examined the milky white skin inflicted with scars that had healed into tiny white circles and lines—a far-away universe whose only visitor was my sister. "You have been good to yourself, haven't you, *darlin'*? You know I hate to see you in the therapy room."

Nix had to be regularly checked for burns and cuts. The first time I ever noticed marks on her was when we were at the orphanage. It was late and I heard her sneak into the room and crawl under the covers. She was only in bed for a moment before she got up again.

"Where are you going?" I asked.

"I have to take a bath," she said. "I have to."

"Right now?"

She nodded. "Yes. Will you come with me?"

I went even though I knew if we should be caught, we would be reprimanded severely.

As she undressed to get in the tub, I saw them lining her arms: the scarred circles and moons of another galaxy. The place she went to soothe her pain. This went on for many years before we were sent to the asylum in 1965. We were just fifteen—the same age our mother was when she became a patient of Dr. Warner's.

Frustrated at Peggy, Nix pulled her sleeve back down and crawled out of bed. I could see the chill bumps on her skin as she slipped out of her skirt and sweater and into the paper thin cotton gown. She pulled up her long socks and wedged her feet back into her shoes. Nix hated her bare feet touching the cold cement floor. She said it reminded her of death because when the dead came to her they were always without shoes. It was something my mother had also mentioned in her writing.

On the way out the door to see Dr. Warner, Nix grabbed the brooch I'd given her. She'd tucked it under her pillow before our nap. When she picked it up, I could see her tighten her fist around it so hard that I feared blood might seep from the cracks between her fingers. My sister held so much hurt inside her but when I think about it, where else could she have stored it? As she shuffled down the hall, I could hear her humming that song—the one our mother always played for us on the piano when Sister Madeline brought us to visit. My sister's voice began to fade, and I tried to hear the words: "...*I'll find you in the morning sun and when the night is new...*"

It was when Nix was gone for only a few minutes that Michael came by to ask about his missing camera even though I knew he was really coming by to see Nix before he left for the day. I told him that she was with his father and he corrected me.

"Dr. Warner? Why?"

I shrugged. "Peggy said it was a routine evaluation. Come over here," I put my book down and playfully patted the bed where I was sitting.

"I don't have time for games, Lux," he reprimanded and my heart tightened into a knot. He looked out into the hall then pulled the door closed. "What else did Peggy say?"

I got up from the bed and moved toward him. I could see flecks of blue glitter on the collar of his shirt. When I was close enough to smell his breath, which reminded me of the only piece of licorice I'd ever tasted, I placed my hand on his chest, picturing the one night we shared a week before when he believed the warm body beneath him was my sister. For a minute, I felt our eyes join—a viscous thread that was cut abruptly when I reached to kiss him and he pulled away.

"I'll tell," I quickly threatened. "Nix. And Dr. Warner. I'll tell them that you forced me." I'd been making similar threats for over a week, and they still held the same effectiveness. When I return to that moment, I don't think Michael was scared. I think he really loved my sister and it would have pained him to hurt her. But I wanted so badly to feel love. To believe that someone wanted me, even if it was a belief I created myself.

Michael flinched but said nothing when I pushed myself against him, pressing my lips into his, my heart racing with excitement. But then I heard the click of the closing door, and I knew that someone had seen us. It wasn't until I opened it and saw the blue sparkly brooch lying on the hallway floor surrounded by drops of blood that I realized it was Nix. She'd caught us. It was a moment for me that was both pleasurable and painful and it caused me to feel suddenly boastful but full of sorrow at the same time. It was a feeling as oxymoronic as we were.

I laughed as Michael pushed past me. It wasn't until I tasted the salty tears in my mouth that I too ran after my sister, searching all the closets on my way to the nurse's station, which, because it was surrounded by a silver fence that touched the ceiling, was referred to as the cage. When I rounded the corner, I noticed the commotion going on with one of the patients who looked as if she was having some sort of seizure. It was Big Mary, the epileptic who pulled on her hair so often that she was nearly bald. She'd had so much shock therapy that most of her teeth were gone. Epileptics were sterilized immediately, and at some time during her stay, Mary had been given an ice-pick lobotomy, or at least that was the rumor, and because of the manner in which her asymmetrical eyes twitched incessantly, I gathered it was true. Mary was probably not yet thirty years old, but she looked like an old woman. Peggy was calling out orders from the cage when I interrupted her.

"Peggy? Have you seen my sister?" She frantically searched the cabinet, pulling from it a small bottle containing fluid—something I knew from experience was to calm a patient—while the other nurses held Big Mary down. Peggy glanced over at me, brows knitted, and for a moment I wondered if she didn't recognize me. Big Mary was screaming, flapping on the floor like a fish out of water. I asked again. "My sister. Have you seen her?"

"No honey," Peggy said out the side of her mouth while dropping to her knees, the plastic cap of the needle wedged in her mouth. She turned the little bottle upside down and inserted the needle into it before spitting out the cap. "I'll help you in a minute, honey, okay?" She jammed the needle into the arm of the flailing woman, and I ran off down the hall, my heart beating madly over the sound of Big Mary's diminishing screams. I sobbed uncontrollably. I had to find my sister. But after searching until lockdown, when I was forced back to my room, there was still no sign of her.

On the edge of the bed I sat and examined the brooch. Three stones were missing, embedded, I imagined, in my sister's palm like some mosaic sculpture. I got up to rinse my face with cold water, catching a quick glimpse of myself in the small mirror that hung crookedly above the rust-stained porcelain sink. It was only then that I realized I was still wearing the long black wig that made me feel as beautiful as my sister. I'd discovered it in one of the boxes upstairs and used it to help me convince Michael that I was Nix. The attic was another place patients were not permitted, but I had a key. Like most of the things I collected, I don't recall how the key came into my possession, but I told no one about it. The power of a secret relies exclusively on its keeper. Nix always told me her secrets, but I never told her mine. I lied awake in bed that night promising to tell her all of my secrets if she came back, but she never returned.

The next morning, Dr. Warner assured me they would find Nix. He told me that he believed she may have escaped through the visitor entrance on the first floor. "The door's buzzer," he explained, "has a short in it and doesn't always sound. We'll find her."

"Have you called the authorities?" I asked judiciously. It's cold. She'll be cold.

"No. Not yet but I will if necessary," he stated with a calmness I found uncomfortably misleading. He began to walk away, his clipboard tucked under his arm like a broken wing.

"Wait," I called "Did you check the tunnel?" As soon as I said it, I realized my mistake, but was too late." The tunnel was an underground railway that once led from the asylum to the penitentiary. It was used to transport prisoners and patients but it hadn't been in operation for many years. Nix had told me about it in secrecy, and though she wouldn't say how she knew, I believed Michael must have told her. Or maybe shown her. How else would she have known? If any of the staff knew about it, they were forbidden to talk about it. Nix said old man Burrows, the groundskeeper, was the only one with the key.

Dr. Warner stopped abruptly. He turned, scrutinizing, his

metal eyes like shrapnel. "And what would you know about the tunnel, Miss Madigan?"

I didn't answer. Instead, in a very shaky voice—one that felt as if I was speaking through another person, I asked to see Michael, but the doctor told me that his son was not feeling well and that he had left.

In my heart, I questioned whether or not Dr. Warner ever looked for my sister. My constant anxiety about her disappearance made me a weekly visitor to the therapy room where I was either given shock treatments or immerged in icy water. In the months to follow, I was sedated so heavily that I'd forgotten how to speak or walk. I don't know for how long exactly I was bedridden because once I was able to function again, there was a gap in my memory. A hole that I learned from Peggy was called a lacuna. A condition, she explained, that usually happens to people who have experienced something traumatic. Strangely, my whole life had consisted of such events but nothing as tragic as what had happened with my sister. I did not tell Peggy or anyone for that matter what made my sister run away, and the guilt festered inside me like an open wound.

I tried to understand how the year after she disappeared had somehow vanished along with her as if she'd taken it with her as punishment for what I'd done. It was as if I had not existed for that entire time. And things were different when I woke from this odd spell. I was different. I felt like another person had taken over my body. My muscles were tight and stiff and I'd gained weight from lack of mobility. I looked old for a girl who'd just turned twenty. It was the first time I felt like I might actually belong at the institution. When I removed the gauze that was wrapped around my wrist, I found these strange numbers carved into the area just beneath my palm. I had no idea what they meant or where they'd come from.

There were other things too. Michael no longer worked at the asylum, and when I asked about him, the staff told me he had accepted residence in a hospital on the East Coast. New York, they believed. Peggy was the only one who confided in me that Michael and his father had a falling out. It was so intense that Michael's mother divorced Dr. Warner and she and Michael moved out of state. To my surprise, Dr. Warner had already remarried.

When I asked about the crying baby I began to hear, the Thorazine was increased to try and stop the delusions that Dr. Warner firmly believed that both Nix and I had inherited from our mother. But the new medication didn't stop the infant from crying, it only made me stop talking about it.

The Inheritance

Cape Perpetua is like a town from a gothic fairy tale. Even in the 21st Century, its foggy, gray atmosphere and dense towering pines are reminiscent of something imaginary. At times, I found myself wishing this were true. It will no doubt disappear one day when the ocean swallows the rocky cliffs that appear as if they'd been carved by a large dull knife. Maybe those people that continue to live here do so because they are fueled by their hopes but also by their fears, believing in some way that because they are at the very edge of the world, they are closer to eternity, that place in the horizon where the water meets the sky.

One cannot pass through this ten-mile stretch along Highway 101 without feeling a sense of obscurity. Those who don't get this reaction right away will, when they discover that most of Cape Perpetua's residents are twins. We are a town of doppelgangers like something out of an Edgar Allan Poe story. And for this reason many people avoid the area altogether; others flock here for the same. It's interesting that more twins have not moved on but maybe they remain because they are incapable of separating who they are from their place in Cape Perpetua's history. To leave would be like losing their identity, half of what made them whole.

There is a certain designation that comes with being a twin. Even if only one child makes it out of the womb, she will always be a twin. It's an identity much like orphan and schizophrenic that will linger even after death. There is no *was* in being a twin. No, a twin is perpetual; I could attest to this.

What I gathered after my release from the asylum was that most people had lost their suspicions about twins and no longer believed they were part of the curse that the city inherited when the *Twin Sisters* crashed into the cape so many years ago. Only occasionally did I catch the Madigan name in passing and it was usually among the older folks who still believed my mother was to blame since hers was the first set of twins ever born to Cape Perpetua. At one time, there was talk of changing the name of the city to better exemplify its inhabitants: The City of Twins, Twinsville, Two Sisters, and Gemini City were all proposals that never seemed to stick.

Twins were still being born at alarming rates in Cape Perpetua. They were all over the city and though they brought a certain character to the area, I feared most were looked upon in the same discerning manner of a carnival sideshow. Some standing on the corners next to one another like bookends, others fused together in crippling distortion. I wondered how the novelty stores with all their snow globes of conjoined twins and dolls with two heads growing from the same dress would continue to stay afloat if the twins one day stopped arriving. Would the tourists still be drawn to a town whose last remaining members, the proof of its ill-fated legacy, had died? Would they still come in hopes of finding a piece of the *Twin Sisters* embedded in the sand or maybe to catch a scent of something ethereal floating like a dream just above the water's edge where the waves clawed the shore? And if we really were cursed by a doomed ship, what would it take for us to become uncursed?

Not surprisingly, Nix and I weren't the only twins at St. Jerome's Home for Orphaned Children but one of the only set to actually be born there. Most had been abandoned, dropped off on the stoop by unwed mothers in the middle of the night or in the case of our mother, orphaned by the death of parents. At one point, the entire orphanage consisted of twins. Some of them were adopted out, others died and those that were left...well if the building hadn't started to crumble, they might still be there, and in some way I believed a part of them always would be.

I cannot remember all as vividly as I recall the Clifton twins. Girls with curly red hair and amber eyes. Their bed was next to mine. They had the misfortune of being welded together at the chest like an iron sculpture of mermaids that shared the same tiny heart, the size of a music box. Sometimes, I thought I heard a dirge in their restless breaths while they slept. It saddened me to watch them be carried around like puppets. They ate together, bathed together, prayed together and coughed together, though Ella a great deal more than her sister. This is how they lived for many years until one day, Ella died and Emma, still fused to her shrinking sister, slowly lost her breath and died a few days later. How horrible to bear the weight of the dead in such a way. My sister's disappearance weighed heavily upon me in the same manner.

Though it is a place that for me will always exist, the orphanage itself is abandoned, used mainly for storage, the chapel rented for weddings and craft bazaars. I'd made several trips to the cemetery behind it since my release from the asylum three years ago; I was saddened to find it in such neglect. It's the living who are responsible for making sure the dead never really die, and as I studied the old graves, I wondered if these souls had just been forgotten or perhaps had no living relatives.

The land closest to the edge of the cliff that formed Heart's Cove, the heart-shaped inlet hundreds of feet below, was unconsecrated. Surrounded by a small iron fence and an a rusty gate that remained locked, it had been a forbidden place for orphans; so overgrown now that the grave markers, most just odd-shaped stones and handmade wooden crosses painted white, were hardly visible. It was the burial place for sinners: the poor, stillborn babies, the insane, and criminals for somehow according to Father Donovan, these poor souls were all condemned. What a dead infant had in common with a murderer and a poor person, I could never decide.

The white stone figure was still there facing the water. It had been there for as long as I could remember. Nix got in trouble once for climbing over the fence to try and see the face of the girl that looked out upon the water. Her hands were extended out in front of her, cupped as if to catch the rain. On her shoulder perched a small stone bird. The sculpture was the largest piece in the entire cemetery and being so close to the edge of the cliff, I imagined it wouldn't be long before the erosion pulled the earth out from under it and the waves carried the girl out to sea. My age did nothing to quell my curiosity about the statue. There were warning signs posted along the fence, but it was my old bones that kept me from climbing over. I had visions of falling to my death five-hundred feet below into the same cove where my mother had fallen in love with the only survivor of a sunken ship. A ghost, some said. It would be an ironic ending for such a blasphemous beginning.

As I looked around, I wondered if any of the children I knew from the orphanage laid beneath the fat round unconsecrated stones I saw poking through the overgrown grass on the other side of the fence. There were too many to count, but when I suddenly felt the overwhelming desire to do so I closed my eyes for a minute as this sometimes helped, then turned and made my way back through the cemetery grounds casually scanning the tombstones for the name, Madeline. I wasn't sure if the Sister had passed or not but I thought of her often and wanted to pay my respects.

Nix and I upon our birth were given to Sister Madeline's charge, and I believe that she somehow felt personally responsible for us. We were the children she could not have and especially because she had watched over our mother, Una, after her parents had died in the fire, she must have cared deeply for us. Because our mother was taken away just after our birth, it was Sister Madeline who gave us our Latin names. Lux, the flaxen-haired child who glowed as radiantly as the sun and Nix whose hair was as dark and thick as the night. Sister Madeline told us when we were older that she chose these names because she knew one could not exist without the other. Somehow, I'd managed to do it for some thirty years. I recalled the nun's words as I continued walking from the graveyard to the asylum, to sit by the fountain and think of the sister I'd lost to the world.

The streets near the asylum had all been named after saints, and my Catholic rearing could not let me pass one without an image instantly surfacing in my mind like a flash card. This practice felt almost like a test, and I feared that if I should one day see an image that didn't correspond properly with a saint's given street, my hand would burn like it had been hit with a ruler. Like it had been so many times before at St. Jerome's.

I continued up Ambrose, toward the asylum, which sat accordingly on Dymphna Court, just a short distance from the orphanage. It was a good hike from my apartment especially because the weather was still quite cool and it made my legs cramp all the more. They ached terribly when I walked around too much. The most logical explanation for this was one that I didn't want to consider: the hole in my heart was contributing to poor leg and feet circulation, which would ultimately lead to my demise. Nix and I had both been born with holes in our hearts, a congenital defect, one of many I suppose, and I deemed this somehow appropriate as if this was an inclination to the pain we'd suffer; we were a metaphor of ourselves. Her hole closed before she was eighteen but mine never did. I had over time expected it to heal, but the last doctor I saw informed me that the chances of it closing naturally were almost non-existent now. He didn't say it, but I could see in his discerning eyes that it would one day destroy me: my death would be caused from a lacuna, something that physically was not there. A hole.

I secured my coat and checked to make certain the letter I'd tucked in the pocket was still there then slipped through the space between the large iron gates in front of the building.

It was strange to want to continually return to the asylum, but it had been my home for so long it seemed to come naturally. Hope was the main reason I returned so often, believing that one day I might find my sister waiting for me. But there was something else that brought me here. It was like some type of invisible magnet that violated the Law of Attraction. Whatever it was seemed to silently summon me but each time I'd leave feeling as empty as when I arrived. I believed this was because the closure I needed would require me to enter the building— something I had not done since the day I was released, for the thought placed me in a state of panic.

The lawns of the asylum had been landscaped recently in an attempt to beautify an institution for the dysfunctional that after so many years of neglect had ironically become dysfunctional itself. It was like a wound that had been sewn over despite the fact that the tissue beneath it had not yet healed. Regardless, I enjoyed walking through the manicured courtyard, and I always stopped to sit at the fountain, which had been dry for many years. At one time, I watched from the room I shared with Nix as water trickled out of the mouths of the angels, an enormous stone pair who rose up out of the center of the basin in what appeared to be anguish.

In Celtic mythology, water originates from the Otherworld where those who inhabit it had the power to control it. My mother had a unique bond with water, and I wonder if the hydrotherapy room at the asylum damaged that bond.

In her journal she wrote that as a little girl she dove into the sea with the belief that she, too, could breathe water like a mermaid. Even then she wanted to know how it felt to live in a different world. When she didn't come up, it was her brother Finn who pulled her to the surface and swam her back to shore. She wrote that the sea was so much a part of her afterward that when she spoke, the sound of the waves could be heard in her breath and no matter where she was from that day on, gravity pulled her towards the water.

It destroyed my mother that she could not follow her brother on his journey into the sea. That she could not save him. On the ship over from Ireland he contacted typhus and had to be tossed overboard. Her sister Kate had died of pneumonia before they left Ireland. Nora and Patrick Madigan arrived in Oregon with only one child, Una, a name that seemed to imply solitude though I know from her writings that my mother was not a lonely child. Lonely for her brother, yes. But, never alone.

The wind stirred and I caught a hint of lilac in its breeze. Encouraged, I looked around for Nix. The scent of lilacs always remind me of her. I began scanning the area for the source of the hypnotic aroma, expecting to find a flowering bush nearby. I saw nothing and I wondered if the mysterious fragrance was a reminder that a great part of a lilac's beauty lies within its transience. The smell always seemed to put me in a daze and today was no exception. Gradually, I was pulled from this spell when I felt the eyes of the concrete angels on me. They were in a sad state of decomposition, much like the asylum. One was missing her hand, an iron rod in its place like Captain Hook. The other looked as if she had developed leprosy or some other kind of erosive skin disease that had ate away at her face, which looked now, as if it had been draped in lace.

The inside of the fountain had deteriorated so horrifically that large patches of the earth were exposed. It was this deterioration, I believed, that gave the angels their humanity, and because they couldn't bear the pain that it caused, their wings were spread up behind them ready to take flight at any minute. I'd seen this same sculpture before in a book of famous cemetery statues, so I knew its inspiration came from the original at Cimetiere du Pere-Lachaise in Paris. I'd developed a fascination for cemeteries after I came to the asylum. Perhaps this was because I feared I might never be buried in one. That my ashes would be stored on a shelf, unclaimed in the library of dust, like a book no one wanted to read.

Soon, the asylum would be demolished or so I read in the paper, and I wondered what would become of the cremains. The same article had mentioned a group of people who were desperately searching for family members of the unclaimed. This group was also trying to come up with methods of honorable burial, though I'd been conditioned to believe *disposal* was a more appropriate word. The ashes were the only existing proof of what had happened at Cape Perpetua's Asylum. Most of the records had been destroyed. I was there the day I overheard Dr. Warner tell Peggy that she was to take certain files to the crematorium. I watched her go back and forth from the Records Room to the basement. Then Big Mary had one of her seizures and Peggy ran to help her, forgetting to lock the door behind her. I still recall the smell of that room. Not a scent that could be easily isolated easily but a fermentation of dust and fading ink and of a delicate existence that had been recorded on paper as thin and redolent as the skin of an onion. Later, when I woke up in my bed with this same scent around me, I knew I'd lost time again. It was something that started happening to me after my sister went missing.

I focused my attention back to the crumbling angels and to the small black plaque with gold lettering that read: *Donated by the Moss Foundation, 1960.* Below that the words of St. Augustine: *If you wish to rise, lay first the foundation of humility.* The fountain was erected the same year my mother died, but I did not know this until I was released because I could not read the plaque from my window. The angels reminded me so much of my sister and me that at times I could see our faces in theirs; they seemed to share the same passionate connection and indestructible desperation that belonged to the Madigan women.

We were just teenagers when we were brought from the orphanage to the asylum. Sister Madeline was against the idea.

She was not a supporter of the Eugenics Movement, I heard her say when begging Father Donovan to keep us at the orphanage. I had no idea then what the term even meant and neither did Nix when I asked her. But we would soon learn.

"Only God should make those kinds of decisions," Sister Madeline spoke sternly on the other side of the door. But Father Donovan claimed it was beyond his control. Our mother, Una, had become pregnant at the age of fourteen he reminded her. This coupled with her absurd notion that she could communicate with the dead was enough to justify her relocation. Just after our birth, she was moved to the Cape Perpetua Asylum, and we did not meet her until we were six years old.

"This promiscuity and instability will undeniably be passed on to her children. Nix has already shown signs of her mother's decadent behavior. Una was a sinner, Sister. Let us not forget."

"Well perhaps she should have been given a scarlet letter then," Sister Madeline snapped as she slammed the door behind her, smiling sweetly the moment she realized we were still waiting on the bench in the hall where she left us. She must have known then or at least speculated what I would learn later from my mother's writings. Or maybe the small round nose we shared with Father Donovan was incapable of escaping her scrutiny.

"Girls, we have to gather your things," the Sister spoke to us calmly on the day we were exiled to the asylum. We had just turned fifteen and by then our mother had been dead for five years.

Upon our arrival, I was identified as having obsessive

compulsive disorder of which kleptomania was a predominant symptom and Nix was diagnosed with schizophrenia. She had to undergo electric electroconvulsive therapy and strong anti-psychotic medication before she was released into a less supervised ward with me.

Because of the manner in which she dealt with pain, it didn't take much for my sister to be reintroduced to shock treatments and increased dosages of medications. Nix must have felt like this was her only connection with our mother, but I knew this was not true as she claimed in her journal that she too was visited by the dead. She wrote that it took her a long time to realize that she was blessed by this and not cursed but this was little or no matter to proponents of Eugenics. For them, the Madigan twins had inherited their mother's genes and this alone was enough to convict us. Our *being* predetermined our conviction. It was unfair. Like starting life as an elderly person and growing younger with each birthday, knowing exactly when you reached two that you only had one year of life left. This is how it felt to me. It was worse than being convicted of a crime. We'd been tried and convicted before we took our first breath.

Sister Madeline had brought Nix and I to see our mother as often as she could when she was still alive, and even now I remember those visits. Her beauty was unmatched by anything I'd ever seen.

There was a dilapidated old piano with chipped enamel keys in the visitation area and my mother would play for us. We'd have to beg her to remove her gloves. She could not read music and often played with her eyes closed. Sister Madeline said that it was a gift she had inherited at birth but that not all things inherited were gifts in society's eyes.

On the last visit I remember, my mother's head had been shaved because of a lice epidemic, but the long auburn hair that may have at one time enhanced her appearance did not have the power to detract from it after it was gone. The room where we met was always cold, but my mother's scarred hands were hot as if the heat from the flames had never left them. She had started the fire that nearly destroyed the city, years ago; the same one that took her parents' life and this must have left her insides scarred as well.

Even now, after so many years have passed, I think about my mother's death. Since lunatics don't merit obituaries, I don't own a newspaper clipping listing her surviving family members or the church she attended or where she donated her time. Her bodily remains, if they exist, are a mystery. I do, however, have one thing of importance. Something I probably should not have. Something I know I must have taken, though I don't recall doing so. It's a death certificate that states that Una Madigan expired on June 18th, 1960, a victim of her own consequence. But, I'm skeptical of this. I believe that Dr. Warner knew more about my mother than he let on. Maybe I feel this way because whenever I'd ask him about her, he'd narrow his eyes and wipe at the little beads of perspiration forming on his brow. He'd rifle through the papers on his clipboard, searching for something that we both knew was not there. Then the cursory assessment of time on the watch that bought him freedom from such questions. He acted this same way when I questioned him about Nix after she escaped. Dr. Warner had his secrets, and in this way we were alike, I suppose.

On the way back to the Guardian, I dropped the letter in the mailbox as I had every week since my release from the asylum in hopes that someone from the paper might help me find Nix before it was too late—before I was consumed by something that wasn't there.

Part Two

Cora Lockhart

The Widow

They were there again and I lost my courage. I sat across the street by the drugstore for an hour watching before I started the car and pulled away, the signs in my rearview mirror shrinking but not getting any smaller as I drove on begging them to do so. For a second, and only a second, I thought I saw her in the backseat, the smear of light that had followed me as a child. I hadn't seen her for years. When I looked again, I realized it must have been the wind blowing around my dry cleaning bag, which was hanging in the back of the car.

I hadn't planned on it, but because I had worn the wood in the pews at St. Anne's and could think of nowhere else to go, I headed into work. Ben had only been dead for three months and my house had since become a casket.

In the employee lot of the *Twin Beacon*, the newspaper where I had worked for seven years, I turned off the engine of the car but made no attempt to get out until Matt, the young parking attendant, obviously concerned about my delay, approached the car.

"Everything okay Mrs. Belmont?" he asked.

I nodded. "Yes. Fine, Matt. Thanks." I furtively wiped at the tear that had escaped from my eye, catching it just before it became visible. People had treated me with such fragility since Ben's death and though I appreciated it, I wasn't sure it was the best thing for me. Instead, it was more like a continuing reminder that I had become a widow at the age of thirty-seven. My first and only husband, Benjamin Belmont had been killed not by Iraqi militants as I had once feared he would be but by friendly fire. The phrase was an oxymoron—something along with hyperbole that in college I was taught to avoid using if I ever wanted to be taken serious as a journalist, but this wasn't the reason it numbed my tongue when I spoke it aloud.

I'd met Ben during my last year at Columbia University where he was studying computer programming. I knew immediately he was special because he filled that space inside me that had been reserved since I was a girl for...for something else. But what? Though I'd been accepted to Julliard, my father would not allow me to pursue my gift for music and after much deliberation and many days of not speaking, we finally agreed on a journalism degree since writing had always come naturally for me. I had always been one of those children in search of answers and this characteristic followed me into adulthood. I was one of those people who would rather hear the worst truth than the best lie.

I didn't tell my father how much I looked forward to the school electives that allowed me to play my cello; music was in my heart, and I would never be able to fully deny it. When I look back I guess I should thank him because if I had not been forced into the path that was chosen for me, I may have never met Ben. Yet, there's that part of me—the part my father would call irrational—that believes in destiny. I'd felt this aberrant pull all my life. A shadow as transparent as a moth's wing that had hovered around me ever since I could remember, always fading when I tried to touch it but never once letting me forget it was there. Eventually, I learned to push it away because my father had warned me that women who are guided by intuition lose their ability to make sound judgments. I didn't want to admit that it was my intuition, that ghost shadow of gossamer light that kept me from my appointment that morning and it wasn't the first time.

When I first received the news about Ben, I crawled in bed and stayed there for days without answering the phone or the door, getting up only to get a drink of water and use the toilet. On one of those trips, my cello called to me from the corner where I kept it. It was covered in a layer of dust. We both were. I sat on a chair and pulled the instrument between my legs, feeling the warm curve of the wood, while I listened for the beat of a heart I knew it must have hidden inside its hollowed body. I wondered if at the same time, it was listening for mine. I wanted her to come find me then, my light but I had pushed her away for so long, she had no doubt forgotten me.

The sound of the cello is like a human voice. With the bow across the strings, we mourned together for hours—my first love helping me endure the loss of my husband, whose ashes I wore around my neck. They were contained in a sterling silver tear drop that dangled from a chain so delicate it was nearly invisible;

yet, so much a part of me that if I removed it, I imagined I would not be able to breathe. Sometimes I wondered what part of him had been captured in that tear. Was it his beautiful green eyes? His enormous heart? His ear? If I didn't monitor my time, I'd spend hours thinking about it.

"Good Morning, Victoria."

"Hey Barb," I greeted the receptionist as I stopped at the front desk to pick up my mail.

"How are you?"

"I'm alright, I suppose."

She nodded, the look in her eye alerting me to her uncertainty. "Do you mind taking these up with you when you go?" she asked, pushing a stack of envelopes over the counter. "There are a few pieces for you, but most of it is for Tom. He's out today. You can just put it on his desk—if you can find room. If not, just drop it on his chair."

"No problem," I said as I took the mail and ran to catch the elevator as it opened.

Tom Irwin had been the editor of the *Twin Beacon* for decades. He was a personal friend of Randall Moss who had owned the paper since it was first printed in the early 1900s. Golfing buddies from way back. Moss was the wealthiest name in town. Their paper mill was well known both nationally and internationally but their reputation was built on philanthropy. Ben used to say that old money has a certain smell—one that seeped into the skin of those it consumed. Ben never cared about money or privilege. This was one of the reasons I'd fallen for him almost immediately. After college, we went our separate ways but we always kept in contact. When he took a job in Cape Perpetua, teaching at the community college, it was as if eight years had never passed between us. We got married the same year I started working for the *Beacon*. He wanted kids so badly. Talked about it all the time. But, I wasn't so certain about the idea. I still wasn't.

As I passed my desk on the way to Tom's office, my phone rang, and I reached to answer it. "Speaking. Yes. I'm sorry. I wasn't able to make it this morning. Something came up. I'll have to reschedule. Let me look at my calendar..." I sat down to flip through my planner but then I noticed Georgina approaching my desk with pastries and coffee. "I'll have to get back with you," I spoke softly into the receiver before placing back in the cradle.

"Georgina. How's the world's greatest assistant these days?"

"Hungover. Here, I brought you an apology." She set the turnover on my desk next to the cup of coffee. "It's apple. Your favorite."

"Unnecessary. But thank you." I didn't have the heart to tell her how upset my stomach had been that morning, but Georgina is a very intuitive girl. She has thick dark hair, cut bluntly in a bob that just covers her ears. In the right lighting, I can often see blue streaks running through it like electricity, which makes her pale complexion look even paler. She stands before me in one of her vintage dresses. It is almost the same color blue as her eyes, which sharpen as she narrows them toward me in conclusion.

"Oh. Looks like I'm not the only one recovering this morning." She contorted her mouth and raised her brows in suspicion.

"Anyhow, I'm sorry I didn't finish the research you requested yesterday. Tom had me doing a bunch of shit for him for his trip. He doesn't understand that editorial assistant doesn't mean *personal* assistant. Next thing you know, he'll have me picking up his damn dry cleaning."

She took a big swig of coffee, her chipped black nail polish a severe contrast against the stark white cup in the same way her dark hair contrasted against her skin. It made me miss being young. And though there was no connection between nail polish and my late husband, it made me miss Ben. I'd come to realize in the last few months that when it came to love, similarities had little to do with association. Love had some type of connection to everything it seemed. For God's sake, the ceiling fan reminded me of him.

I never got to tell Ben how much I loved him during our last conversation, but what haunts me more is that I never had the chance to say I was sorry. We had argued when he called. He wanted to start a family as soon as he returned from duty and he wanted me to think about taking a leave of absence from work—something I had not yet felt ready to do. The conversation escalated and I hung the phone up, regretting it immediately but not being able to do anything about it since I could not call him and tell him I was sorry. Three days later, they were at my door. Those uniformed officers who exude the unmistakable scent of grief that still lingered in my house like a dense fog.

The phone startled me from my thoughts. "Victoria Belmont," I answered soberly, to project a strength I wasn't sure existed anymore. It was my father's nurse alerting me to a change in his medication.

"Hi Victoria. Just wanted to give you an update. We've increased your father's morphine. This will make him a little more comfortable but a little less alert. Dr. Brightman wanted me to let you know so that you wouldn't worry when you came by. Your father's been asking for you quite a bit today. Will you be by?"

My 86-year-old father was in the final stages of pancreatic cancer. I used to visit him daily, but since Ben's death, I'd not gone as regularly as I should have, and the guilt was slowly but certainly taking its toll. With this remorse came a little bitterness. I loved my father, but at times, I felt the burden of being the only caretaker. Hiring a nurse certainly helped, but mentally, I was exhausted. My half brother lived in another city, but proximity didn't have much regard in his relationship with Dad. They hadn't been close for years. In fact, I'd only met my brother a couple of times, the first not really counting since I was traumatized. I was just five years of age when my mother was killed in an accident. I'd been in the car with her, the scar that ran just under my ribcage and down to my hip, my only memory of what had happened. When I became old enough to understand, I'd run my fingers along the raised ridge that not only divided me in half but also seemed to separate me from the rest of the world. I'd stare at the scar for hours in the mirror, trying to picture the mother I'd lost, someone who resembled the photograph my father kept on his bureau, but not once did she ever manifest. Instead,

I'd be overcome with a feeling that I'd misplaced something very valuable and only the girl in the glass knew where to find it.

My brother and his mother attended the funeral and I'd seen them only a few times afterward. It felt odd having a brother that was twenty some years older than me. Outside of the same skin tone, the shape of our face, and the intensity of our deep brown eyes, we seemed to have little in common. Yet even so I sensed a certain familial bond with him that I knew might fade if I soon didn't do something about it—at least then I could say that I tried to be close with him. I realized of course that we might have been closer had he and Dad had an amicable relationship.

"Okay. Thanks for letting me know Janice. I'll be by after work."

"Oh, one more thing," she added. "He's been asking for your brother. Do you want me to try and reach him?"

"No. I'll take care of it," I said competently, my stomach twisting at the thought of asking my brother to arrange a visit.

Only when I was off the phone did I realize that I'd inadvertently opened most of the mail in front of me, including Tom's. "Shit. This is Tom's mail," I spoke in a loud whisper as I held the letter in front of me. The script was tiny and moved in slow, methodic curls. "This looks personal."

Georgina moved behind me, the hint of stale clove cigarettes wafting from her hair. "No. I don't think so. I recognize the handwriting. It's that nut who writes him about her missing sister. I've never actually read the letters but everyone knows about them. They've been coming for a couple of years. For some reason Tom shreds them all as soon as he gets them. Not sure why," Georgina spoke while reading over my shoulder. "Oh," she said with reserve. "Maybe that's why." She pointed to the name Dr. Warner.

"Well that's odd," I responded uncomfortably. "It seems like I should have been the first to know about this."

"I wouldn't worry about it. She's just some old kooky lady that got booted from the asylum by state budget cuts—thanks to our new governor. There's a whole mess of them at the Guardian House. I pass by there on my way home sometimes. They're always standing outside panhandling and talking to themselves. Sad."

"Yeah," I said quietly, still disturbed by the contents of the letter.

"I should get back to my desk. Lunch?"

"Maybe."

"Alright, I'll stop by later."

"Georgina?" She turned and I waved the letter. "Let's keep this between us for now, okay?"

She nodded, zipping her thumb and forefinger across her lips.

I read the letter once more before stuffing back in the envelope and slipping it in my purse.

Proof of Existence

It wasn't like I was given a choice in the matter, but when I discovered that the apartment that had been chosen for me at the Guardian did not have a tub, I actually felt less nervous about living there. The idea of sitting in a bath was not one I associated with being clean or warm. I'd had enough baths and none of them had been relaxing. The hot water in the building wasn't very good and when it began to run cold, I immediately got out and got dressed then boiled some water in the only pan I owned for a cup of coffee. It had been nearly a week since I mailed the last letter to the paper, and I was almost certain I was out of stationary to pen another.

With my cup in hand, I went over toward the bed, reaching under it to pull out the suitcase that once belonged to my mother in hopes that I might find some blank paper and an extra envelope inside. The case contained my mother's remains. Not her bodily remains—I have no idea what became of her after she died but the things she held in her possession before she left this world, for this is what truly embraces the meaning of existence: the things that remain after we are gone. These things are proof that we once existed. My sister and I were proof that our mother existed and also, in the eyes of society, a testimony to her sin.

Some sins are easier to see than others, I suppose.

My mother had few possessions: photographs, a tarnished St. Brigid medallion, the gloves she wore to hide her scarred hands, a rosary, and her writings, which none of the staff realized I'd had in my possession at the time I was turned out from the asylum along with the others who were forced into a world but not taught how to be accepted in it. I also kept some of Nix's paintings and a few other items in the case.

I'd come across my mother's things by chance one day at the asylum when I snuck into the attic. Though I can't be sure, it occurred to me that I must have taken the key from Michael's key ring on one of his late-night visits to see Nix.

Nix knew all the forbidden places in the asylum, but she claimed Michael wasn't always the one to tell her about them. I wanted to believe her about the dead. I really did, but at times, it was difficult. If she could see them then why couldn't I? We were practically identical. Cut from the same fabric. I wondered if she shared the same ghosts as our mother or if ghosts were buried with the people they haunted. It bothered me that I was different from my mother and sister, but I also understood that it wasn't necessary to see a ghost in order to be haunted.

Over time, the attic became my refuge at the asylum. I'd spend hours hiding up there going through the racks of boxes and suitcases that lined the wide-planked wooden floors. Even in the summer it was a cold place with dust dancing in the pinched light that broke through the small boarded windows. Sometimes, I could hear conversations funneling up through the vents as I tried on bright scarves and long fancy gloves with pearl buttons and flipped through old worn albums of yellowed photos—people and places that summoned my imagination. I even found a tea pot and two tiny rose-vine cups, badly chipped but still functional.

Rats had made nests in the mound of shoes that grew in the corner like a sculpture. It reminded me of an article I saved from a newspaper someone had left in the TV Room. It was the story of how Auschwitz had been liberated, but it was the image of the shoes in the accompanying photograph that haunted me. They were piled so high they nearly reached the top of the crematorium. The shoes were the only proof at the time that these people had ever existed. The survivors may have been liberated, but much like wards of the state, they'd never be free. I kept the article. I don't know why. Maybe it's because of what my mother wrote about the dead never wearing shoes when they came to her. I imagined the amount of ghosts the Holocaust generated, and I wondered how many of these lost souls were in constant search of their shoes.

I spent many days in the attic before coming across the ragged red leather suitcase. I didn't realize it was my mother's until I saw the initials U. M. written in thick black marker on the flowered viscera of the case. The ink had bled into some of the flowers. It reminded me of those little blotches of blackness doctors used to analyze people.

Little by little, I managed to sneak the contents into my room until the case was empty. I would have overlooked my mother's journal had I not spotted the loosened lining and began to pick at it—more from my curious nature than from the obsessive compulsive disorder I had been diagnosed with. I kept the journal hidden in my secret tear in the mattress along with my other treasures. To make certain no one came across my hiding place, I made my own bed each day.

When I was released from the asylum, I fetched my mother's red suitcase from the attic and used it to pack the things I brought to the Guardian with me. I had to beg my case worker, who I've only seen a few times since my release, to go back for the books, which filled three large boxes. With my small monthly income from the state, I often chose to buy books rather than food, for literature quelled my hunger in a way that food could not.

I took my mother's journal from the suitcase and moved over to the chair by the window so I could read the story of how my sister and I came to be. I'd read it many times before with the understanding that some of it had been fabricated, a fairy tale created by a woman who was forced into reality at a very young age. The Irish are born storytellers. They know that even the greatest fiction holds an essence of truth.

In order for her to survive as she did, my mother concocted a marvelous story in which her twin girls had been the offspring of something unworldly—a story in which she had been impregnated by a specter—a handsome young man who had been on board the *Twin Sisters* when it met its fate. This must have been her only escape from the painful reality that her brother was never coming back and that her girls were not actually fathered by a spirit but a man of the cloth who put his faith in another kind of Ghost.

Nameless Day

In the Latin language, Una means one. But this couldn't have been my father's intention when he chose my name. I often wondered if he in some way felt responsible for the death of his other two children by giving his only living child a name that in great irony implied such singularity.

It's November 1958 and cold. For eight years I have been a patient at the Cape Perpetua Asylum for the Insane. I'm twenty-two years old but feel much older. My beautiful twin girls are in the care of Sister Madeline who brings them to visit when she can. I trust that she will keep them safe though I realize she cannot protect them from their inherency. She has a kind soul and part of me feels she knows who fathered my girls but is not permitted to disclose it in order to keep her position in the Church. Or maybe it is her position with faith she fears losing.

I have been diagnosed as a schizophrenic by Dr. Warner who chooses to believe that I have a personality disorder rather than acknowledge that my visitors exist and have existed since I was a little girl. I started this journal in hopes that I will be able to leave a record of my own existence even if it is never discovered. If I do not hide the journal, the staff will confiscate it. But if I do not write it, I leave my girls with nothing but the reality of who they are. I fear I have little time left as I have begun to see myself in my shadow, and I am always without shoes. The dead never wear shoes. I don't know why.

The day my family arrived on the Oregon Coast was a day without a name. December 22, 1944. For the Druids who formed a secret language based exclusively on trees, this was a day of darkness. There was no tree for this day. It was the shortest day of the Celtic calendar year in which the Dark Queen held the sun captive, but for the Madigan family, it had become the longest. This did not detract from its darkness though. It was custom to fast on this day to appease the queen so that she would return the light to the world. We had run out of food on the ship two days before, and my father said that certainly by now, the queen must have been satisfied. But she wasn't, and I had a feeling she never would be.

This secret language called Ogham was said to be path to the Spirit World and as my brother Finn's body was lowered into the ocean early that morning I hoped Grandfather would be waiting to welcome him. Finn, like many others on the trip from Ireland that began over eight months before, developed typhus. He once saved me from the sea when I believed I could breathe water like a selkie. But I could not save him from it. And more than ever now the sound of the ocean swelled in my breath. It seemed to beckon me like a siren's song to a seaman, and I knew one day, it would claim me as its own.

I had been reluctant to leave Ireland, the land where I was born, the land of all the legends, and I pleaded desperately with my parents to let me stay on. "It is not possible, Una," they explained to me. "You are just a *cailín beag*, a little girl. Besides, Finn is not going to stay. You will be all alone." And though I knew this was not likely, I acquiesced for the thought of being by myself did not intimidate me, but the thought of being without my brother was something I could not bear. And now, I was forced to do so. I was the only child left to Patrick and Nora Madigan when they arrived in Cape Perpetua.

Though I loved my sister Kate, I did not share the same bond with her as I did with Finn. It wasn't because Kate was younger or because she always took my things and hid them, and it wasn't because she played tricks on me all the time or ratted me out and made up lies about me. It was something deeper than this— something that could not be extracted or even identified. For as strong as my bond was with Finn, my bond with Kate was as weak. But Kate was a tenacious child, always trying to be close to me as if she could tell that I did not need her as much as I needed Finn, and this made her vie for my attention more desperately. Even after her death from pneumonia just before her fourth birthday and six months before we left Ireland for America, Kate remained true to her character for there was rarely a day that passed that she did not come to me.

Sometimes she would show up with our grandparents or uncle, who had all passed in the years previous and other times she would appear with people who because I recognized their photos from the walls of the entrance to St. Brigid's Well, could not be considered complete strangers. People, who despite the fervent appeals their relatives had made to the saint and her healing water, had died regardless. But mostly because she was still seeking my undivided attention, Kate came alone. She was there on the ship the morning Finn died, the same day my only photo of him disappeared from the cabin, and I could not be sure if Kate lingered on the deck that morning for support or simply because with no sibling competition, she felt in some way victorious—that she had somehow been able to finally capture my attention. Though if Kate believed competing with her own brother when he was alive had been an arduous task, his rivalry in death would prove even more difficult because I would be forever consumed by loss, so preoccupied with my constant search for Finn's spirit in the thinness of the air around me that Kate would continue to be almost as transparent to me as she had been alive—even as I grew into a young woman.

Finn developed the fever a few days before we reached the Oregon shore. As he slept next to me in the upper bunk, his skin became so hot that I myself began to burn like fire, and I rubbed my St. Brigid medallion and prayed to the goddess, whose healing powers were immersed in water but also in fire. But, by then his cough, a deep sodden hack had established itself in the bilge of his lungs like a ship taking on water and within hours the rash had spread over his torso, masking his birthmark, a distorted red star on his neck.

My brother was sequestered in a small dark room under the galley, a place so much like a coffin that it was not possible for light to burn his unnaturally sensitive eyes. After a day passed, his deliriousness turned to despondency and I sat outside the latched door listening for his shallow breath. On the morning of his death, I pushed so hard against the wood door in an effort to hear him that the grain became embroidered on my ear while I waited for the sounds around me to subside. When I no longer heard the water beneath us or the creaking sway of the hull that surrounded me like the giant ribs of something that had swallowed me; when the only thing I could hear was the quiet emptiness of my heart as it waited for the sound of Finn's breath so it could beat again, I felt the tears slip from my eyes and hit the floor with the weight of lead coins that broke the loudest silence I'd ever known. It wasn't until later that I noticed his photo missing from the wall above my bunk—a bizarre reinforcement that he truly was gone.

Finn wasn't the first to be tossed overboard for fear of infecting others, but because my father Patrick had gained the respect and friendship of the captain during the long months of traveling, Finn was the only victim that wasn't dropped directly into the water. There were no doctors on board, but when the captain confirmed Finn's death, my mother dressed her only son in a white undershift and his swollen body was placed into a dinghy and lowered into the blackness of the icy Pacific like a great Viking warrior, like a solitary star in the deep violet sky. The water, I hoped, would take him back to Ireland, back to *Tir na nog*, the land of eternal youth, where dead children live again but never age. Finn would always and forever be twelve years old.

I watched the small white boat, one the Captain said was

meant for saving lives, float away with the effortless grace of a flower on the waves then disappear into the glowing morning horizon. I could feel the pull of the water. It called to me as I stood on the rail. It even knew my name. I'd learned as a child that the sea was apathetic. It was not to be trusted and yet at that moment it held all of my faith. But as I looked back at my grieving parents, whose tears drowned out the sound of my name, I stepped down from the rail and embraced them. The sea would wait for me. I truly believed this.

Though it was a day that had no name, it would forever be known as the day I myself died, the day I became as thin as the veil of lace that separated the living from the dead during Oiche na Sprideanna, Spirit Night. And somehow I managed to continue living even after four years had passed without my Finn.

Heart's Cove

I watched as my mother Nora kneaded the dough. Though it was the most demanding part of making bread, it was also her favorite part. For the one hour she folded her fingers into the pliable mass she became non-dimensional. She told me that during this time, she thought of nothing behind her and nothing in front of her. There was no past. No future. It was just her and the dough and the solitary moments it loaned to the air around her as she lost herself in its unstructured obedience. But on that December morning, almost four years to the day of our arrival in Cape Perpetua, the temperature dropped drastically and the air outside began to wheeze like a person whose lungs were slowly filling with water. My mother stood motionless at the kitchen counter for a moment and listened carefully, not with her ears but with her heart, for a true Irish girl knew when a gale approached even if she was a blind mute.

She wiped her hands on her apron on her way over to the window and when she pulled the yellow flowered curtain aside, she saw the purple bruises framed in the sky: a storm was rolling in off the Pacific.

"Una," she said as I finished my breakfast. "Make certain ye wear *yer* rain boots to school today. There's a storm coming." She tightened her apron strings and went back to making the bread she planned to sell at the holiday festival the following day.

By late afternoon, the entire city was blanketed in a low fog that seemed to coagulate the air into a strange wet warmth. The storm hit during the night and carried over into the next morning. Through my bedroom window because the rain was so heavy, the entire city appeared as a page of smudged ink. The coast was used to precipitation during these months but even so it was not difficult to see that this was a very peculiar storm, one that weighed upon the city long after the *Twin Sisters* smashed into the rocks of Cape Perpetua early that morning. The only thing left of the ship other than the boy was a distressed piece of wood bearing the vessel's name. In the years to come, the legend would swell like the waves of a stormy sea until it became known as a curse—one that was said to have begun with me.

When the storm was over, the city was littered with overturned tables and decorations that had been placed on the main street in preparation for the festival. Dolls made of straw and husks and wrapped in white fabric dresses floated like ghosts down the foggy streets and became wedged into the rocks and mud where they stayed, their featureless faces haunting those that passed by. Loaves of saturated bread left on doorsteps went untouched and the birds disappeared from trees and bushes and later washed ashore with the waves. And the boy.

It was the first year my body had begun to behave differently. I started to feel a slight sway when I walked as if the earth was moving beneath me, but I believed this was just the sea calling to me as it had always done. It was painful to ignore because it was as if I was abandoning my brother, Finn, by not heeding the call, but I was so sure that since so many others had found me, he too would one day come. I had read in one of Hemingway's books at my father's store that man could live a full life in seventy hours as easily as seventy years, and this is exactly how I felt without my brother. It was like my entire life consisted only of the moment I'd lost Finn.

The day after the storm when the rain had finally ceased, I sat on a rock overlooking Heart's Cove and took out my drawing pad. Drawing was something I could lose myself in entirely for hours without the urge to eat or drink or think. There was something about creating those images that let me live in the pages of shadow and light and because of this, my favorite medium was charcoal. I felt guilty that I had never once used the colored pencils my mother gave me for my birthday a few years back. My pictures were grays and blacks, and I saw my life defined in these flat monochromatic colors. Though I was not color blind, most things appeared to me in black and white, including the day with its white soft fog floating eerily above the calm black endless ocean, and the dark rocks growing from the alabaster sand.

I searched through the fog for Face Rock and when I found the Indian maiden, whose stone glare forever searched the sea for something she lost long ago, I began to sketch. Though what she had lost, she may never find, she continued to search for it in the horizon, and I didn't need to know of the legend to see this. I prayed to St. Anthony for both of us. When I finished the drawing, I could see it was my own face I'd drawn.

The sea lions were barking in the distance. The sound made me want to slide off into the water and swim back to Ireland, but I knew if I left, Finn may not ever find me. I waited for him every day but he had not yet shown himself even after four years. Maybe he was angry with me for letting him die. Dead strangers found me but never Finn. I laid restless in bed at night in hopeful anticipation of each sound. The creak of floorboards, the rattle of a window pane, the sound of dust settling on the sill; these were all worthy of further investigation. I don't think I'd ever really slept since the day my brother died.

The leaves stirred beside me like one would expect upon the arrival of a ghost, and I felt my sister's presence behind me. I did not turn around when I asked, "What do you want, Kate?" But Kate didn't answer. She rarely spoke at all and when she did, it was short sentences composed of single words that were often so distorted, they were unrecognizable as if she had been immersed under water.

"Go away," I told her. "I don't feel like company right now." But Kate never listened because though my sister had been gone for many years, she had not aged. She was still an impish four-year-old child wearing the same dress she was buried in, a white lace gown with a high neck and wide satin sash in which her long curly red hair graced like a whisper. Oddly, she looked like a miniature version of a bride or a sepia photograph of a fairy that had lost her wings in the same storm that tangled her hair. However, the dress, unlike her, had aged so it was torn and dirty around the bottom. She was barefoot even though I distinctively remember the shoes she wore in the coffin: small brown boots with buttons as delicate as vertebrae along the side. The spirits that visited me were always barefoot and I wondered why. Grandmother wore a hat with a big flower on it and a long velvety dress, but no shoes. Grandfather showed up in his favorite dark suit (was it brown or blue? I can't remember) and he continued to carry his hand-carved cane with an ivory handle though he didn't need it anymore for walking. He always smiled and said my name slowly with the lilt God gave him, Oooo-Nah and it sounded just like the ocean. It made me happy when I remembered the way his laugh filtered through his back teeth and gurgled like water pushing through the rocks along the shore. He still wore socks and there was always a hole where I could see one of his buckled toes, usually his pinky, but not once in all the times he visited me had he ever been wearing shoes.

Grandfather's accent made me think of Clare County and the people whose voices, so similar to mine, echoed in the walkway of the well over the cries of the desperate who dropped prayers like coins in the medicinal water in hopes that St. Brigid would answer. In America, the girls at school made fun of my voice, the way I pronounced things, so eventually I stopped talking to them and only spoke when I was required to. On occasion, I was scolded by my teacher for talking to Kate and the others who were believed to be imaginary.

"In Ireland, people who see the dead are revered," I relayed with great pride, one day.

"Well here in America," Miss Hudson retorted, "they're feared. Considered evil. The spawn of the devil," she added. "So please stop it."

But I couldn't tell her that *stopping* wasn't that easy. It would have been like trying to stop breathing.

Kate disappeared as quickly and mysteriously as she appeared and marking the spot where she stood was a brown velvet ribbon. These ribbons had been tied to the tree for the festival but the storm must have loosened this one from the branch where it was tied. Missing was one of my favorite charcoal pencils. "Kate," I cursed under my breath then picked up the ribbon and ran my thumb over its soft wet nap.

When the fog lifted, I could see large pieces of wood immerging from the sand like broken bones poking through skin. The shore itself was littered with unrecognizable debris though I could see the festival dolls at the tip of the water's reach. They seemed to be dancing with the waves that stretched to receive them, pulled one by one gracefully and inevitably toward the sea, a movement that looked choreographed. They floated eerily toward the diminishing horizon, and I felt the pangs of jealousy stab at me. The sight made me yearn for my brother, who I expected would one day walk out of the water and find me.

With the scent of salt and oil in the air, I suddenly became aware of the figure of what I believed was a boy, standing as still as a statue along the water's edge. I rubbed my stinging eyes in disbelief.

He didn't seem to notice me, and I wondered at that moment if he were real. I quickly gathered my things and headed down through the brush toward the purring water, keeping my eyes glued to the motionless character the entire time—even after losing my footing on the sodden earth and scraping my elbow.

The boy, I was certain it was a boy, now, was standing just a few feet away from me staring out into the immeasurable ocean. He did not turn and yet I had a feeling he knew I was there. He was not wearing shoes. The thought made my heart constrict into a knot, one as deftly tight as a sailor's.

I kept quiet and continued searching the boy for a sign of the living. Those that visited me regularly always materialized in browns or black and white and the boy with his soggy and ragged clothes was no exception. He appeared without color as if he had just stepped out of one of my drawings, a picture of fatality. It was his hair that fascinated me. It was so blond that it was white and seemed to glow as if it was backlit by a sphere of light even though the sun hadn't broken through the sky for days. The boy finally turned, and I stared uncontrollably at his skin, which was so white it was like flour sifted into a graveyard seraph. He appeared metaphorically, as if he were a premonition of his own death, his beauty petrifying. With this white skin and hair, he reminded me of a burning candle, and I wanted to touch him to see if he was flesh and blood but I was afraid. Not frightened of death or the idea that he might be dead, but fearful that he would not be of the living, and I desperately needed him to be. At that moment, I felt my whole life depended on it.

I took a step closer then stopped in order to preserve that feeling of hope that radiated outward and filled me with a stinging sensation that tingled through the course of my limbs and caused me to fold into the wet sand. I was sure that it was the first thing I'd felt since the day Finn died and because I did not want this feeling to dissipate, I sat quietly for a long period of time before I stood and spoke.

"Are you hungry?" I asked. If he needed food, he must be of the living, and this is why I began with this question. It was the most important thing I'd ever asked.

When the boy turned to face me, I realized that the question of his hunger, this question of his existence was no longer relevant because his eyes were the only part of him not lacking color. In fact, they glowed with a glaucous waxy green that was so transparent it had the same forbidden energy as the phosphorescence I'd seen laced in the waves at night through my bedroom window.

Believing that he may not have registered my accent, I asked him again, slower this time. "Are...you...hungry?" I pointed to my mouth while rubbing my stomach.

He nodded and I dug in my bag for the bread slices my mother packed for me that morning. The air was cold and damp and the boy was not dressed properly for December weather yet I could feel the heat from his body when he took the bread. His skin was like an open flame. I was always cold and I attributed this to my close continuous contact with the dead.

The boy thanked me and accompanying this gratitude was a small spray of warm air emanating from the insides of his body, a gossamer-like fog that looked to be made of the same fiber found in the wing of an insect or a spider's web. It was as soft and sheer as lace.

"What's your name?" I asked him before he could finish swallowing the slice of bread.

He tilted his head slightly as if he didn't understand and I asked him again.

"Hoyt," he spoke softly. "My name is Hoyt." He said nothing else but he didn't need to. I had already heard it: the familiar lilt of the Celtic tongue.

"Where do you live?"

"Nowhere. I live nowhere," and when he said this, he looked out toward the ocean like it was a distant relative he had not seen in a while. I knew then that the boy whose Irish name meant *spirit* was a gift. My brother must have sent him to watch over me in his absence.

"You must live somewhere. Where's your family?"

"Dead, I guess. They're all dead," and he held up a large piece of broken wood with the words *Twin Sisters* branded into it. "This is all that's left of my home. I live nowhere, now."

He moved toward me in a paradoxical stride of inelegance and grace as if he were not at all comfortable maneuvering on something as resolute as land. As he walked, I could hear the sound of wings beating in the wind like sheets hung on a line to dry. When he was directly in front me, his pupils grew from small to large then back again as if he'd just been awakened by a bright light. He seemed both familiar and strange—a memory I'd never actually experienced or a dream I was not able to recall entirely.

We stood facing each other for a long time before I reached for his hand. It was like holding onto a hot coal. There was something about touching him that day made me want to live forever. It was at that moment that I changed inside, and I felt he was responsible for this feeling, this unsettling joy in the pit of my stomach. It was as intoxicating as the freshly printed pages of a new book. It took me in and I was swallowed by its immensity, its ability to suddenly remind me but also make me forget. In this elation, I had the urge to don a bright colored dress but I did not own any clothing of color, preferring the blacks and grays associated with those in constant mourning. Since Finn died, I'd lived in an air of despondency and solitude, doing only what was necessary to get from one moment of life to the next because this is what people from Ireland did. We carried on even if we didn't want to. "The Irish," my father told me, "have always been professional mourners."

I don't know how long we sat there on the sand listening to the water before the wind began to turn icy and the sky darken; my parents would be angry if I was late for dinner.

"I'll be back," I told him. "With food and blankets." But when I returned late that night with the stew of cabbage, roast beef and carrots and the wool blanket as promised, he was gone. It occurred to me then that I never even told him my name. I wouldn't see him again until months later, after the fire that made me an orphan.

When I spoke of the boy to my parents days afterward when Cape Perpetua filled with the news of the shipwreck, they believed that it had to be a mistake. "Are you certain, Una?" my father asked. I can't imagine that there could have been any survivors on a ship that was crushed by the rocks. Maybe the boy was playing a trick on you? A visiting relative of one of your classmates?"

"No Da. He was from the ocean. I could see it in his eyes."

Every day I looked for Hoyt, sometimes for hours in and around Heart's Cove. He had disappeared as quickly as he appeared, and I feared our paths would not cross again. I longed to feel the heat of his presence. That burning glow that exuded from his skin and warmed the cold that had settled inside of me since the death of my brother. It was the reason I first started with the matches. They were a misguided proxy: an attempt to feel what I knew was possible from a warmth I'd not known before. The flame allowed me to have control over something. I could make fire then extinguish it, a power I felt belonged only to the gods and goddesses of mythology. The more I created this magic, the more I craved it. I never once expected what I sought would kill my parents. And as I write this with these monstrous hands, their faces come to me, but much like Finn, their spirits do not, and I am left wondering if they, too, are angry with me.

Una Madigan
The Cape Perpetua Asylum for the Insane

The Patron Saint of Lost Things

I skipped lunch and left work early, the contents of the letter sitting in my stomach like a layer of spoiled milk. After poking around the downtown bookstore, I found myself in front of the five-story brick building on the corner of Castor and Pollux. I knew The Guardian well because it had been in the news so often over the last few years since funding was cut for the asylum and those who were supposedly unfit for society were suddenly a part of it. Some of the more fortunate ones were taken into places such as the Guardian; I tried not to let my mind wander to the whereabouts of the less fortunate.

There was a woman sitting on the sidewalk out front trying to make eye contact with passersby as if whatever she'd lost could be gained by their simple acknowledgement. Her profile—a narrow sharp nose and prominent chin reminded me of the legend of the Indian maiden whose face was a rock that grew up in sorrow out of the Pacific Ocean. She had lost her only love. I wondered if my profile warranted the same grief.

I crossed the street with the intention of hurrying inside but before I knew it, I was standing a few feet from the woman on the sidewalk who had in the time it took me to cross the street, discovered the butt of a cigarette someone had tossed on the ground. The man on the cell phone ignored her request for a light, and she tucked the cigarette into the pocket of her coat, a beige fake fur, which was matted like a worn stuffed animal. The coat was the kind a hip young person, one of those who are intrigued by the dead, might find potentially cool but very few others. My eyes casually inspected the rest of her attire which consisted of some type of sequined party dress from the Seventies, black tights and gray New Balance sneakers that were a few sizes too big. The woman looked like you would expect an unsound person to look, and I hated myself for thinking this. Of all people, I should have been more sensitive about this.

There were two old men, twins, sitting on the glider out front and between them, a tan wrinkled woman in a short copper-colored wig and coordinating eyebrows that looked like they might have been drawn on with a crayon by one of her grandchildren. Irritated, she kept swatting away the cigar smoke the old man beside her was choking out through a face that resembled a gargoyle. I couldn't tell if his eyes only appeared half-opened because he was so distended, or because he was simply dozing, an inflated doll with a short brown stogie wedged in his mouth like a cork. When it started to rain, I darted into the building, thankful that the door had been propped open with a broken cinder block, probably nabbed from the construction site across the street. Once inside the lobby, I was accosted by a wave of hot dry radiator heat that had managed to preserve the vinegary smell of its inhabitants.

I glanced around the room. There was a small desk near the

back but it was unoccupied. The entire place must have been run by a small thread of volunteers, none of whom were available today. There was a gaunt young man in a torn blazer tapping at the keys of the out-of-tune piano. He stopped to wipe his mouth with the sleeve of his jacket then resumed without noticing my interest.

When I refocused my attention I noticed an elderly lady staring vacantly but curiously at me. She sat in a high-back chair, the wings of the chair somehow making her seem parenthetical, a side note to actuality. Her eyes appeared wet as if they had just been poured into her sockets and did not yet have a chance to set. Except for her, nobody else seemed to care that I was there. It never occurred to me then that because I'd become so lost and empty over the last three months, they might have thought I lived among them.

I was anxious to find the woman who wrote the letter so I dug in my purse for the envelope I'd tucked there earlier, hoping her apartment number was listed, which it was just under her name in the top left corner. The envelope I noticed had a distinctive smell to it—a scent I knew but could not place. Smells had only recently started to affect me, and I immediately became nauseated at the first scent of dampness in the elevator. Relieved when the door finally opened, I stepped out quickly into the hallway, which was lined with dark gray carpet that obviously had not been cleaned in a while. A stale moldy odor permeated the air and I soon realized it was not the carpet but the lingering stench of fresh paint—a green I could describe only as medicinal had been applied to the walls in an attempt to cover the dirt and scuffs but I wasn't convinced; I knew that the renovations of any institution were generally a distraction.

Outside of apartment 237, I stood and waited. I knocked again then bent and slid one of my business cards under the door. I'd only taken a few steps when I heard the door open. I turned and headed back.

"Miss Madigan?" I didn't wait for an answer. "I'm Victoria Belmont. From the *Beacon.*" She remained quiet. "The newspaper." I stretched my arm out to greet her but she stood still in the shadow of the door, her intense blue eyes glowing like a nocturnal animal paralyzed by the light. Her appearance caught me off guard, a peculiar sort of beauty characterized by delicate features and fine white hair that reminded me of the angel we had as a tree topper when I was a girl. Her eyebrows however were dark, as were her lashes, further accentuating the iridescent blue of her eyes. We were close in height, but she was much thinner than I'd ever been. Her pore-less skin had few wrinkles, which in my opinion looked to be more the result of sorrow than age. She did not reach to take my hand; awkwardly, I dropped it. "I'm here about your letter."

"Oh." She smiled only slightly. "Come in. Sorry. I don't get many visitors." After closing the door, she guided me over to the chair next to the bed and in front of the curtain-less window. The rain had stopped and light filtered in through the broken slats in the blind, motes of dust dancing wildly in its stream. She casually swatted at them and then confessed to me that they gave her the urge to count.

I was a bit surprised to find that the room was filled with books. Great literature—things I had always planned to read but never made the time, all neatly organized in distinct piles. "Please. Sit." She grabbed a pile of books off the seat and set them on the window sill. "I like to read," she spoke in odd defense then sat on the bed, tucking her shoulder length hair behind her ear. "Would you like some coffee? It's instant. Or I have tea."

"Tea would be great."

"Is Lipton okay? It's all I have."

"Yes, fine. Thank you."

"I don't have any milk. Never developed much of a taste for it. We didn't get much of it at the asylum. Powdered, mostly. It was really lumpy and watery." She moved toward the tiny kitchenette, which was equipped with a small stainless steel sink, a miniature fridge and a hot plate that sat dangerously close to the edge of the counter in order for the cord to reach the outlet. The hotplate reminded me of a camping trip that Ben and I had taken a few months before he was deployed, and I placed my hand on my stomach, feeling sick at the memory.

"Miss Madigan. About the letter you wrote. I wanted to ask you a few questions if you don't mind."

"Lux. I like to be called Lux." She filled a tarnished pan with water then turned. "Have you come to help me find my sister?" There was little emotion in her voice. I suspected this might be because of meds or possibly from practicing this question over and over so that she had become deadened to its effect.

I didn't know how to answer her question. I was probably the most honest journalist in existence, but the reason for my visit had more to do with finding this woman's sister. "I would like to help you find your sister, yes. However, I need some more information from you."

The water began to boil and Lux removed it from the burner. She brought over two rather antique looking tea cups perched on matching saucers. One of the cups was chipped. When she placed the other on the small table beside me, I noticed the scar on the inside of her wrist, which I thought was a burn until I realized it was a series of numbers. A tattoo? I couldn't be sure. She would have been just an infant during WWII. I had come that day to hopefully find answers for my own selfish reasons and to think that this poor woman had managed to survive the Holocaust. How could I possibly feel good about myself if I continued to probe into her past life, drudge up old sorrows and who knows what else. It would only cause her more grief; maybe push her over the edge. She was, after all, a mental patient who couldn't have been very stable, though I would not have gathered this from her appearance.

"What kind of information?" She sat back on the bed and drew the chipped tea cup to her lips.

I pulled out my note pad and the Montblanc Meisterstuck pen Ben had given me for my birthday the year before. It was my favorite pen, the only one I carried with me at all times. Under the circumstances, I suddenly felt guilty using a German writing instrument to record my meeting with a Holocaust survivor even if she hadn't noticed. "Well, to start, I'd like to know the exact day your sister disappeared from the hospital—"

"Is that what they're calling it now? A hospital?"

I didn't know how to answer this respectively so I went on. "I also would like to know why you believe Dr. Warner had something to do with your sister's disappearance?"

She sat for a moment, sipped on her tea. "Do you believe in intuition, young woman?"

It would have been a lie to say I didn't since intuition is what brought me to the Guardian that day. "Yes, sometimes."

"Well, my heart tells me that Dr. Warner knows what happen to Nix—that's my sister's name—whether or not he had anything to do with it. He was—is—a man with many secrets. I know he's still alive. A woman at the library helped me check for his death records and there are none."

She sat in reflection for a moment then spoke again. "He was the last person to see my sister that day—our birthday. October 13th, 1969. He said he thought she may have escaped through one of the doors—the one with the broken buzzer."

"In your letter you mentioned that you and your sister are twins?"

She nodded. "Yes. We are. This isn't very good," she said as she set the cup and saucer in the window sill. "I'm out of sugar."

Only about 200 out of 3,000 twins survived the Holocaust. I jotted down the word *twins* next to the date of Nix's disappearance and then wrote *sugar* off to the side. I needed to stop by the store anyway to pick up a few things for my father.

"Do you have any idea why your sister would have run off—I mean, was Nix—"

"Crazy? That's what you want to ask me isn't it?"

Again I was caught off guard. "I didn't mean to offend you. I just need to know as much as possible in order to help you."

"Nix was diagnosed as a schizophrenic...but," she hesitated. "But that's not the reason she left. She was angry with me. I'd taken something of hers. And not that it matters now to anyone but she wasn't."

"So, both you and your sister were patients at the Cape Perpetua Asylum?" I chose my words carefully. "And you had a misunderstanding of some sort?"

She nodded. Her hands were now folded in her lap, her thumbs rubbing together.

"Did you ever contact the authorities about Nix's disappearance?"

She shook her head slowly and I realized how ridiculous a question I'd asked. What authority would believe a mental patient even if she had been able to contact them?

"Well, can I ask about your parents or how it was that you became patients of the hos—asylum?"

"Nix and I were brought from the orphanage to the asylum in 1965 because of the inheritance. We were fifteen."

"The inheritance?"

"Yes. What was bequeathed to us by our mother, Una."

"Forgive me. I don't quite follow."

"It had to do with eugenics. Do you know what that is?"

The mention of the word sent a shiver up my spine. Ben and I were huge opponents of the Eugenics Board. I'd written many articles demonstrating my opposition to the horrific idea that a movement so atrocious could not only gain popularity in the modern world but go on to inspire Nazi Germany. It was the state of Indiana I detested the most. They were the first to enact a sterilization law in 1907. By 1970, there were over 60,000 victims of sterilization. Suddenly, I felt ill.

"I do. So your mother was also a patient at the asylum?" My mind was racing with thoughts of the Bell vs. Buck Supreme Court Case, which upheld the eugenic sterilization of Carrie Buck, who'd given birth to an illegitimate daughter, Vivian, who was a product of rape. Both mother and daughter had proved to be highly intelligent, but by then it was too late for Carrie. She would not be able to have any more children.

"Yes, but she died before we were institutionalized there. Well, that's what we were told by Sister Madeline."

This made the numbers on Lux's wrist even more curious. Was she Catholic? They were the least persecuted during Hitler's campaign. "And when was that? Your mother's death? Do you know?"

"She died in 1960. I don't know what became of her afterward. I've always wondered." She smiled a sad sort of smile. It was painful and distant.

I felt that taste in my mouth, nausea working its way up the back of my throat. "May I use your restroom?"

She pointed toward one of two doors that were adjacent to

each other. I thanked her and pulled the bathroom door shut behind me, immediately turning on the faucet to mask the sound then dropping to my knees in front of the toilet. I lifted the seat and purged as quietly as possible, hoping that she had not heard. When I came out, she was sitting in the same place. She looked up at me with such sympathy—the kind that borders on empathy. As if she somehow knew. It made me a little uncomfortable. I picked up my note pad and shoved it in my bag. She stood. Her eyes were kind, yet lost, and when she thanked me, I could see they were damp.

"I'm sorry about the tea, Miss..."

"Victoria. It was just fine. Thank you." I walked toward the door and she followed. A discolored newspaper article about the liberation of Auschwitz was taped to the wall and again I wondered about the numbers on her wrist, which I could now see more clearly.

Next to the clipping was a Saint Anthony prayer card, held in place by a tack. The ditty I learned as a child came to mind: *Saint. Anthony, please look around; something is lost and must be found.* Oddly, some of the sympathy cards I'd received after Ben's death had this same prayer card enclosed. Most of the envelopes were still sealed because I could not bear the thought of losing Ben each time I read over words that were meant to comfort me but instead served as a reminder that what I'd lost could never be regained. I'd shoved the cards in a box, out of sight on the top shelf of my closet with the intention of tossing them in the fireplace. My mind was yanked from these thoughts when unexpectedly Lux recited the same little phrase I'd remembered from catechism, throwing my Holocaust idea out of perspective.

"Saint Anthony, please look around; something is lost and must be found. Peggy gave me that to me when she retired."

"Peggy?"

"She was a nurse at the asylum. A beauty queen once. Almost."

Uncertain how to respond to this, I nodded respectfully. "Thank you for the tea. I'll do what I can to help you find your sister."

She nodded then opened the door. "Wait," she called as I made my way down the hall toward the stairs. She cocked her head. "Do you hear that?"

I wasn't sure if she was referring to the TV blaring from one of the apartments or the woman's shrill voice climbing up the elevator shaft? "Hear what?"

"The baby. It's crying."

The elevator dinged opened, and as the tarnished silver doors were drawn back together like a pair of metallic curtains, I saw the distorted image of myself, blurred almost beyond recognition.

"No. I'm sorry. I don't," I responded uneasily then placed my hand on my stomach, wondering if this woman I'd just met somehow knew I was pregnant and planning on having an abortion.

Missing Pen, Missing Twin

My father's house sat in seclusion at the end of Morning Star Drive, a street that ended at what seemed like the end of the earth when I was a child. It was a modest Cape-Cod home, shingled in gray asbestos with lots of windows trimmed in white wood. My back yard overlooked the ocean and when my father would push me on the swing, I would pretend I was a bird, flying high above the rocks and waves. It's where I first spotted the face of the Indian maiden carved deftly into a large rock in the middle of the water. I'd asked my teacher at school about it and she was the first to tell me about the legend of the young Indian girl whose lover never came back for her so she sat waiting for him for so long that she turned to stone. I didn't know anything about love or have any idea that one day, the loss of mine would immobilize me in the same way.

I was an intuitive child, a loner who'd always felt something missing from her life. Our nearest neighbor was a half mile away so I learned to entertain myself. I remember feeling alone but never entirely by myself. My father always discouraged me from indulging in the arts for too long. When he noticed me painting or drawing, he would bring me the dictionary or an encyclopedia. He also frowned upon any make-believe friends, and it wasn't until later that I understood that this was probably because he had spent most of his life around people who talked to their imaginary friends.

He was a good father, and though he did not nurture my creative prowess, the nanny he hired to help care for me always kept me supplied in paper and paints without him having too much knowledge of it. But that was before I discovered the cello. Or maybe in actuality, it discovered me. I was only ten at the time. Miss Lillian had kept me at her house one weekend when my father was out of town. A storm had knocked the power out so we lit candles and told ghost stories. I wasn't a child who was easily frightened. I liked the idea that there could be a world beyond the one we knew. A world where my mother and much later my husband lived until the day I could come and join them.

It was when I used the candle to go get a glass of water that I saw her hovering near the cello case. The gossamer glow of light that looked to be made from the skin of a jellyfish, a milky iridescence in the shape of a human. She was moving so effortlessly, it seemed as if she was immersed in water. I walked towards her; I wasn't afraid. In fact, I was comforted, believing it was my mother. But when I was close enough to touch her, she vanished, and I was left standing next to the instrument that Miss Lillian said had once belonged to her grandmother who had played for the symphony. With permission I opened the case. It was like a coffin, the cello inside a body. I pulled it out. When I look back, there was no choice in the matter. Lillian and I were both surprised when I straddled the instrument and began to play a song that I didn't know I knew. Miss Lillian knew it well. She said that Billie Holiday sang her favorite version of that same song, and she hummed along, occasionally offering a word or two.

The sound the cello made was one that I imagined belonged to the world where my mother had gone. It was haunting and beautiful at the same time; the saddest sound I'd ever heard and yet mysterious and compelling. As I drug the bow across the strings, the cello told its own story, but instead of words, the notes lingered long after they'd been stroked like a ghost that had lost its way.

I set the grocery bag on the counter while I searched for a vase for the flowers, and when I found one in the cabinet under the sink, I filled it with water then arranged the lilacs. My father wasn't really a fan of flowers, and in his state he might not even notice them, but lilacs had been a part of me for as long as I could remember. As a girl, I could smell them even when they weren't in season, and this hypnotic scent lingered behind me like a lilac-scented shadow. I began to unpack the groceries.

"Janice?" I called.

"In here," her voice called softly from the back of the house. She was folding laundry in front of the muted television.

"No sound?"

"Not really necessary with the shows they broadcast today." She smiled. "Besides, your father has been too weak to speak so I have to listen for the bell."

"Has he eaten anything, today? I brought some soup and

pudding—vanilla, his favorite."

"I haven't been able to get him to eat since his soft boiled eggs this morning. Maybe you'll have better luck."

Nodding, I headed up the narrow staircase to my father's room.

"Hi Dad," I spoke quietly as I placed the flowers on the bureau. His skin was even more yellow than the last time I'd visited, so much that it seemed to cast the room in an eerie golden glow that when bounced off the green walls reminded me of an aquarium. The gurgling sound of the I.V. machine further established this. My father joked the last time I was here that he had no idea that this is what was meant by the Golden Years.

He had never displayed much of a sense of humor, and I always believed this was because a man in his position had to be taken seriously at all times.

He whispered my name before his eyes opened completely. "Torie. I've missed you." He closed them again but kept on talking. "How are you?"

He was the only person I allowed to call me Torie besides Ben. "Alright, I guess."

"Just alright?"

"Yeah. Shouldn't I be asking you that question?"

"Come sit by me. Can you stay a while? I've been thinking about you."

I moved over to his bed and sat next to him remembering a time not that long ago when there was barely room for me there. I set my purse on the floor then took his hand in mine. His jaundiced skin was hot, and I reached to touch his forehead. "You're burning up. Let me get you a cool rag." When I returned from the bathroom, I placed the cool cloth on his head. His eyes were closed.

"I'm sorry I didn't make it to your concert that year," he whispered in a voice that sounded as if his throat was full of broken glass.

"Concert? And what concert was that?"

"Seventh grade. You had a cello solo."

"Oh Dad. Why do you worry about such nonsense?" The truth was that when I looked out into the audience that day and didn't see him next to Miss Lillian, a hole formed in my heart, but it had healed and broken open many times since then that it was of no consequence. My father was not one to make apologies, and I wondered if he did so now because he knew he had little time left, in which I imagined that all the old ghosts come out. It has always been my belief that we all have them, but only some of us choose to see them. "Honestly, I wish you wouldn't waste your energy," I told him. "It was such a long time ago."

"I suppose," he breathed out.

"Do you want something to eat? I brought vanilla pudding."

He shook his head. "I'm not hungry."

I reached for his water and held the straw to his mouth then dug in the nightstand drawer for the Carmex and used my finger to rub it over his cracked lips.

I was hesitant to ask because my father never spoke of the asylum. The subject had always been completely off limits. When

I became a journalist, we had heated discussions about the Eugenics Movement, but he never once divulged any information about his days at the Cape Perpetua Asylum, which was a breeding ground for the study of Eugenics. It was like some secret society of Masons that couldn't be penetrated, and it really pissed me off.

I briefly glanced at the gold plaque hanging on the wall by the window. *The Lieber Prize for Schizophrenic Research presented to Dr. Warner by NARSAD,* an agency dedicated to mental health research. It was one of many awards my father had earned over the years.

"Do you know a woman by the name of Lux Madigan?" I asked him. "From the hospital," I added. He remained silent and for a minute I thought he had fallen back asleep. "Dad?"

"You know I don't like talking about that place." He started coughing and I wondered if it was meant to discourage me.

"I know. I haven't forgotten. It's just that I'd really like to know."

His illness must have softened him some. "Yes," he spoke acquiescently. "The woman you speak of was a patient of mine at one time. Why?"

"Well, she believes that you know what happened to her sister years ago. She wrote to the paper asking for help. She claims her twin sister, Nix, disappeared under your care back in..." I reached in my purse for my notes. "Nineteen sixty nine."

His breath was labored. "Lux Madigan. She and her sister were both patients of mine." Nix had a multiple personality disorder and Lux, she had nervous ticks and OCD. Obsessive—"

"Compulsive Disorder," I finished for him.

"Nix escaped from the asylum and was never found. I filed a police report to no avail. Lux never got over it. She would often pretend to be her sister."

"What do you mean? Role play?"

"I'm tired."

"I know. It's important."

He coughed. "Miss Madigan's unstable mind could not come to terms with the disappearance of her sister. They were twins, a cross between identical and mirror—one with light hair and pale characteristics, the other with dark hair and the same pale features. Among other things, they shared a room. After her sister escaped, Lux took to wearing a long black wig—some ungodly thing she must have found somewhere—and the clothes her sister left behind. She became much more unbalanced after her sister was gone. I took a short leave not too long afterward but I feared then that Lux would never be released. Regardless, I wouldn't take much stock in what she claims. Though not as unstable as her sister, she still has serious issues." His eyes remained closed.

I hesitated but finally spoke, not without thinking of my own mother who had been gone so long she seemed more like a myth. "Did you know the twins' mother," I glanced at my notes, "Una?"

His eyes snapped opened and in them I saw something I was sure was anguish, though I couldn't be positive since it was not an emotion my father had ever felt comfortable displaying. "Dad?"

He closed his eyes slowly as if it hurt to do so then drifted off but not peacefully, a furrow carved deep into his brow. I did not wake him again.

I laid in bed that night thinking I should just let it go. I had enough to occupy my mind without worrying about a woman I didn't even know, but even if she wasn't in her right mind there was something about her that evoked in me the kind of sympathy I knew I couldn't walk away from and still look at myself in the mirror. My reflection had always seemed so unfinished to me so I did my best to avoid it. But, I couldn't let this go. I wondered if I felt a certain connection with Lux because we both projected such an enormous aura of solitude? Or maybe I just felt guilty that because she had been a product of the Eugenics Movement, she didn't have a chance in the world, though it occurred to me not for the first time that we both had been raised by the same man. I dosed off thinking about the strange numbers on her wrist.

The next morning, after breakfast, which consisted of half of an English muffin, two sips of coffee and a swig of grapefruit juice, I headed for the library to do a little research on the Holocaust and also the Cape Perpetua Asylum. Normally, I would have used the *Beacon's* library to do my research, but I didn't want to take any chances with the letter I'd basically stolen from Tom Irwin. And if word were to somehow get back to my father that I was gathering research about the asylum...well, it wouldn't be good. There was someone I could ask. My brother Mike. He worked with Dad at the asylum for years. But, that was before they became estranged, and involving him just didn't seem like the right thing to do.

I'd brought my laptop to the library to take notes but I forgot to charge it beforehand so I dug in the oversized bag I called a purse for my pen and notebook. I panicked when I couldn't find the pen. I must have looked like a mad woman in my search, dumping out the contents of my purse on the table. It made an obnoxious noise, which warranted an irritated glare from Mary the librarian who had been at the library since I was a little girl. "Sorry," I mouthed and went back to searching, smacking at the pockets of my jacket to no avail.

After coming across a full-page obituary commemorating the life of the architect, Gray Lamb, who designed the state hospital along with quite a few other government buildings, I learned of the labyrinth of tunnels that connected the asylum to the penitentiary. At one time they allowed trains to pass back and forth carrying freight and supplies. The freight I assumed was patients and prisoners. The railroad and the tunnels had not been used in years. Both were closed in 1960, oddly the same year according to Lux that her mother died. I asked Mary to help me locate the newspaper records from that year. She suggested I start with microfiche since the library's database for news from that time might be limited.

"What exactly are you looking for, anyway?"

"Anything written about Cape Perpetua's Asylum, but mainly I'm interested in the underground tunnels. Have you ever heard of them before?"

"No, afraid not. The only thing really significant article I remember about the asylum was the poisoning accident."

"Poisoning? When did that occur?"

"Apparently, a patient working in the asylum kitchen confused rat poison with powdered milk. A real tragedy. Even some of the staff were affected and ended up dying. Let's see...I was just out of college. So about—and don't you dare tell anyone how old I am—the late Thirties. Why are you so interested in the asylum anyway?" she asked as she continued to feed the machine with microfiche. "Are you writing an article on it?"

"Not sure yet."

The machine clicked, a sound I heard it my sleep while in college and occasionally still, often interchanging it with the sound the doorknob made when Ben was trying to surprise me while home on leave.

"Here it is," she said.

Just then a group of children begin laughing loudly by the water fountain. They were taking turns spitting water at each other. "Excuse me, young people," Mary whispered loudly as she sternly marched off in their direction. "If you need anything else, just let me know," she told me over her shoulder then turned back to reprimand the kids.

"Thanks, Mary" I responded though by her strategic march toward the children, she couldn't have heard me. I focused my attention on the microfiche, scrolling the pages of the *Twin Beacon* for what seemed like forever until I found a small piece citing the closing of the underground system, dated June 1960:

Asylum Tunnels Close after Death of Inmate

The mysterious death of Jack Fairbanks, an inmate from the

Oregon State Penitentiary has prompted the closing of the underground system that connects the prison to the state mental hospital. The narrow gauge railway was used to transport supplies and, occasionally, prisoners and patients between the two institutions. A report by the Cape Perpetua Police Department has proved inconclusive though it is suspected that Fairbanks may have been hit and killed by one of the rail cars. Further details pending.

I searched all the way through to the end of 1960 and even into the first few months of the year following, but I couldn't find any more about the asylum or the inmate's death so I made a copy of the article then turned off the machine and put the microfiche behind the counter with a note of thanks to Mary.

In the car, my stomach was in knots over my pen. Had I last used it at home? I didn't remember doing so, but the way my mind had been lately, anything was possible. It could have fallen out of my purse when I stopped to see Dad. I'd call Janice as soon as I had a free moment. I felt like crying and throwing up at the same time. It was just a pen, but the most important pen I would ever own. Every time I caught a red light I began a frantic search under the seats and along the console of my Volvo wagon. It was said to be

one of the safest cars out there and I hoped this was true as I continued searching as I drove on.

I stood outside Lux's apartment, sipping a ginger ale, trying to swallow my nausea while contemplating whether I should knock or go home and look for my pen when the door opened and startled me. I choked.

"Hello," she greeted me solemnly.

I couldn't tell if she recognized me or not so I reintroduced myself. I twisted the cap back on the plastic bottle. "I came by yesterday," I replied after telling her my name. I motioned toward the paper bag I clutched in my grip. "I brought you something."

Her eyes lit up and I wondered if maybe she thought that the bag might have contained information regarding her sister. I felt guilty to have given her false hope. "Oh yes. The lady from the newspaper. I remember you," she spoke. "I was just about to take my walk." She held the door open for me then removed her worn wool coat. It was beige and wrinkled but very well made. She caught me staring, and I felt awkward. "People donate things," she said. "This was in the box downstairs. I chose it because I found a grocery list in the pocket, and...well, it made it seem more real, I suppose. Keats believed that without experience nothing could be considered real. This coat has what I believe to be, experience."

What she said made me think of my favorite childhood story, *The Velveteen Rabbit.* I didn't know this woman, but I suddenly felt an odd parallel between her and the rabbit. She had spent most of her life in an asylum where she was made to feel unreal—not part of society. Not loved. An outcast like the rabbit had been initially. But it wasn't experience that made the plush rabbit real. It was love. According to the Skin Horse, *it was painful sometimes but love made you real*—something Lux probably didn't have much familiarity with in her life.

I put the box containing the sugar cubes on the counter then dug in the bag for the assorted teas, which Lux immediately and curiously inspected when I handed her the black box with gold writing. "Oh, this is fancy tea," she said with excitement before a sudden worry took over her eyes. "I'm sorry. I don't have any money to pay for this."

"It's okay. It's a gift. Earl Grey is my favorite but the English Breakfast is also very good," I reassured her.

"The woman next door is from England."

"Oh, is she a friend of yours?"

"No. Not really. The walls in this building are very thin. I like her accent." She continued to study the tea box. "Let's try the Earl Grey." She put the water on to boil and I made my way over to the same chair I'd sat in the day before, casually taking in the surroundings, uncertain if I was in journalist mode or just incredibly curious about this woman's life.

"You sure do a lot of reading," I commented to break the silence as I continued to take in the room. Once again I was in utter awe over her collection of books.

"Among other things, it's something I believe I inherited from my mother," she spoke grimly. After a moment of uncomfortable silence she turned and smiled. "Would you like sugar?"

"No. Thank you. So your mother was a reader?"

"She was. A writer as well. I suppose stories are in the Irish blood." Lux continued wiping the counter, the same spot over and over, I noticed. She carried my cup over to me then went back for hers but not before wiping the counter once more. "Her father, my grandfather, owned a bookstore here years ago. I read about it in her journal. It was destroyed in the fire."

"Your mother's journal?"

"No. The bookstore."

"Oh. I see. My brother has a bookstore. In Spokane."

"I've never been to Spokane. I've never been anywhere, really." She sipped her tea. "This is good."

"I'm glad you like it." We sat in silence, and I tried to muster up the courage to ask her what was on my mind. "Your mother's journal? Did she leave it for you?"

Lux shook her head. "I found it. In the attic at the asylum. It was in a suitcase, but I don't think she wanted anyone to have it."

"Why do you say that?"

"Because it was hidden behind the lining."

Now I was more curious than ever. I waited for her to offer to let me read it, but she didn't so I tried a different approach. "Did your sister get the chance to read your mother's journal?"

"No. She didn't know I had it. I kept things from her," and with this her eyes swelled with tears so that they looked like glass beads. "I shouldn't have."

I reached in my purse for a tissue remembering my vow after Ben's death to invest in Kleenex stock. I handed her one then laid the small packet next to her on the bed where she sat.

"Do you know how bad it feels not to be able to apologize to someone?" she asked, a solitary tear slipping from her eye and rolling down her face until she caught it with the tissue.

The truth was that I *did* know how it felt not to be able to say sorry. I lived with this horrible feeling every day and at that very moment I wanted nothing more than to go to the bar, any bar, and get tanked, but because of my condition, this was impossible. I don't know why it mattered since...well, since I wasn't planning on having the baby, but it did. It just made it all seem even more unethical if that was possible. Not just socially immoral, but a type of immoral that my heart found unbearable. I didn't realize I had even needed one until Lux pulled a tissue from the pack and handed it to me.

"Thank you," I told her, blotting at my eyes and nose. "I just recently lost my husband."

"I'm so sorry," she said, and I could see the grief in her eyes, feel it in her touch as she reached and gave my hand a quick, tight squeeze. It was difficult believing that Lux Madigan was unstable. She seemed—not exactly normal—but not deranged either. The woman had been institutionalized for most of her life; I couldn't expect her to be normal, even though I didn't know exactly what defined normal. Was I normal wearing the charred pieces of my dead husband around my neck? My father, a man who supported genetic cleansing: Was he normal? A city of twins. Normal? Hardly.

Lux excused herself and walked into the bathroom, closing the door behind her. The ring of my cell phone startled me. It was Georgina checking on me and reminding me about a co-worker's birthday party that night. I, of course, had no interest in partying but I told her I would try and stop by anyway.

"Liar," she said. I loved her for this.

"Guilty as charged," I relented.

"Oh well, I guess I'll have to drink enough for both of us, then. See you tomorrow," she laughed then hung up.

The water in the bathroom was still running, and I took this opportunity to have a closer look around the room. After picking up a few books and flipping through them, I noticed a small trash can next to the closet door, which was opened slightly. It was an invitation I accepted. I peeked inside, being careful not to make any noise. Just then, Lux came out of the bathroom and I was forced into a lie, my eye twitching rapidly.

"I was just coming to check on you to make sure you were okay."

"I'm fine," she spoke. "But I think I need to lie down for awhile. I'm sorry. I tire very easily these days."

"It's okay," I reassured her as I walked over to collect my purse. "I'll come by another time. I'd like to talk to you more about your sister. And your mother."

She nodded then told me to wait. I watched her pull out a suitcase from under the bed and when she returned, she held a stack of papers gathered by a piece of string. She was hesitant; she took a deep breath. "These are my mother's writings. I've never shown them to anyone before. Maybe it's time I did. After all, she was the one that people held responsible for the curse."

"The curse? Are you referring to Cape Perpetua's twins?"

She nodded.

Though I hadn't heard it referred to as the *curse* in a while, I remembered how the students from high school were always taunted as more than three-quarters of them had a twin. I suddenly recalled hearing the Madigan name in passing in the halls. I didn't really believe in the ridiculous notion of a curse. There had been some speculation that the cargo of yams on board the *Twin Sisters* was to blame from the increase in twins but like everything else not capable of being proven, this was just a theory. Lux handed me the bound papers and I felt a slight reluctance in her release.

"You will be sure to return them?"

"Of course. I'll take very good care of them. I promise."

On the drive home, I carelessly plowed through a red light, thoughts of my missing pen continually being interrupted by the image of the long black wig I'd seen hanging in Lux's closet. Had she worn the wig because it made her feel real? Though it solidified what my father had told me about her instability, I knew it wouldn't keep me from her. I'd felt a strange connection with Lux Madigan the moment I'd met her. She'd lost something that made her feel complete and even though I'd had a good life, I'd always felt empty in a sense; as if something I should have had at birth was somehow mistakenly left out by my creator. I imagined one day, during some routine exam, the doctor would discover this missing part and I'd become a medical miracle in his amazement that I'd lived so long without it. Of course, my connection with Lux could have been because we harbored so much pain and guilt, but it also didn't escape me that we'd both been raised by the same doctor—something I did not want her to find out about. At least not right away.

As I pulled in the garage, I realized that the inside of my car had taken on the scent of the old papers Lux had given me. It was identical to that of the envelope she used to write the letter to the *Beacon*. I recognized it now. That smell. It was a mixture of vitamins, rubbing alcohol, and soap. And if it's possible, the scent of memories was also there, absorbed into the fiber. My father used to smell exactly the same way when he came home from work, and I found it curious that he was a lot like paper in the way that he became ingrained with the lives of others. It was their scents that I smelled on him and not his own. I suddenly had the desire to go through all of Ben's letters. He used to write me almost every day. Instead I stayed in the car in the garage and leafed through the pages that Una Madigan had written, while being a patient of my father's at the asylum.

The Curse

The gloves intimidate me. Normally they are given to St. Jerome's novitiates but since my hands were so scarred, I was issued a pair my first day at the orphanage where from the bureau they stared at me as if they were aware that they symbolized things I could no longer represent. A soft white cleanliness I could not imagine being a part of anymore. I began to have dreams where I was wearing nothing but the gloves and they were soiled with ashes and the blood of my parents who I could not rescue from the flames.

I had told no one that I was the one who started the fire. I'd been lighting my matches while sitting on the bed and suddenly the quilt became engulfed. I tried to subdue the flames but they spread so quickly, and I found it difficult to breathe. The bookstore was just below our apartment and I knew for certain if the fire reached it, the whole building would burn very quickly. I ran for the stairs but they glowed in flame and so I climbed out the window and dropped from the ladder to the ground. I didn't notice my ankle had been turned until later at the hospital when I woke alone in a room and was told by the nurse what had happened. Both my hands and my ankle were bandaged. Though I don't remember doing so, the nurse explained that I had tried to save my parents and that's how my hands were burned. And when I asked where they were, my parents, her eyes filled with tears and she slowly shook her head from side to side. Not yet a week later, in the first few days of February 1950, Sister Madeline from the orphanage came for me.

She was strict but kind as long as she was always shown respect. The orphanage was in a bit of turmoil when I arrived. Father Browning had died unexpectedly just a month before and Father Donovan had taken his place. My intuition told me that Sister Madeline didn't care much for him and only followed his orders out of respect. I had only been there a short time when the Sister caught me scolding Kate. At first, she did not seem too concerned when I told her about my sister occasionally visiting me but then one day as I helped out in the kitchen things changed.

Father Browning, a round happy man with a fatherly demeanor who had twice before came to me my first week at the orphanage, stood near the large drawer, which held the potatoes. He pointed so that I would know where to find them. When Sister Madeline asked how I knew where the potatoes were kept, I made the mistake of telling her that Father Browning had shown me. "We do not speak of the dead, in this way," she reprimanded, her hands firmly planted on my shoulders. I had no idea his appearance would make her so angry and yet she still did not tell Father Donovan about my visitors. Of course it was only a matter of time before he discovered on his own and this is the reason he said I had to be punished. It started out with bare-bottom spankings and progressed to weekly late-night visits to his private quarters. And all along, I felt because of what I had done that I somehow deserved it. He said that in order for my sins to be forgiven that our time together would have to remain secret. Not even Sister Madeline could know. I was so afraid of going to Hell that I went along with his inappropriate behavior until the time came that I would be punished for it as well.

I was no longer permitted to draw and my reading was limited to lives of the saints and Latin dictionaries. I didn't realize that I had a talent for the piano until I sat down one day and began to play. Sister Madeline enjoyed listening but became very concerned when she discovered that I had never had a lesson. Not one. She made me promise never to tell Father Donovan about my natural talent.

"Inherent gifts often frighten people, Una. If anyone asks, you most certainly had lessons before you came here. Understood?"

Was she asking me to lie? I didn't understand but I nodded anyway to be respectful.

Every chance I got I would sneak down to Heart's Cove and look for Holt who had miraculously survived the wreck of the *Twin Sisters* but had since disappeared. There was a secret path that led from the orphanage to the shore. It was just beyond the blackberry bushes, which were dense and made for an easy escape though not a painless one.

I'd begun to think that I'd imagined Hoyt. Maybe he really was one of my visitors who had deceived me into thinking he was of this world. But then one day, as I tossed rocks out into the sea foam, I saw him walking toward me on the shore. He was wet as if he had just come from the ocean. When he reached me, he put his warm hands firmly on my shoulders and whispered in my ear. "Everything will be okay, Una. Everything will be okay." I wondered if and how he knew about Father Donovan.

At my reluctance, Hoyt gently removed my gloves and closed his hands around mine like the petals of a flower protecting the bud within. Maybe because he didn't see the scars, I did not see them either when he released my hands from his. They looked as they did months before when we first met in the very same spot.

That day we laid together unclothed, our bodies pressed in union, and I was not shy over my nakedness. What I feared was that he would judge me because I was ruined. But if he knew, he said nothing. His skin was so hot that when I touched it with my cold fingers, little white marks developed on his body, quickly evaporating like prints on a frosty glass pane. I placed my head on his chest and traced the outline of his frame, allowing my hand to rest firmly on his hip bones then travel toward the stiffness between his legs. Our hearts tapped together in sync with the waves, and during that time I forgot who I was and what I'd done.

Hoyt waited for me daily at Heart's Cove. When my stomach began to grow, he did not fear it. He would put his head on my swollen belly and hum a song I grew to love. He said the captain played it all the time on the ship.

I knew something was wrong after my cycle stopped and I was concerned but not frightened. Sister Madeline of course could tell by looking at me that I was pregnant and when she questioned me, I told her about my secret meetings with Hoyt.

"Who is this Hoyt?" she asked scornfully. "Answer me." She shook my shoulders.

"He's from the *Twin Sisters,*" I told her. "The only survivor."

"Listen to me, young lady. There were no survivors from that ship," she said, a sharp look of fear in her eyes.

"I know. He's not of this world. He's different." I knew this would keep her from looking for him.

After our words, I was forbidden to leave the orphanage even for fresh air. I pictured Hoyt there on the shore waiting for me, and I was consumed by his despair. After the birth of my girls in October of 1950, I was taken immediately to the asylum where I remain today, still wondering if Hoyt is there by the cove awaiting my return. If I close my eyes I can smell the salt and oil of his skin.

It took me a while to understand exactly why I'd been brought to the Cape Perpetua Asylum for the Insane. I did not feel unsound yet I knew that because of my visitors, it might seem like I was, which is why I was hesitant to speak of them even though by doing so I felt somehow disrespectful. But from one of the other patients, I learned that the reason I was brought to the asylum is because as a fourteen-year-old mother I was deemed unfit for society. A moral degenerate. She knew this because she was there for the same reason. We had *undesirable* genes that would without a doubt be passed on to our children. I scoffed at this absurd notion, not sharing with this patient or anyone else for that matter who had truly fathered my twins. Many women at the asylum had stories similar to ours. We were sterilized to prevent any further contamination of society. It did not matter that some of us had been contaminated by it. None were told about the procedure beforehand and when I discovered what had been done to me unknowingly, I cried feverishly. What they took from me and the others was not theirs to take. They were thieves.

Father Donovan must have told Dr. Warner about my visitors and this is the reason he started treating me with chlorpromazine, which was intended for schizophrenics I later learned. I fell into a deep depression without my girls and this was referred to as hysteria, which required hours upon hours of water therapy. But I never once complained being wrapped in icy sheets or immersed in the frigid baths for long periods of time. I was used to being cold and truth be told, it was the thought of my girls that kept me sane from the torture of it all. I daydreamed that we would one day be together as a family but in my deepest heart, I knew this was just a dream. I broke down at the thought that I'd never even held my girls after giving them life.

One day a letter arrived from Sister Madeline, in which she explained to me that she had chosen the names Lux and Nix for my girls. I felt a little jealous over this but since the names were so incredibly appropriate, the feeling quickly subsided. As I studied the photographs she had enclosed along with the letter, it became perfectly clear why she had selected these particular names. They were completely opposite in appearance and yet both unimaginably beautiful. I hoped that one day they would show the world the balance that lay between them.

Sister Madeline said she would bring the girls to visit as soon as she could. By then they were already six years of age. It pained me that they did not recognize me, but how could they have? After many visits, they found their way next to me on the piano bench as I played and sang the song Hoyt used to hum to them while they were still in my womb, safe from the world. It was the song he'd last heard on the ship just before it met its fate. Not a day passed that I did not think of Hoyt. In my mind, he'd always be on the shore waiting for me to return.

The Sister came to visit me alone one day and brought disturbing news with her. She told me that many of Cape Perpetua's residents believed the ship that crashed into the cape cursed the city, which since the birth of my twins had now become infested with other twins. Sister Madeline said many of these twins were deformed and people blamed me for this. Said I was wicked. The Sister said there were malicious rumors about me spreading as rampantly as the yellow gorse flowers that graced the coastline and that because of this Father Donovan had forbade her to bring Lux and Nix to visit me anymore. When I asked her about the rumors, she said that people feared me and that I was nothing more than a Lilith, whose spawn belonged to Lucifer.

"And you?" I asked softly. "Do you fear the same?"

"I believe no such thing about you. As for the father of Lux and Nix, yes, I believe that yes, he might be evil." She lowered her eyes and it was then that I suspected she knew about Father Donovan but like me, she was helpless in the matter. "I will not keep your girls from you; however, I must be furtive. We can no longer visit weekly but I will do my best to bring them to you every month on the day Father Donovan conducts business away from the orphanage. Be well, Una. May God be with you, child." She made the sign and I followed though not without hesitance.

In November of 1959, not too long after my 23rd birthday, I got a new roommate. Alice was a few years older than me and extremely beautiful. I don't know what became of my last roommate but one of the nurses told me Linda would not be coming back. I later learned through talk among the patients that she had drowned in water therapy after being left unattended and suffering a seizure. This sort of thing was common at the asylum, which was often short staffed. I said a prayer for Linda and greeted my new roommate.

Alice was different than anyone I'd ever met. She was tall and thin and wore extravagant ball gowns and fancy jewelry that sparked under the green fluorescent lighting of our room. Patients weren't supposed to have possession of these sorts of things, but Alice put up a battle when they tried to take them from her, threatening to call her father about the funds they were receiving from him. I liked her even more after I'd heard she slapped old Nurse Foster, a wretched woman who I believed actually enjoyed subjecting patients to water therapy. Alice laughed when I told her she was the envy of the entire ward, me included.

A radiant red-haired beauty with skin that looked liked it had been borrowed from an expensive glass doll, my new roommate would dance around the room as gracefully as a sheer curtain blowing in an open window. She would take my hand and guide me along. And late at night, we would sneak into the community room and I would play the piano. Alice would sit on top of it in one of her gowns and pretend to be a lounge singer. Her infectious laugh filled the room and in turn made me laugh as well. Of course, when we were caught, we both had to endure various types of treatment that was meant to "tame us," Alice said. Her father, she told me, had sent her to the asylum for just that reason and as soon as her younger brother returned from his studies overseas, he would come for her. Alice said that her brother had no idea that their father had sent her away but that when he found out, he would be furious. I felt comfortable in telling her that I was also waiting for my brother.

"I will not be *tamed*, by their definitions of it," she told me sternly one day. "And when I leave this place, I'll be taking you with me." I believed she really meant this too—not because she was affluent or pretentious but because she was my friend. The only one I had.

Even though she had plenty of it, Alice didn't care about money. Other than the gold necklace she kept secured around her neck—refusing to remove it even for water therapy, Alice continually gave away her jewelry. Just a month after her arrival, she gave her favorite nurse, a young black woman by the name of Adele, a beautiful blue brooch after she commented to Alice that the pin was the most amazing thing she'd ever seen. Adele had polio as a child and she walked with a limp. Alice had always felt bad for her and when the nurse told her that she was not permitted such gifts, Alice assured her that nobody would ever know about it. She was good that way: kind, generous, funny and well-educated. Often she would rattle off sentences in other languages. French, Latin, Italian. And she was clever too. She'd hide her pills under her tongue and trick the staff into thinking she'd swallowed them. This became more difficult of course with the syrups we were occasionally given, but Alice always seemed to find a way. She couldn't escape the shock therapy treatment, however. None of us could. Not long after she started receiving it, small blue bruises developed on her forehead. I was familiar with these marks; many of the patients in our ward had them, myself included. They left little indents in the skin that reminded me of bruised fruit. Alice claimed they didn't bother her, but occasionally I would catch her staring in the mirror, trying to conceal them with the powder she kept in an antique silver compact, embellished with the scripted initials, A.E.M. With faint blue lines running just beneath the surface, Alice's skin was like finely pressed paper, and I remember finding this a bit ironic since I'd learned from one of the other patients that she was an heiress to the paper company her father had inherited from his own father.

I often wondered how long it would be before her smile was affected by the shock treatments and she started losing her back teeth. From my own experience, I never understood how shocking a person until their teeth loosened and fell out could be good for anyone. But those who questioned these methods only invited more sessions. On more than one occasion, I'd see a tooth on the floor in the hall and once when I was talking with a patient, a young quiet girl who stuttered when she spoke, one of her teeth loosened and she nearly choked to death. These type of occurrences were common but I refused to be numb to them.

Over the past few months, I'd begun to experience visitors like none I'd ever seen before. They terrified me with their blue lips and eyes that appeared to be filled with blood as they crawled across the floor and reached for me. There were so many of them I'd close my eyes and pray for them to leave but even this did not discourage them. They cried for help and one, a young woman dressed in white, a nurse's uniform with a nametag that read, Nurse Birch, tried to speak to me but when she opened her mouth, only vomit spewed out and it smelled like rotten eggs and maple syrup.

My sister Kate and my grandparents did not come to me during this time, and I worried that these new visitors had scared them off. At times, I'd wake up in a cold sweat in the middle of the night calling for Grandfather and in his place, Alice would comfort me.

"It's okay, Una. I'm right here," she'd tell me as she stroked my hair. I felt at ease speaking with her about my visitors; I even told her about the frightening ones and she never flinched. The last time Dr. Warner examined me, they came crawling across the floor towards me as I lay on the exam table as if they knew their presence would send me into a panic. I tried to push them away but they just would not go. I held my hands out to keep them back.

"Una. There is no one here in the room but Nurse Peggy and I," Dr. Warner spoke austerely. As he said this, he casually walked around me as if to prove to me that because he could not see them, I shouldn't either.

"They are here, Dr. Warner," I pleaded. "You must believe me." But I knew that he didn't. Perhaps he wanted to because we had grown closer over the years and it bothered him to see me in such distress. Only recently had he started referring to me by my first name. At one time, he was so cold and impassive that I feared he must certainly have hate towards me, but I wasn't sure now. When speaking to me as of late, he had a tenderness in his eyes. He almost looked repentant for his indifference towards me in the past. I think he wanted to believe me but his science mind would not allow him to do so. He became much more compassionate and often tried to comfort me when I had flashbacks of the fire.

Over time, I had changed too. In the beginning I spoke freely of my visitors because I didn't realize that the truth was so detrimental to my being. It didn't take long though to understand that the more I mentioned them, the more therapy and medication I received and the less I was liked by the doctor.

Maybe Dr. Warner felt that since I no longer talked to him about those who came to me that I had somehow been healed by the treatments he prescribed. In reality what these treatments taught me was how to keep secrets; how reality was not always the best solution. But this idea was not foreign to me. I grew up understanding that fiction was often much easier to accept.

"Peggy," the doctor ordered the nurse, a woman I had not seen before. She had a peculiar accent—not like any I'd ever heard before. "Prepare Miss Madigan for ECT."

"Wait!" I called. "They're real. She's real," I said adamantly, referring to Nurse Birch. "She wears one of the uniforms of the asylum. Her name is Birch. Edna Birch." With this announcement, Dr. Warner's brows grew together like a thick dark caterpillar and he began to stroke his chin with his thumb and forefinger. Then, Peggy quickly addressed him.

"Doctor. Edna Birch *was* a nurse here. She was accidentally poisoned when a patient helping in the kitchen confused rat poison with pancake—"

"I'm quite aware of this, Miss Gifford," he said reproachfully. "But I also know that people around here talk too much and that is most likely where Una heard the name—from one of the staff. Now, please ready the machine."

"Yes, Doctor." As she turned to leave, the nurse's eyes momentarily locked with mine, and I believe she realized that I was telling the truth. But what I couldn't distinguish was whether or not she was frightened or intrigued.

There was a way I could have convinced Dr. Warner that I was telling the truth, but I was not ready to disclose it to him yet for fear that he would become angered by what I had learned from his mother who came to me months ago with the slices in her wrists as fresh as the day she made them.

Una Madigan
The Cape Perpetua Asylum for the Insane
122

Bones

When I woke in the middle of the night, I was so cold my fingers were numb, my neck pinched and tingling from the headrest of the car where I'd fallen asleep. Every bone in my body ached. Una's journal lay on my lap, the interior car light creating a foggy golden glow that made everything around me seem like an old photograph. It would have been so much easier to finish out the night in the garage—not to have to go into the sarcophagus that life had hand delivered me, but I craved a hot bath and a cup of tea to calm my stomach so I gave in.

Immersed in the soapy water of the tub, I tried not to think of the water therapy my father advocated during his practice. Forcefully being submerged into icy baths for prolonged periods of time was not something I could imagine enduring. There was a more accurate name for this procedure now. Water torture. A form of military questioning that Ben refused to support. And yet, my father had somehow believed it was a cure-all for hysteria and schizophrenia. How was that possible?

I had never felt extremely close to my father as a young girl. As he aged, he seemed to have more time for me but by then, I had established the independence a young woman craves from an early age. I wondered if this independence is what kept me from wanting children now? Or was it because I felt that a child raised without a mother could never be a good mother herself? Was it fear of failure or just plain fear? At least I had a choice. Sterilization was mandatory at the asylum in the years my father worked there. Women were not given a choice about children. Thinking about this overwhelmed me with guilt. I couldn't make a decision right now to save my life, but at least I had a choice. Not a choice but *my* choice. *My* decision. The ultimate embodiment of independence and my right as a human being.

I crawled into bed with one of Ben's dirty tee-shirts and quickly fell asleep. I felt like I had only been asleep for ten minutes when the phone rang. It was 9:30 in the morning; I'd slept through the alarm again.

"Victoria? It's Tom."

I must have sounded groggy.

"Irwin. From the *Beacon*," he spoke louder and slower.

"Hi Tom. Is everything okay?" I could count on one hand, two fingers really, the times Tom Irwin had called me at home. I sat up, immediately.

"Normally, I wouldn't ask you—especially not now, but I need you to head down to the old state hospital. Doug and Martin are out on assignment and Laura's out sick."

"What's going on?"

"Well, early this morning, a demolition crew found human bones beneath the fountain. I was hoping you could get down there and see what's going on. I know it's not your beat, and like I said, I'm sorry I have to rely on you but I'm in a pinch." His rambling voice carried that tone that let me know that because I was a grieving widow, I was his absolute last choice. He'd probably asked the janitor of the building just before calling me.

"I'm on my way."

Fallen Angels

The angels were silhouetted against the orange glow of the sky and in the minutes before I realized where I was, I believed to be caught in the midst of some type of apocalyptic dream, one in which I was awakened from with the ring of the Angelus bells from St. Anne's across town, alerting me that it was six in the morning. How long had I been sitting there on the edge of the fountain in front of the asylum? I could not recall the steps I'd taken to get here or even remember getting out of bed. I'd lost time again. Where did it all go, this time that disappeared? Was it really just gone forever or was my mind storing it so that one day it would be flooded with memories that would destroy me with their weight? I wasn't sure if it was this thought that made me shiver or the coolness of the morning air.

After peeking inside my coat to find that I was still in my sleeping gown, I looked down at my feet, to my mismatched shoes. One dark brown oxford, untied and one black Mary Jane with a tarnished buckle. My socks if they were not a pair at least appeared similar, ivory and wool, a cable knit stretching nearly to my knees.

It's when I reached to tie my shoe that I saw it. A little glint of gold that caught the morning sun. It glittered like I imagined the skin of angels might do, and I leaned forward in curiosity. I used my fingers to extricate it from the soil where it was embedded, then held the necklace close to examine the long red hairs tangled in its chain. I thought immediately of a mermaid, a selkie, my mother would have said. There was something very familiar about the tiny gold heart. I'd seen it before somewhere. Uneasiness settled over me like a light layer of dust, and I closed my eyes. Just then I was startled by the sound of slamming doors from the trucks pulling up just outside the gate. I'd been warned in the past not to be on the property and when I saw several men in yellow hats approaching, I got up from the fountain and quickly ran to the first open door I could find without any rational consideration as to where it would lead me. Before I realized it, I was inside the asylum—a place that caused me such pain I feared I would collapse right there on the spot. Fear had brought me inside and now it kept me from breathing or moving. Outside, the voices of the men surrounded the door.

In my coat pocket, I instinctively fingered the necklace I'd found as if it were a rosary. I counted the decades of imaginary beads to try and calm myself. My caseworker usually brought my medications by the Guardian but I had not seen her in over a month so I did my best to control my urge to count, which seemed more imperative when I was nervous or scared. It was a mystery even a rosary could not placate.

Unlike my sister and mother, I did not possess the ability to see a ghost; though, as I stood there in the hallway of the asylum with its damp fetid odor I knew exactly what it felt like to be one.

It occurred to me then that I was not haunted by the asylum as much as it was haunted by me and by those who would in some way always be trapped inside its walls. And maybe this is why as I stood in the vestibule, it was as if I had stepped inside a catacomb that with the exception of a few stray pieces of old, dysfunctional furniture, appeared to be abandoned. The leaky roof had rusted parts of the threadbare carpeting—so much that I could see stains surrounding the impressions from where the furniture was once positioned. The dampness of the building gave it a human characteristic as if water had settled in the bones of someone who was arthritic and no longer mobile.

After taking a few steps forward, I stooped to examine the skeleton of a small bird, embedded into the moldy carpet. It looked like a finch or something of that same delicate frame. Nix would have picked it up and buried it, or kept it, but she was much better with the dead than I. She had amassed quite a collection of small bones and insect wings she stored in a shoebox under her bed.

I startled when I heard a shrill behind me. It was accompanied by the frantic flapping of wings that reminded me of a flag waving in the wind, and only then did I realize that this section of the hospital was not totally void of life. Two starlings darted from the exposed rafters and as they brushed past me, the stale air stirred by their wings caught in my throat. Their cries were human-like and haunting. In the newspaper I'd read a story on how the starlings had taken over the old crematorium chimney, giving life to something that had become a symbol for death and indignity. I imagined each bird carrying a spirit from the chimney away from this place to the Cloud Cuckoo Land, a city in the clouds where Aristophanes believed everything was perfect. But he was a dreamer.

Without realizing I'd done so, I found myself in the hallway that led to the room I once shared with my sister. As I slowly moved forward, I began to count the squares on the floor. Twenty five would bring me just outside the door. I remembered this. *One. Two. Three, four, five, six. Seven...*and as I passed the hall that led to the examination room where most of the procedures took place, I again heard the screech of the starlings. It halted my numbers. Once my counting was interrupted, I would have to go back and start again. The sound grew louder, more intense and only as I reached to cover my ears did I realize that it was not the birds I heard but an infant. Crying. How was it possible? A child here? Inside the asylum? Why, who would bring a baby here? To this place. But as quickly as it started, the crying stopped, and I stood with my hands over my ears afraid to take another step. When I gained the courage to finally drop my hands, I startled at the voice behind me.

"Ma'am, you really shouldn't be in here," a man dressed in blue cautioned me. He had a large ring of keys on his belt and a box of light bulbs in his hand. "It's not safe."

"I'm...sorry. I—"

"How'd you get in here, anyway?"

"The door was unlocked." I paused. "I...was looking for someone." I began to twist the button on my coat like a knob on a radio.

"Well, the main entrance has been moved to the other side of the building, but I have to warn you, it's a maximum security level and you won't be able to get in without special clearance. We only keep the criminally insane here now. One ward. The rest have been placed in other homes. Who is it you're looking for? Maybe I can help."

I stumbled over my words, and I'm sure he must have gathered that I was lying, but he was polite and gave me no indication. "I was trying to find an employee by the name of Peggy. A nurse. She was a friend of mine." The button fell from the coat, and I heard it hit the ground and roll like a coin. Without losing eye contact with the man before me, I knelt and started patting the floor around me like a person with limited sight.

"I don't believe I know of any Peggy, ma'am. It's over there," he said as he pointed to the floor near an old broken chair. "Your button. Ya see it? Over there."

"Oh, yes." I moved a few steps sideways and squatted to pick up the button, my eyes still focused on the man before me. If he noticed my mismatched shoes, he pretended not to.

"You could ask at the front desk, but you might want to call first. It can be kind of hectic in there sometimes, if you know what I mean."

"Oh, sure. I'll do that. Thanks again. Sorry for the intrusion." I headed back the way I came through the doors by the angels.

"Good luck. You can go out the door at the end of the hall. I just unbolted it for the construction crew."

He pointed to the door at the other end of the hall—the same door Nix had escaped from on the night she disappeared. He couldn't possibly expect me to leave the same way. The fingers of light that crawled underneath taunted me; I couldn't bring myself to move. The man stood behind me, patiently waiting for me to begin my exit.

"Ma'am? You alright?"

"Yes. Fine. It's just that, well, I came through those doors over there...by the fountain."

Well, they're blocked now, ma'am. They have it roped off out there in preparation for the demolition of the area just outside. You see, this building is going to be razed in a few months. Don't worry, that door down there will let you out near the fountain, just not directly beside it like the door you entered through. You'll see the front gate to your left."

Except for my breathing, which quickened so that I felt as if I was hyperventilating, I remained still.

"Are you sure you're alright? Do you want me to show you?"

"Oh, no. That won't be necessary," I choked over my shoulder as I willed my legs to move. "Thank you." I began to wring my hands in front of me as if they were made of terrycloth; something I had perfected in this same building. It had been my fault. My sister leaving like she did. There was no doubt in my mind, even then. I had broken Nix's heart and I hated myself for it. But there was something else—.

The starlings seemed suddenly angry at this end of the

building. It was as if they somehow felt my apprehension as I edged toward the doors. *One, two...three.* Even if by some miracle, Nix appeared right now, how could I ever expect her to forgive me when after thirty years, I could not forgive myself?

He was still watching. The man in blue. I could feel his concerned eyes, heavy upon my back as if I'd been cloaked in some kind of thick cloth. I took a deep breath and continued. *Four, five, six, seven, eight...nine.* I hurried through the door, swiftly making my way left toward the entrance gate trying only to concentrate on my numbers, but the grounds were full of men with big hammers and loud voices. It was so noisy, I couldn't think. I couldn't count. Then I saw the angels in the fountain move forward. At first I thought my eyes were tricking me but it was no trick. The stone seraphim both tumbled slowly and gracefully toward the ground as if their maker had purposely adjusted time to prevent them from being injured and in that split second I wondered if he had intended to do the same for me with all the time I'd lost over the years. The sight of their fall caused such a pinch in my heart that I screamed out. But, I heard nothing. The air around me was silenced, and everything—the men, the angels, the leaves floating from the trees—moved in a motion so slow it appeared as if the world before me was submerged in water. A quiet cold water that left no room for sound. My knees buckled and when I hit the ground, my eyes locked into the desperate stone stare of one of the angels. She had broken apart from her sister and now lay immobilized before me.

Maternal Instincts

There were two police cars, an unmarked van and, oddly, an ambulance in front of the asylum when I arrived. Through the double iron gates, I saw the massive stone angels broken into pieces on the ground, and off to the side a small circle of men surrounding someone or something I couldn't distinguish. To the right, I saw Joe Larsen and a few other familiar faces from the police department. They were gathered around the center of the fountain and when Joe spotted me, he waved me over.

"Victoria. Long time no see. How are you?" He addressed me, politely and professionally but not in a way that anyone listening could deny the longing in his voice, a certain nostalgic pull that called him to another time. He had not and would probably never forget that we had once been intimate. Our relationship had ended on a sour note years before, but I never took the time to think about why anymore. When people asked, though no one had in a long time, I'd always tell them the same thing. We were too young to be that serious.

"Good to see you, Captain Larsen," I answered playfully. Joe and I had gone to high school together. We dated for two years though I couldn't remember at that moment if it was during my sophomore and junior year or my junior and senior year. He'd broken up with me, and I'd blocked most if not all of that year out. Joe was a big man but had kept the soft features of his boyhood, the intense blue eyes and wispy blond curls of a giant Danish cherub. He had turned down a football scholarship to become a part of the Cape Perpetua Police Department. It was big news at the time. His father and grandfather had mapped out this road for the Larsen boys, though Joe's oldest brother had been killed in a traffic accident his first week of duty. I realized only then as I saw how he looked at me that his heart had never healed. It would have been arrogant to think it was because of me that he emanated with such sadness so I chose to believe his brother was to blame. Or it could have been something that was not as easy to identify—not one separate event but many continuous events. His misguided football career, his ailing mother, and/or his widowed ex girlfriend, which no doubt made him question why I chose Ben and not him. Perhaps it was life that had broken his heart. Whatever it was, I felt he must have noticed the same thing in me.

"I'm sorry that I haven't been in touch, sooner. About Ben, I mean. I—"

"It's okay. Really," I interrupted then quickly moved around behind him to have a closer look. "What do you have here?"

"Well, the fountain was scheduled to come down today—you know Larry Hutch, right? Hutch Construction?"

I nodded; we'd graduated with his sister. "There's really not much left to demolish," I said looking at the angels before me on the ground.

"Yeah, the rain and snow have seen to that. Anyhow, Larry and his crew arrived early this morning and started right in with God's girls there. When they finally came down, they brought with them part of the concrete basin and inadvertently a big patch of the ground." He pointed to an area that had been sectioned off by white dividers where two investigators hovered taking notes and photos and another—most likely, the osteologist continued digging around in the dirt. "They halted demolition when they saw finger bones. At first they thought it was a joke, a prank left over from last Halloween, but when they moved around some of the soil and saw the skull they called us."

"Any idea of who it is?"

"No, but it's definitely a woman."

"Why do you say that?"

With his head, Joe coaxed me over in the direction of the discovery. "Didn't take a genius or even a CSI expert. Have a look."

I peered into the sunken patch of ground at the bones that with the team's careful excavation had exposed most of the skeleton, which they were preparing to box up and transfer to the lab. My stomach let me know right away that I was not prepared. The woman was on her side, in the same fetal position as the skeleton of the child cradled in her womb. I clutched my own child with a pain I didn't know existed then turned away from Joe and vomited.

"Oh, Victoria. I'm so sorry. How insensitive of me." I sensed a little facetiousness in his voice. Did he know I was pregnant?

How? But when I looked at his face, I knew Joe Larsen didn't have a malicious bone in his very big body. He dug in his pocket, pulled out a hanky and began to gently dab at my mouth. No, Joe Larsen's heart was the size of a wheelbarrow.

"I'm the one who should be apologizing. Did I get your shoes?"

"No."

But I could see that I had. "I should go clean up. Will you call me when and if you find out anything? Irwin personally asked me to look into this."

"It might be a few days, but I'll let you know as soon as I hear anything. I'm really sorry about—"

"It's alright, Joe. Thanks." I turned, still horrified by what had happened yet relieved that it had been Joe and not one of the others who would no doubt joke about it the rest of the week. As I walked past the angels, I caught sight of the crew still huddled around what I could now see was a person. I called back to Joe whose eyes had never left me—I could feel them. "What's going on over there?"

"Unrelated. Some woman coming out of the hospital took a tumble. She's alright, I guess. Just a few minor scrapes. She seems a little confused but other than that..." He shrugged.

Most of the building was off limits to the public. I wondered why and how this woman managed to get inside the building. As I looked closer, I could see now that the woman was Lux. She was being helped to a standing position by the paramedics who each had an arm. She looked disoriented. I noticed then she was wearing a nightgown under her open coat and two completely different shoes. "Oh. I think I know her," I said, forgetting my embarrassment and quickly walking in the direction of the group.

"Lux? Are you okay? What happened?" It took her a minute to register my face. She seemed to be in some strange trance.

"I don't know. I fell, I guess."

"Are you hurt?"

One of the paramedics spoke up when Lux didn't answer. "She appears to be fine. No apparent broken bones. She does have an irregular heartbeat, but that could just be the excitement from the fall. Still we'd like to have her examined at the hospital just to make sure."

"No." She spoke adamantly. "No hospital. I just want to go home. Please."

"I'll take her home," I told the paramedic who had filled me in. "If she changes her mind, or I notice anything that needs attention, I'll bring her down."

In the car, Lux was quiet when I asked her why she was at the asylum that morning. I was even more curious why she'd been inside though I was hesitant to inquire.

"I go there because it makes me feel close to my sister," she finally said. "I wait by the angels—Nix was very fond of them—in anticipation that one day she will be there. Now that they are gone I..." Her thoughts trailed off momentarily then she spoke again. "I know it seems odd that I should want to return to that place—you must think that I am more unstable than I appear—but it was my home for so long and..." She looked over at me then quickly away.

"What is it, Lux?" Her eyes found me again and I could see that they were fearful. I didn't feel that she was necessarily afraid of me but perhaps frightened of what I might think. I reached across and placed my hand over hers to try and comfort her. Our hands were very similar; thin fingers nearly the same length. I half expected her to move away but instead she looked down at what I'd done and a slight ease fell over her face.

"Sometimes I'm brought to the asylum against my will."

"What do you mean?" I asked gingerly not wanting her to think I was in any way assessing her mental faculties.

"Well, it's like I don't have a choice in the matter." She hesitated, took a deep breath then went on. "You see, I can't always recall all the hours in a day and on more than one occasion I've opened my eyes and found myself, just as I did today, there. By the angels." She looked wistfully over her shoulder in the direction of the asylum. "But today was the first day I've been inside since I was released. The thought of going back inside has always terrified me. I know it sounds strange, but I feel that the only way Nix will return is if I go inside and release her—not the physical her—I know she is not actually there in body form anymore, but the memories of her for it's these memories that bind us both to that place. They will not let us leave." She looked at me as if she was the one assessing my mental faculties. "This may not make sense to you but what I've come to realize is that my sister cannot forgive me until I have forgiven myself. Until then, I don't think she will be coming back."

During our first meeting, Lux had told me that she had taken

138

something from her sister. Whatever it was, it had obviously left her consumed by guilt. Wasn't there a way she could give this thing back to her sister back should she ever return? But then the reporter in me kicked in, that small light in the corner of my mind lit mainly by reality. The chances of Nix Madigan ever returning were pretty slim. I knew this even when I first read the letter. It had been too long. She had either gone on with her life in an effort to forget about what and who she'd left behind or she simply wasn't able to return because she was incapacitated or quite and most possibly, dead. But I couldn't share with Lux my feelings on this because a big part of me—the part that wasn't rational—the part that believed in destiny and sleeping girls who could be awakened by a magic kiss wanted to believe that her sister could one day return. There was still that spark of hope as slight as it was that Nix was alive and staying away for reasons I was unaware of. Maybe Lux was correct in assuming my father knew more than he was letting on. As much as I didn't want to believe this, it was very likely. Something about Nix's disappearance had not settled with me right from the beginning.

I walked Lux up to her apartment, making sure she had not changed her mind about the hospital and that if for some reason, even if it was in the middle of the night, she found herself in delayed pain to call me and I'd come and take her. Before she went inside, Lux made a gesture toward me and for a minute I thought she was going to embrace me. Instead she took my hand in hers, looked me directly into the eyes and thanked me. It was only then that I realized that she might have felt the same peculiar connection with me as I had with her. Apparently, sorrow created an unspoken but prevalent camaraderie and we were joined by the invisible and viscous threads of grief.

Because I was anxious to begin working on the identity of the woman discovered earlier, I grabbed a sandwich from the deli and took it back to my desk at the *Beacon*. Tom would no doubt want an update, but since he was not at his desk, I typed up my findings in a small paragraph with indication that the story was still unfolding and there would be more information following. I left no room for a photograph though the image of the mother and child skeletons, a morbid set of nesting dolls, had been ingrained in the emulsion of my mind and would probably not be leaving for a while, if ever. Who was this woman and how had she and her unborn infant ended up under the fountain? How had she not been reported missing—unless. I stopped myself. The asylum couldn't have been so careless with its patients. Or could it have been? It had already crossed my mind that the female skeleton might belong to Nix Madigan. The thought of relaying this information to Lux sent chills up and down my arms. Not only would I have to tell her that we found her sister but also that she was pregnant at the time of her death. Was it possible that Lux already knew this and just didn't to tell me? Maybe my father wasn't the only one with secrets.

Later that afternoon, I pulled Joe's card from my desk drawer and gave him a call.

"Joe Larsen," he answered austerely.

"Hey Joe. It's Victoria."

He was silent.

"Belmont."

His voice softened. "I know. Feeling better?"

"My stomach is. My ego…not so much. I know it's early but I was wondering if you'd heard anything back from the lab?"

"Not much. I can tell you the victim was a pregnant female, which you are already aware of. Mid to late twenties, blunt head trauma. We're sending out for dental records but it could take a while. We've hit—excuse the pun—a dead end in finding her dentist. And apparently whatever crushed her skull knocked out quite a few of her teeth and damaged the jawbone so even if we are lucky enough to find the records…"

"Do you think she was murdered?"

"Well, I can't say for sure but it's looking that way."

"How far along was she?" Again, I felt the need to place a hand over my stomach to protect what was growing inside despite the fact that less than a week ago I'd planned on destroying it. The swell was bigger, more rounded. My time was running out. I had to make a decision whether or not I wanted to be a mother. Whether I could be a mother.

"About six months give or take a few weeks. We're checking our missing persons' archives but since we really don't know how long she's been lying there, that will take some time, too. I'm looking at the years before nineteen sixty since she would have had to have been there before the fountain was put in. In fact, it's good that you called. I was wondering if you might be able to help me out?"

"Me?" I asked surprised.

"I need to get a hold of the state hospital records, specifically those before nineteen sixty, which apparently have been stored off site. Do you have any idea where?"

"No, but I'll find out and call you back."

"Much appreciated. My home number is still the same, you know. I mean, in case you can't reach me here or on my cell."

I didn't know how to respond to this so instead I blurted out a question that had been on my mind since I'd spoken to my father about the Madigans. It was a question I had not intended to ask for fear of implicating my father, but it came out in an unexpected and somewhat relieving breath.

"Joe, this is totally isolated but would it be possible to find out if a missing person's report was filed on a patient who disappeared from the Cape Perpetua Asylum in nineteen-sixty-nine?"

"Sure. I can look into it. You want to tell me why you're inquiring?"

"Not really. I mean...Not yet, anyway. It's just an instinct for now."

"Okay. No problem. Give me till tomorrow. I'll do what I can. What's the name?"

"Nix Madigan. N-I-X. M-A-D-I-G-A-N." I could hear him scratching the name onto paper with a pencil. As long as I had known Joe, he had always written in pencil, and I believed it was because he was afraid of commitment, but now I wondered if it was simply because it was a way for him to change the past. Go back and erase the things that he felt were unfair. "Thanks, Joe."

"You got it."

What I soon discovered about the Cape Perpetua Asylum records is that they indeed had been moved to a storage facility but because of HIPAA, the privacy act, which was passed in the mid-nineties, I would need permission to access them. The records were actually in the process of being transferred to a database, which was great news, but the woman at the office in charge of the transfer made it clear that even so, I would need the written consent of each patient.

Each patient, I thought. Impossible. "What if the patient is deceased?" I asked her.

"HIPAA applies even after death. You would have to be the executor or hold power of attorney to access the individual's records," she explained.

"I see. I'm actually doing some research for Dr. Warner who's bedridden right now. He was at the hospital for over thirty years. Because he is incapacitated, he has given me temporary power of attorney. Would that apply in this case?" I could feel my eye twitching, something that happened when I lied. Thankfully, this wasn't detectable through the phone lines though I wondered if she could hear it in my voice. I tried to comfort myself with the idea that it wasn't all a lie. I truly was Dr. Warner's executor but that's where it ended.

"Yes. That will suffice. Just bring a state-issued ID and the proper documentation with you to our office. The POA must be signed and you have to make an appointment. Do you know where we're at downtown?"

I wrote down Gemini and Venus, the intersection where *Bridewell, Turner,* and *Associates* was located; the first available appointment wasn't until the following day. The pen I'd plucked from my collection of cheap plastic Bics reminded me that I still had not found my Montblanc, and I pushed the thought from my mind, knowing damn well that in my current state, I could start crying or puking at any minute—two things I would like to keep my coworkers from witnessing as either would only fuel already established sympathies and quite possibly foster other speculations regarding what I was still referring to as my *condition.*

On the way out, I learned from Barb at the front desk that Randall Moss, the owner of the *Twin Beacon* had been hospitalized. "Another heart attack," she said, shaking her head slowly. "Doesn't look good. Irwin's been at the hospital all day. Their son Jacob is flying in tonight." Barb raised her eyebrows and twisted the corner of her mouth slightly, which enlightened me to the fact that she was aware of the rumors about the elusive son being incredibly handsome.

Jacob lived abroad somewhere—Paris or England and visited infrequently. In all my time at the paper I had only seen him once during my first week. We'd taken the elevator up or was it down? He smiled and nodded toward me but never said a word. I wasn't even sure who he was at the time. He was dressed in a worn pair of jeans and simple cotton t-shirt. We weren't alone. The entire graphics department—all women at the time—had been standing behind us, their dreamy eyes I could see in the shiny interior surface, focused on the man next to me who either did a marvelous job of pretending he didn't notice or was just that modest about his good looks. He'd been the talk of the lounge for the entire month following his departure. I'd heard that he and his father were not that close and this had stayed with me most likely because it reminded me of my own father and brother. Sooner or later, I was going to have to call Mike about Dad.

That night after stopping in to check on my father, who slept peacefully through my visit, I went home, opened the windows and curled up in bed with Una Madigan's journal.

The Truth about Secrets

The hours following a shock treatment are often debilitating and require a great deal of bed rest at least for me anyway. It seemed as if each time, I was pulled further into a hole that I feared one day I would not awaken from. Alice was by my side each time I opened my eyes or got up to use the toilet. During this time, I seemed to be in some strange trance as I was not entirely unconscious, hearing the rain outside and conversations in the hallway. It was like being only half alive and I wondered if in death I would always only feel half dead. Would I come back and visit those like my daughter, Nix, who had the ability to see beyond life? I hoped not. I wanted to be whole in life and whole in death as well. I did not want to be half of anything. It sounded too painful.

One morning the day following a treatment, with the sun beaming through the windows and warming my face, I awoke to an empty room; Alice was nowhere in sight. It was about the time breakfast was usually served in the large noisy cafeteria and I assumed, though she despised the weak decaffeinated coffee, that Alice must have went to eat.

I washed my face and dressed in the clean frock I found folded on the chair. One of the nurses must have placed it there for me and I wondered if it was the new nurse, the one with the strange accent, who'd done so. I vaguely remember her checking on me more than once during the course of the night.

"Oh honey, don't wear that drab thing," I heard Alice's voice behind me. "The state needs to invest in a new designer. Put on one of my dresses. We have to celebrate." She was wearing a floor-length green gown made of a silky thin material. The hemline was loose and soiled with what looked like mud. She took me in her arms and we began to glide around the room, twirling so much I felt dizzied from the rush. I plopped myself down on the bed.

"Celebrate? What are we celebrating?"

"You can keep a secret, right?" She giggled when she asked this since we had over the time we spent together shared many secrets. "I'm in love." She put her hand across her lips to try and conceal her girlish smile then sat next to me. I felt weak and nauseated from all the movement but too excited to care. I envisioned Hoyt on the shore with his arms held out for me to join him. I took Alice's hands in mine.

"In love? With whom?"

Blushing, she leaned over and whispered a name in my ear even though we were the only two in the room. The truth about secrets is that they are rendered powerless unless somebody has a desire to know of them. In our particular case, nobody cared about our secret. Somehow because we were considered afflicted women, our words had little value. The power of Alice's secret took manifestation in the whisper and yet still because no one was there to wonder what it was she had entrusted me, its meaning became deflowered in a sense. But, I held onto it hoping to give it strength.

"A prisoner? Well, how'd you meet *him*?" I asked her, surprised that she had gained access to a place that was strictly forbidden.

"Oh honey, it was easy. I met him my first week here. All I had to do was flirt with Clarence the groundskeeper. You see, he has a little crush on me. I can tell. I only have to bat my eyes and show him a little cleavage; he'll do just about anything—except let me out of this hell hole. I've already asked him several times. I know he has the keys to do it. Now if only he had the balls."

And with this, we both laughed hysterically until we were interrupted by Dr. Warner, who silenced us with his cough.

"Well, I see you are feeling better Miss Madigan," he spoke to me, ignoring Alice's presence.

"And I'm fine too, Doc. Thanks for asking," Alice said sarcastically. She blew him a kiss and he left almost immediately following. I didn't tell her but I felt sorry for Dr. Warner. I knew things about him that no one else did. Things about his mother. I imagined Dr. Warner spent hours staring in front of the mirror vowing to never be like her. I wondered if this contempt he held for her fueled his desire to become a doctor—one with enough power to, if not control the gene pool, at least contain it. But all his success had not fixed the hole he had inside of him. It only masked it. I believe that the thought that he shared genes with his mother not only disgusted him but frightened him as well. And I suppose he is fortunate that the Eugenics Board wasn't around when he was a child or he may have found himself a patient at the asylum.

In the weeks after Dr. Warner came by, I saw very little of Alice. She floated in and out of the room at all hours and we rarely had any time together at all. I missed her—our long talks, her laughter, her outrageous style. But I understood. About love. How it fed you when you were hungry and made you feel not just full but complete. I had felt this way only once in my life, and I was still living on its nourishment, though I was beginning to weaken at the thought that I might never see Hoyt again. My life was here now, and I knew I had little chance for escape. Lux and Nix were growing into young ladies. Sister Madeline had kept her promise and they visited when they could, but they were there with me every single day though not physically.

I've kept it to myself that I have not been feeling well as of late. I'm exhausted most of the time, but it is the flutter in my heart that concerns me most. I wonder if during my sleep I swallowed one of the moths that roam the building. They are everywhere. Alice laughs when I tell her they are the souls of those who have died here without ever finding the light. I have never been afraid of death and yet I am not ready.

Lately I've been dreaming of myself again. It is always the same dream. In a dress I recognized from my childhood, a brown Sunday dress, which has somehow grown with me, I'm running toward my girls but they don't see me. Instead I run right through them. When I look back at them, I see that Nix, my dark haired beauty is aware of my presence. She reaches for me, but Lux does not have the sight.

As I'm still immersed in this dream, only seconds from waking, I look down to find that my feet are bare. I'm not wearing shoes. It's a sign for certain. Then I jerk awake with fear for my girls. What will become of them after I'm gone? I pray that they will not be brought to the asylum to serve as part of Dr. Warner's vindication towards his mother. But I knew that because of me, they were instilled with genes that infected them and they could in his eyes be nothing less. We would be talked about in one of those doctor meetings as valid points: Examples of how society's degenerates should be *handled*.

Una Madigan
The Cape Perpetua Asylum for the Insane

Lost and Found

I checked in with the receptionist, a young round-faced blond who couldn't have been a day over twenty at *Bridewell, Turner,* and *Associates* and took a seat to wait for Tracy Hayes, the woman I spoke with the day before about researching the patient records from the asylum. Minutes later, a tall wiry brunette came to collect me. In her black fitted suit, the skirt just a pinch too tight so that it crawled as she walked, the woman reached to take my hand. After she introduced herself, I caught a glimpse of familiarity in her wide cheekbones and narrow bird-like nose, both of which seemed too powerful for her diminutive eyes. It took me only a moment to realize that she looked exactly like one of the tellers at my bank.

"My sister," she admitted after I inquired and as we walked towards a room in the back of the office. "We're actually twins. I was born first, but Tara smokes and colors her hair so she looks a little older."

I felt a little awkward hearing such personal information, especially about someone I knew; I guess I was under the impression that disclosure of any information in a law office was breach of contract. Apparently not when it came to age. "Oh," I said thinking that I'd never once smelled smoke on her or noticed dark roots. "She's very nice."

"It's just back here," Tracy let me know as she marched on, looking over her shoulder every few seconds to make sure that I was still with her. Through her neutral colored hose, I could see the faint traces of some type of vine, a tattoo that circled her right ankle. I wondered momentarily if she regretted it. Its indelibility made me think of my last conversation with Ben and the argument we had. In the near future there would most likely be some time of magic potion—there was already some type of laser—that dissolved unwanted tattoos. But there was no type of potion that could permanently remove my regrets. Booze was a temporary fix though drinking myself into oblivion was not an option for me at the moment. At least—and I thought it again. In my condition.

Tracy motioned to a long cherry wood table where we both sat. Stacks and stacks of manila folders were organized neatly into rows on the left side of the computer, a big bulky thing which was positioned in the middle of the table. I showed her my license and the power of attorney papers I possessed regarding my father. I also showed her the note I'd forged, feeling immediately the twitch in my eye as I handed it over. To avoid eye contact, I looked down at the paperwork before me—a Release of Records form, "a common procedure," she said to me, when medical records are involved. I signed where she noted by the X and slid the paper over to her.

"So what exactly are you looking to find?" she asked abruptly but skillfully so that I couldn't tell if I was under scrutiny or if she was just curious. I wasn't prepared to be questioned. When I made the appointment over the phone, the day before, I pictured myself sitting in a room alone rifling through piles of paperwork and scrolling through the computer's database. "Well, Dr. Warner was part of the Genetics Board. Before he became incapacitated, he was studying twins. Specifically, a set of girls, the Madigans, who were but are no longer under his medical care. I'd like to find out as much as I can about them so he can complete his research before—" I didn't want to say it for fear that my voice would give it strength, and I was thankful that Tracy was astute enough to take my silence and slight shrug as a euphemism for death.

"I see. I'm all about twin study especially since I have nothing in common with mine." She smiled facetiously. "Well, I'd like to stay and help you but I've got a few appointments lined up this morning. They will probably run on into late afternoon. But, I've got you all set up. The files are in alphabetical order." She pointed to the folders on the table with her hand and another vast collection on the floor against the wall. "Those over there have been put into the database. These on the table have not. Feel free to search both, but please don't confuse the piles and try to keep them in alphabetical order if at all possible. Oh and you are not permitted to photocopy or print out any of the records but please feel free to take your own notes." Tracy logged me onto the computer and stood to leave. "That should do it. If you need anything else, just ask Rosie at the front desk. The restroom and water fountain are down the hall to the left."

"Oh," I called to her just as she reached the door. "Would it be possible for me to return tomorrow if necessary?"

"I don't see there being any problem with that. Just let me know what time you might be coming by so I can reserve the room; we feel that one person at a time in here will help minimize the chance of information being displaced."

This caught me by surprise and it must have shown on my face. "Someone else has interest in the asylum's records?"

Tracy remained quiet for a second as if she was assessing the proper way to answer my question without disclosing anything she shouldn't. "Yes," she finally answered. "A gentleman. He actually started calling a few months ago but has not yet been able to keep his appointment."

I could tell by the look on her face that this was all the information she was going to give me. I could also tell that she probably wanted to tell me more—it was in her nature—but she dared not.

"Good luck, then," Tracy said to me. "Perhaps, I will see you again tomorrow."

I nodded, wondering if she could sense how far away my mind was at the minute. Who else would be interested in the records? It had been a few years since the majority of patients were released. Who'd want to know now? It couldn't be anyone at the paper. And my father—he was too sick to even think about the asylum anymore.

I stared at the task before me and tried to focus, which was pretty much impossible since I really didn't know what I was looking for. Joe said to try and find patients staying at the hospital before the fountain was erected in 1960. The remains, if they belonged to a patient at all, couldn't have been placed there after the concrete had set. I couldn't decide whether to start with the folders or the computer. The folders would take much longer but then I'd have them out of the way so I dove right into the S's, which is where Tracy had left off.

I took out my pad and pen and took a deep breath. After each female name I came across in the folders, I wrote down the date of birth in one column, the day that patient entered the asylum in another column and a release date, if there was one, in the last column. If I could find no release date, I looked for the absolute last record available, whether it was a visit to the therapy room or a date in which medication had been administered.

From my previous research with eugenics, I had learned that the asylum at one time housed over 2,500 people. It was supposed to hold no more than 1,500. Each time, I went through another folder, another name, I tried to picture that person and what their life had been like before and after the asylum. Some of the folders had photographs, black and white and faded, others only contained terse descriptions that left much to my imagination. It took me over two hours to get through the S-Z folders and even though the building held twice the amount of women compared to men, there were only a few possibilities that might be the unidentified woman. I put checks by their names: Betty Sands, Erma Sharpe, Diana Shaver, Frances Tate, Lucy Thompson, Linda Tillman, Wanda Tulls, Louise Vaughn, Kathleen Velasco, Barbara Vines, Janet Wade, Vivian Walker, Mary Wall, Enid

Walsh, Kimberly Weaver, Elaine Williams, Malena Woods, Kitty Yates and Mable Zabrowski. Off to the side, I jotted down the weight and height of each woman if I could find it. Most were underweight, which made me painfully aware that I was beginning to show.

My father's signature stood out on each document listing the sterilization procedure these women—some as young as thirteen—were forced to endure. Obviously none were likely candidates for the Jane Doe under the fountain. My father had missed one, apparently. Unless, of course, she was already pregnant when she came to the asylum. What would he have done then? It was horrible to think about, but I couldn't help it. I'd always tried to separate my father from the god-like choices he made as a doctor. It had been difficult but what made it easier was that since we never spoke of it, I never knew for certain what exactly he did at the asylum. My questions were always shunned but my intuition at times took over. I wonder how he would feel if I told him I'd been considering an abortion. I could sit next to him on the bed and tell him that for weeks I'd sat in the parking lot of the abortion clinic and contemplated killing my child. I wonder if he could separate me from the death of his grandchild. Would he understand if I told him it was out of my control or that it was for the good of everyone?

I stood to stretch, using both my hands to massage the back of my neck. What I really needed was caffeine. When I opened the door and saw it was clear in the hall, I ventured out to the reception desk to ask Rosie for a cup of coffee. After answering a call and writing a name on the yellow message tablet in front of her—one that I was sure held the identity of the man calling about the records, she was kind enough to show me to the lounge where I filled a Styrofoam cup with coffee, thought about asking her for a look at her message book, thanked her instead and headed back to start going through the files on the computer. This would take up the rest of the day if I even came close to finishing.

The computer was much more efficient, names and dates were organized in Excel and I could arrange them accordingly, making sure I returned them to their regular columns. Half way through the B's, I began to notice or rather decipher a name listed on many of the records just beneath or next to my father's signature. Peggy Gifford. I remembered Lux mentioning a Peggy, but I couldn't be sure it was the same one. I scratched her name down on the corner of my tablet and kept on going through the hundreds of names, many of which were marked as deceased. Sadly, a good portion of these folks had never been claimed by relatives and this was noted by the letters NC in the very last column. It took me only a short time to figure out that this meant Not Claimed. As if they were luggage in the lost and found at the airport.

Long before I became a reporter, the *Beacon* had published a story on a Jewish woman who was able to locate her grandfather after years of searching for him due to an organization of volunteers known as the *Reclaimers*. Unfortunately, the old man, who had suffered with dementia, had already been cremated, which caused all kinds of problems, resulting in the closing of the crematorium at the asylum and an impending law suit. I knew about this because the *Reclaimers* were still around and they worked hard not to let anyone forget. They were desperately trying to find relatives for the cremated remains of over 5,000 victims whose ashes were still stored at the asylum, which would soon be demolished. I was grateful for all their effort, though most of them knew my father, had an extreme distaste for me and refused any offer I made to volunteer. Maybe someone from the organization had called about the records?

As I began my search in the N's, I suddenly realized that I had worked all the way through the M's with not one Madigan. How could that be? I started again at the beginning of the M folder and ended up with the same result. Not one record for Una, Lux, or Nix. It wasn't possible. It was as if they were still living their lives in the shadows of others even though Lux may have been the only one of them for certain that was alive. I thought of a time Miss Lillian had taken me to the beach and we watched as the water erased my footprints, leaving no trace that I had ever been there even though we both had seen the prints because we were there.

At six, Tracy knocked and entered before I answered. "How's it going in here?"

"I'm just finishing up," I said as I straightened my notes and tucked them into my bag. "I was curious if perhaps some of the files had been...I don't know, misplaced?"

"I don't believe so. Actually, I know so because I'm the only one who has had contact with them and I am pretty particular.

Why do you ask?"

"Well the M folder on the computer doesn't contain the names I'm researching. The Madigan twins aren't in there. Anywhere. Their mother isn't in there either. And I am most certain they were patients at the asylum."

"Well that's odd. Let me have a look." She sat down at the computer and opened the M file. M-A-D-I-G-A-N."

"That's it."

"Maybe it's just misspelled in the system. I've been working late on this and perhaps it's my fault. I'll go through it again, tomorrow when I come in. Does Rosie have your number?"

"Yes, I believe so."

"Alright, I'll call you if I find anything."

I was too tired to stop by my father's on the way home. Besides, it was getting harder and harder to visit with him and not question him about the asylum. He didn't watch the news so he wouldn't know about the bones that were found under the fountain and yet part of me wanted to tell him myself so I could see his reaction.

As I pulled in the drive, my cell phone rang. It was Joe calling to tell me that there was never a police report filed on Nix Madigan. My father had lied to me. There must have been a reason why. I gathered my purse, umbrella and laptop from the front seat of the car, trying to push aside the notion that Lux was right about my father. Maybe he did know what had happened to her sister. This thought left an empty sick feeling in my gut.

Just as I opened the car door, the garage light sparked on

something wedged in the crack of the front passenger seat. I reached over expecting to grab hold of a quarter or dime but after fishing around, I was surprised to pull out a dainty gold locket on a delicate chain. When I looked inside, there was an old black and white photograph of a young man. I had no idea where the locket had come from or who it might have belonged to. The man in the picture looked to be in his early twenties with thick dark hair. There was something oddly familiar about him. His eyes or nose. I couldn't be certain. I tried to remember the last person who sat in my car besides Lux. Ben's funeral? Did I even have my car that day? I reached for my own necklace, the permanent tear containing Ben's ashes. Running my forefinger and thumb over the smooth surface, it became warm and animated—alive with death, an irony that not only consumed me but also the time. Before I realized it, forty-five minutes had passed. I took a deep breath, draped the locket I'd discovered over the mirror, and went inside to get some much needed rest.

My instinct told me that Tracy was not going to find the Madigan files; they weren't there.

In the middle of the night, I got up and emailed Georgina, asking her to try and locate Peggy Gifford, the nurse who had worked at the asylum. Peggy would have certainly seen the footprints just as Miss Lillian had seen mine that day on the shore.

I asked Georgina not to mention this to anyone. Our secret— one that I felt held a great deal of power though I couldn't be sure why.

For the Good of All

It had been a few days since my fall, and I had only twice left the apartment: once to go to the library and another time to escape the sound of the crying baby that had pulled me from my sleep and lingered until I was driven away from the Guardian. I wasn't sure if it was just my weakened state or if the crying seemed to be getting louder as if I was somehow getting closer to the source.

Several times I had reached for the suitcase that held my mother's writing, remembering as I pulled it out that I had given her journal to Victoria. I hoped she would soon return it as my mother's words comforted me in a way I did not understand until they were not there. It was like not knowing the importance of air until it was unavailable. What was it like to be a mother? I'd never told anyone—not even Nix, of my desire to know of motherhood. What good would it have done? This maternal pull came about for me when I was still at the orphanage. I think it might have been because there were so many children without mothers that I somehow wanted to make it right. Whatever the reason, I longed for a child for years after Nix and I were sent to the asylum. It is only when I discovered my mother's journal that I realized that any child of mine would not really belong to me but to the asylum so I pushed the idea as far out of my head as possible.

I pulled out the old suitcase from beneath the bed and took out some of the things I'd kept inside: the rosary, some photographs and artwork that I had saved, mostly Nix's finger paintings of angels. I could not bear the thought that the angels that guarded the fountain were no longer there. Instead they were lying on the ground, separated from each other as Nix and I had been. How could I go back to the asylum now? It had been a place for me to sit and think about my sister and that I would no longer be able to see our faces in those of the angels made me feel more lost than ever. Soon, the entire building would no longer exist, and I had not yet gotten what I needed from it though I couldn't say exactly what that might have been.

As I emptied the suitcase entirely, setting all the contents in a pile on the bed, I heard someone at the door, and I got up to answer it.

"Hi Lux," Victoria greeted me as I opened the door. "I came by to see how you're doing. And to bring you this." She held out a shiny silver tea kettle.

For a moment as she stood before me with her dark hair pulled away from her face so that the shape, a long narrow heart, was outlined in the peculiar green glow of the hallway light, I saw something in her that made me think of my mother, and I spoke the name Una in a loud whisper. This took her by surprise I could tell by her discerning eyes, which did not seem judgmental but confused instead.

"Victoria," she corrected though by then I already realized my mistake.

"Of course. It's good to see you." I reached for the kettle, which trapped my distorted reflection and made me dizzy. Stumbling, I suddenly recalled the silver dome above the surgery table at the asylum. I tightened my grip on the knob then held the door open for her to come inside, hoping she had not seen me lose my balance.

I started the water for tea as she took a seat in the chair next to the bed. While I waited for the water to boil, I pushed to the side the items I'd laid on the bed, not wanting to appear slovenly then sat on the edge with my hands knotted in my lap until the whistle startled me. "Sorry. I've never had a tea kettle before. I've seen them in advertisements though." She smiled and a feeling came over me like I had known this woman for a long time. As I got up, one of the pictures Nix painted of the angels floated gracefully down to the floor as if it had wings.

"Did you paint this?" Victoria asked as she leaned to pick it up. I watched her eyes intensify while as they studied the image of the angels.

"Nix painted it. Along with many others," I spoke over my shoulder while soaking the tea bags. "She was captivated by the angels in front of the fountain at the asylum. We had a clear view of them from our window, and sometimes I'd wake to find her with her forehead and hand pressed firmly against the glass, staring at them, their faces and wings glowing in the moonlight. You see, I have not told you everything about my sister. Both her and our mother could see things that I *could* not, and I'd be lying if I said I did not feel like an outsider because of it."

"Your mother speaks of this ability in her writing. Your sister had this same gift? This connection with the dead?"

"Yes, though I'm not sure it was truly a gift. I used to think it was, but not now. And yet, still, it has made me somehow unworthy of being a Madigan." I could see Victoria trying to process the information. She was skeptical. I couldn't blame her. I'd never been sure myself, but I feel that was only because I didn't possess the same abilities.

"I don't mean to be disrespectful but did you ever doubt them? Your mother and sister?"

"Well, never my mother because I didn't know of her claims until I found the journal, the one I loaned to you. But, I must admit. I often doubted Nix. This may have been because I was jealous. I'm not sure. I felt as if she and our mother were connected in a way that I was not. But now, when I remember some of the things Nix said to me about her visitors, I believe she may have been telling the truth."

"What was her fascination with the angels in the fountain?"

"Do you believe in ghosts?" It was a question I'd wanted to ask Victoria from the first time we met. Her response surprised me.

"Yes. I do," she told me. "What do the angels have to do with ghosts?"

"I'm not sure but Nix told me that a woman beneath the angels came to her. A woman with a baby. Sometimes, I swear I hear that child crying. Dr. Warner used to tell me that it was just my mind playing tricks on me and that if I took my medication regularly, the crying would stop. Eventually, I told him it did. But that was a lie, a way of protecting myself from the shock treatments, Dr. Warner believed were necessary. It has been over thirty years and I still hear the infant's cries. Can you imagine hearing a child cry for so long and not be able to comfort it? To hold it so that it wasn't afraid. To wipe its tears and press its soft head over your heart so that the beat might quell its apprehension."

"I can't say that I do. I don't have any children. Not yet, anyway. Did you ever want to be a mother?"

"For a long time, yes. But the asylum changed things for me. Not just my mind; my body as well. They altered me so that I could never bear children. I don't remember the procedure, but I remember being told about it. Even though by then I had changed my mind about being a mother, I still cried for a month over the finality of it. Permanence is always difficult to accept, I suppose."

"Oh Lux, I'm so sorry. So, so sorry. Those bastards. They had no right."

"*For the good of all*, Dr. Warner said. *It's best to keep undesirable genes from spreading.* I've tried not to hate him over the years but I've had to try really hard. I'm not an evil person, I hope you understand that." I could see then that I had upset Victoria. I had not meant to, and I could not tell if she was sad or angry, but I apologized profusely. Saying *sorry* and *thank you* were symptomatic of my obsession with keeping things in order. I handed her a tissue, hoping that she was not annoyed with me. She tried to collect herself, her hand on her stomach the entire time, her voice waivered.

My talk of ghosts had stirred something in her, and I hoped it wasn't fear for it was not my intention to frighten her.

"Can you tell me more about this woman under the angels? What did she want from Nix?" she asked.

"She wanted her to know that—" I stopped suddenly, feeling as if I was once again betraying my sister. Victoria was waiting for me to finish, her brows high, her eyes wide and focused on my lips as if this would somehow coax the words from me. But I couldn't. They wouldn't come. Instead, we sat across from each other, both agape in the silence we shared until it was shattered by a noise I could only describe as some type of alarm.

"It's just my phone," Victoria said as she began to search her purse until she pulled out the little black and silver box. "Excuse me for a moment, please. *Hello. Victoria Belmont. Oh, hi, Georgina. Okay. Will do. Is everything alright? Okay. See you soon.* Sorry about that. It looks like I have an urgent meeting I must attend shortly but about your sister and this woman. Did Nix ever mention a name?"

"No." I shook my head trying to recall any names my sister spoke of and only remembered one. Abigail, the coffee heiress who was murdered. Nix was never really good with names even amongst the living. "I don't think she knew her name."

"And what do you think this woman wanted with Nix?"

I looked away.

"Lux. If we are to find your sister, you must learn to trust me. It's the only way I can help you. I can't imagine how difficult it must be for you, but you have to try. I can't do this alone." Victoria's dark eyes pleaded with me. They were kind and honest and for a split second, I felt the tug of my past, pulling me back to the asylum. Back to someone I had nearly forgotten about. Was it their deep brown color or depth that brought me to him? Michael, who I had not thought of in years. It was a disturbing feeling, not at all what I expected. I had not loved him, even then I knew. I merely wanted to him to love me liked he loved my sister. "Lux," Victoria called me back from a time that I wish would be lost but wasn't. "Are you okay?"

I studied this woman, Victoria. There was something about her that I felt I could trust. It was strange to believe that it might have been our pain that connected us: a stranger, a widow who recorded the events of history onto paper and an aging mental patient, whose time was often unrecoverable, the events of her life not easily recaptured. Both of us searching for answers, we were bonded by what was missing from our lives. And in this emptiness, this desire to know, I found that I no longer felt alone, so once again I betrayed my sister.

"Nix said that the woman wanted her to be aware that one of the cans was empty. And that she couldn't rest until it was found."

"The cans?"

"Yes. In the Cremains Room where the ashes were stored. Nix spent a great deal of time in there. Too much time. Like our mother, she was comfortable with the dead. And in all honesty, they seem to be much more harmless than the living."

"I have to run to my meeting, but I'd like to talk to you more about this later if you don't mi—"

Victoria stood and I watched the smile on her face slowly fade as she looked over my shoulder at the pile of things on the bed—the things I'd unpacked from my mother's old suitcase.

She leaned in, her face twisted in confusion. "My pen. You have my pen?"

Retracing Footprints

I left Lux's both ecstatic and upset. Had she taken my pen or had I just dropped it and she put with her things not knowing where it came from? She apologized profusely and swore to me that she could not remember ever seeing it. Either way, the important thing was that it was in my possession again after I feared it was gone forever. Like Ben. I had to remember that Lux was not normal. She was afflicted with certain mental disorders that I wasn't sure happened before or after she was brought to the asylum. I couldn't be too angry with her especially after what my father had done. How could I ever talk to this man again? What gave him the impression that he could play God? My father was not the man I wanted him to be, and it wasn't the first time this thought came to me.

My pen was still clutched tightly in my palm when I arrived at the *Beacon,* and though I had already made up my mind about my unborn child, after talking with Lux today, the pen seemed to somehow help solidify the decision that I would keep my baby. It was a choice I made without underlying principles. I was terrified but I wanted to be a mother. I *would be* a mother.

"There you are," Georgina called to me as I hurried into the kitchen to grab a quick a bottle of water before the meeting.

"What's going on?"

"Moss died early this morning. Irwin is a mess. Looks terrible. I mean, he can be a jerk, but I still feel bad for him. He's taking a bereavement leave for an undetermined amount of time. I guess his son, Jacob, is going to fill in for him. Are you wearing lilac perfume?"

"His son? But he doesn't know anything about running a paper. You know I don't wear perfume."

"Who cares if he knows about the paper business? He's hot as hell. Besides, he has a Ph.D in French Literature, you realize. That's pretty sexy."

"Great. So, are they going to change the name of the paper to Le Beacon?"

Georgina laughed so hard she began to snort. It was probably her only noticeable flaw. "Oh crap. We have to get a move on. People are taking all the good seats in the conference room."

"And by good seats, you mean the seats next to Jacob, right?"

"You know me so well."

After the meeting, Georgina pulled me aside to tell me that she had located Peggy Gifford. My eyes lit with hope.

"She lives in Beaumont, Texas, wherever the hell that is. She sounds like an elderly southern belle. Except she swears like a sailor."

"You spoke with her?"

"Why of course I did. What kind of research assistant do you think I am? I had to make sure I had the right woman."

"Well, what did she say?"

"I told her I was doing a story on the demolition of the Cape Perpetua Asylum and that I was contacting all the former employees. She told me, rather hesitantly, that she had once been employed by the asylum but had retired before the decision was made to shut it down."

"What else did she say?"

"Well she went on to tell me about the beauty pageant she was hosting at the retirement center and that she had the hots for her neighbor who recently had a stroke. What a character. I had to cut the conversation short because people were showing up for the meeting and for some reason decided to gather around my desk. I told her a representative from the paper would be in touch. Here's her number and address."

"Thanks Georgina. *You* are incredible."

"I know," she said playfully while she examined her blood red nails. "But it's nice to be appreciated."

After everyone cleared out for lunch and the office was relatively quiet, I sat down at my desk to give Peggy a call. The phone rang several times and I was just about to give up when a woman answered. Her southern twang was a cross between a debutante and a trucker.

"Hallo."

"May I speak with Peggy Gifford, please?"

"This is Peggy. Are you calling about the pageant?"

"Oh. No, ma'am. Actually, name is Victoria Belmont. I'm a reporter from—"

"The *Beaumont Gazette*? My word. You're calling to do a story on my Belles of Beaumont contest, aren't you, darlin'?"

"Not exactly Ms. Gifford. I'm calling from Cape Perpetua, Oregon. I work for the *Twin Beacon*. I just wanted to ask you a couple of questions if you don't mind. About your employment at the asylum, to be more specific." It got so quiet on the other end of the line I thought we'd lost our connection. "Ma'am? Are you still there?"

"Yes. I'm sorry. I'm here. It's just that I haven't recalled my life there in so long, I thought I'd forgotten it. But that's impossible, I guess. What is it that you need to know, honey?"

"Well, just to clarify: You were employed by the Cape Perpetua Asylum for the Insane from nineteen-forty-nine until you retired in two thousand, correct?"

"That's right. I was a young thing—just shy of twenty when I started there. I only planned on staying for a few years but all of a sudden, I was forty, then fifty and...well, I felt a little lost when I left to be perfectly honest. But one thing I knew for sure. I missed the sunshine so I came back home."

"Well you sound like you're very happy."

"I sure am, sugar. I just got my hair done and now I'm watching my neighbor water his roses. It's a fine sight. A little slow but a real good looker." She laughed and I was instantly reminded of Flo from Mel's Diner.

"Was Dr. Warner your employer at the asylum?"

"Yes he was."

"And how was that? Working for him."

"Well, he had his good days and bad days I suppose. I can't

say we always shared the same opinions, but he treated me with respect most of the time. Don't get me wrong: We had our disagreements about things."

"What kind of things?"

"Medications, patients, sterilizations. That sort of thing. Oh, and I just thought that shock therapy was a bunch of bullshit, honey. Pardon my language."

Trying to muffle my laugh, I continued. "Do you remember a set of twins by the name of Madigan. Lux and Nix?"

"Well for heaven's sake, I sure do. I tried not to show favoritism but those girls were something special. They had the most beautiful eyes. Like drops of seawater. I knew their momma too. A real tragedy. You know, I never felt like they belonged at the asylum, well, at least not Lux. Nix maybe. She had some issues but most of these started only after she became a patient at the asylum. She was smart as a whip, though. Read all kinds of books. Knew Latin. Even after her shock treatments when she began to lose time, she'd still quote things from books. Lux was different than her sister but sweet as honey glazed ham. She was still there when I retired. Leaving her was difficult because I knew I'd never see her again. Do you know if she is still alive?"

"She is. Actually it's the reason I'm contacting you. The asylum is scheduled for demolition soon. Most of the patients were released a few years ago and placed into group homes. Lux is at the Guardian, downtown." It occurred to me that Peggy had certain details about the girls mixed up. Lux was the reader but it wasn't something significant enough to mention.

"You see her, then?"

"Yes. She wrote to me at the paper asking for my help in locating her sister, Nix, and this is the reason I'm calling you."

"I remember the day she disappeared. Lux was never the same afterward. She blamed herself, you know. I prayed Nix would be found but she never was and Dr. Warner—I know he felt bad about it—he told me so, but he was hesitant to report her missing. In fact, I'm not sure he ever did."

"Can you tell me what happened that day?"

"I can. It's not something I like to think about anymore, but it's something I will never forget as long as I live. Dr. Warner had me prepare the procedure room that afternoon right after lunch. Nix was to receive a treatment—one of those dreadful shock therapy sessions, a step above torture if you ask me. Poor dear, just the week before she went through a bilateral salpingectomy— that's the sterilization surgery. I fought bitterly against this to no avail. Originally Lux was supposed to be the first to be sterilized but Dr. Warner thought it was important that Nix get the surgery right away due to her affliction."

"Affliction? You mean because she claimed to see the dead?"

"That's right. Just like her mother. Dr. Warner believed they both suffered from multiple personality disorder."

"Did you believe Nix's claims?" Again there was an awkward silence. "It's okay if you did."

"You see, I knew the girls' mother had a special ability—I experienced it firsthand. So when Nix came to us, it wasn't hard for me to accept that she may have inherited this gift from Una.

That was their mother. Una. A beautiful tragedy, that one. So, yes. I believed. Dr. Warner was skeptical even though I do feel towards the end he believed Una was telling the truth about her gift. With Nix he was adamant that it was a part of her psychoses, which also involved cutting her arms and starting fires. She also stole things from the staff and other patients. Well, now that I think about it, maybe it was Lux who was always taking things. No, it was Nix. That's why she was scheduled to receive shock therapy the day she disappeared. She had taken something from a nurse, an expensive piece of jewelry. I'm almost positive. Anyhow, I prepared the room that day as Dr. Warner instructed and after nap time that afternoon, I went to get Nix. He made me tell her it was a routine exam; I hated lying to her. She was more reluctant than usual and I felt as if she might have known something was not right. All these years and I still feel guilty about lying to that child. Normally, I was the one who usually assisted Dr. Warner in the procedures, but there was a problem with a patient just as we started that afternoon and I left Nix alone with him. A little while later, Lux came running down the hall looking for her sister but she was wearing a long black wig. It looked so real that for a moment I thought it was Nix."

"Did Lux always pretend to be her sister?"

"I don't believe Lux was schizophrenic. Nix may have been. It was difficult to tell with her. I think Lux wore the wig because she wanted to look more like her sister—Lux's hair was almost white, you know. I don't think she was trying to be Nix as much as she was trying to be like her. Lux may have had some jealousy issues—a completely normal reaction for sisters in my opinion. Nothing to be institutionalized over. I should know. I used to have one. Anyway, I don't ever remember seeing Lux wear the wig again after her sister disappeared."

"Did Dr. Warner tell you Nix had disappeared?"

"Yes, but not until a few hours after it happened. He said she had probably escaped through the front door, which wasn't working properly but..." she hesitated.

"But what?"

"Well, I don't know if I should say or not."

"I assure you Ms. Gifford that our conversation is private. If I use any of the information you provide me, I will never reveal your name. You have my word." She hesitated for a minute then spoke.

"Well the front door buzzer had been broken for weeks, but I hired an electrician to repair it that day, and he was there all afternoon including the time Nix supposedly escaped through the door."

"There was no way she could have passed by him unnoticed?"

"Well, she could have only he'd locked the door so that folks wouldn't be going in and out while he tried to locate the short in the wiring. If she escaped, it wasn't through that door."

"And what about Lux's sterilization. Were you there for her procedure?"

"No. I was on leave. My sister, God rest her soul, got sick. Cancer. I was gone for about seven months, give or take a month. When I came back, Dr. Warner had already sterilized Lux. I felt so bad for the poor thing. She looked really pale and for the first time, unhealthy and withdrawn. Can you believe she forgot how to play the piano? Not only that but she could no longer write with her left hand. She forgot she was ambidextrous. And, probably the oddest thing was those numbers carved into her wrist. They'd become infected and had to be treated. She told me she didn't know how they got there, but I immediately thought of Nix. She'd always been the one who marred up her arms so I was surprised to see this on Lux. In fact, I was surprised by a lot of things when I returned."

"What kind of things?"

"Well, some of the staff had left and the doctor was going through a divorce. I figured this was what made him act so strange. He even asked me to destroy some of the files in the Record Room. Can you believe it? Medical records. All the M's. I told him I would even though I had no intention of doing so. I planned on taking the documents home and hiding them but when I went to retrieve them, I noticed many of them were missing. Can you hang on a second? Someone's at the door. I sure hope it's my neighbor." She giggled like a girl.

I waited for her to return, catching bits and pieces of the conversation I heard in the background. My father was not a man I felt I could respect or trust any longer. I'd learned too many things about him that I knew would not dissipate. How could I face him and not say anything about what I'd learned? Not ask him how and why he could do the things he did. Things that could not be changed. Not now. Not ever.

"I'm back, honey, but I got to run. I just learned that one of my contestants is thinking of backing out because she is insecure about her walker. I need to get over to the assisted living facility and give her a talking to. It's been a real pleasure chattin with you. If you need anything else, don't hesitate to call. And do me a favor. Tell Lux I wish her the best. Always have. In all honesty, I'm thankful she made it out of that place. Didn't think she would."

"Thanks Ms. Gifford. Just one more thing. Do you think Nix could still be alive?"

"Honey, I have wondered that same question for many years. I don't know. I want her to be. For Lux. I really want her to be. We used to say the St. Anthony prayer in hopes that she would return even though a part of me had always felt that Nix Madigan was lost—even before she vanished."

"I appreciate your time. And hey, good luck with the pageant."

I'd only replaced the receiver back in its cradle when the phone rang, startling me. It was Janice, my father's nurse. She sounded panicked.

"Victoria, your father has taken a turn for the worse. I didn't want to do it but his blood pressure dropped drastically; I had no choice. He's at St. Joseph's. I'm sorry."

"Thanks, Janice. Don't worry. I understand. I'll be there as soon as I can."

"I'll wait for you. Oh, and I've already left a message on your brother's voicemail. Again, I felt it was the right thing to do."

"Well, don't expect him to come, but it was nice that you tried. I'm leaving right now. I have my cell phone if you need to reach me."

I would have to face my father whether I wanted to or not.

Tremors

Janice was waiting for me when I arrived at the hospital. She looked exhausted, and I forced her to go home and get some rest. My father hadn't been coherent since the day before and she was very distraught about it.

"His temperature was so high and his skin so jaundiced," she said. "I'm sorry I didn't notify you sooner. I was hoping he'd pull out of it like he always does. Then his blood pressure fell and—"

"Janice. You don't have to apologize. I appreciate all your concern. Now, go home and get some rest. I'll call you tomorrow after I speak to the doctor."

The next day turned into the next week and the next month and before I knew it my father had been at the hospital for nearly three months. I took another leave from the paper. It was going through such chaotic change that I felt I wasn't missing anything, and though I stopped by to see Lux a few times, most of my days and nights were spent at the hospital with my father who floated in and out of consciousness. If there was one good thing about it, it was that he was too out of it to notice my growing stomach. The doctor had little hope of him pulling out, but since he was not comatose, he said it could go either way.

I'd spoke with my brother Mike only once regarding our

father. He said he would try to come and to keep him posted. His mother was having heart surgery and he felt he needed to stay with her, which I totally understood. And then there was the book store that didn't run itself. But even if that wasn't the case, he probably wouldn't have come anyway. Whatever happened between him and my father was enough to make him quit the medical field permanently and move away. He never married or spoke of a girlfriend. At times, I wondered if he was gay. I used to blame both him and my father for what had happened but the more I'd learned about my father, the more I was certain he had done something to Mike. Something that could never be amended. But what?

Joe Larsen came by every couple of days to check on me. I'd given him the names of the women I pulled from the attorney's database but all of them had been accounted for either in graves or still alive, some of them in nursing homes.

The first time Joe noticed my swollen belly, I thought he was going to cry. He didn't have to ask whose child I was carrying; he knew—unlike Georgina who actually asked me if I'd been seeing someone. She was the only person from the *Beacon* who knew about my pregnancy and she swore to keep it a secret. With the way my stomach was growing, I imagined the entire office would soon know.

As we sat in the cafeteria one morning, Joe and I talked about the unidentified remains of the woman found at the asylum. He had no leads and he'd been swamped with a string of burglaries he explained as we ordered breakfast. Not much time to focus on finding the identity of our Jane Doe.

"Are you limited for time since the asylum is on the city's demolition list?" I asked him. "I thought for certain, it would have already happened."

"That's been put on hold for a while. They can't legally tear it down right now because it's the scene of an unsolved crime. We don't know who that woman is, but we do know she died a violent death." He watched as I ate a stack of pancakes, eggs, toast, bacon, a side of fruit and a muffin. My appetite was as big as my abdomen. "Have you picked out a name, yet?"

"No. Not yet. I was hoping it would come to me but it hasn't so far." I rubbed my silver tear drop between my fingers as if this would somehow help a name materialize.

"When are you due?"

"Two and a half months."

"Your father has no idea, does he?"

I shook my head. "I'm kind of glad he doesn't." Joe didn't ask and I didn't offer to explain why I felt this way.

"I'm sorry," he said to me. "Life is not always what we expect it to be. I've harbored some ill feelings toward my own father for a long time but thankfully it has never affected my love for him." His radio sounded and he lowered the volume but not before I felt the weight of many eyes around us. "Accident. Another earthquake knocked a tree onto a passing car. Sounds pretty bad. I have to go."

In the past month or so, we had experienced several tremors at the hospital. One even affected the power for a few minutes and the staff had to activate the back-up generator. "I understand. I appreciate you coming by to check on me. And the baby."

He stood to leave—a gentle giant who captured all the eyes in the cafeteria. I stood as well, having a much more difficult time wedging myself from under the table. I suddenly felt like a door jam then momentarily lost my balance. Joe tenderly gripped the top of my arm, bracing me and for a minute we were back in high school and he was helping me down the stairs in my foreboding prom dress. I'd tripped because my shoes were too high, but he had saved me then, and I could tell now that he was still trying to keep me from falling. He surprised me with what he said next. "I've always wanted to be a father. Do you mind if I..."

"Go ahead." I inched closer to him.

Reaching toward my belly, he placed his enormous hand over it and my stomach was suddenly dwarfed. He smiled when the baby kicked.

"He likes you."

How do you know it's a *he*?"

"Women's intuition."

"Of course. I should have known. If you need anything at all, Victoria. Anything. Just call. I'll keep your father in my thoughts."

I went back to my father's room and sat in the chair next to his bed. He was breathing peacefully, his lids closed but moving slightly, and I wondered what a man like him dreamed of. It was almost fearful to think about. I tried to close my own eyes but couldn't so I reached inside my bag for Una's journal. I had brought it with me, reading it during the spare moments when I was not too tired. After I retrieved it from my bag, I repositioned myself so that the light from the window shone over my shoulder, lighting the words before me as I scanned for the place where I'd left off.

The Memory of Sound

Alice was missing. She hadn't been back to the room in days and the staff was in a frenzy over it. Peggy was the first to ask me about her.

"You wouldn't happen to know where Alice is, would you?" she inquired one morning as she changed the sheets.

"No," I said practically swallowing my tongue. Initially, I had not spoken of her disappearance because I did not want her or me, for that matter, to be punished.

"Everyone is looking for her, Una. If you know where she is, please tell me so that I can try and help her—prevent any unnecessary therapy. Dr. Warner is very upset. He doesn't want to have to call the authorities."

"I don't know where she's gone to Peggy. I swear on the Lord." And this was the truth. "But I, too, am worried about her. I miss her."

"She never mentioned plans of escape to you? Or perhaps she's gotten herself in some sort of trouble? I can't help her if I don't know what's going on."

I lied, suddenly feeling the power of Alice's secret strengthen inside me like an ocean storm, heading for shore. "I don't know anything." I felt horrible lying to Peggy. She was a kind lady, and

I know she only wanted to help but I couldn't risk it. Alice may have found a way out. Maybe she finally talked Clarence Burrows into opening the door. Or maybe she eloped with her new love, the prisoner she'd met in the tunnel. His name graced my tongue and I swallowed it back down. Though it pained me to think that Alice had left me behind, I was happy for her if she indeed escaped. I wanted out, too. But even if I were released that day, where would I have gone?

I awoke the following morning with a pinch in my chest. It was sharper than usual and it caught me off guard as I got out of bed. Peggy found me on the floor and took me to the infirmary. Dr. Warner said that I had a heart murmur. I didn't tell him that my heart had bothered me on and off for as long as I could remember. I thought the ache was caused by life. He drilled me about Alice but I revealed nothing to him. He had a threatening tone in his voice and though he didn't come right out and say it, I knew that he would punish me if and when he found out that I had lied to him.

I hid my journal very well so that there was no chance of anyone discovering it. I'd sliced the lining of my suitcase and tucked the bound pages inside of it. If it should by chance be discovered, I wasn't sure what would become of me. I put myself in danger each time I write in it, which is almost always in the middle of the night after the staff has made their rounds. Often it is difficult to see since the lights are out and I cannot bear to think about lighting a match; I have not touched one since the accident. But the moon is good to me. She shines through the window behind me; I feel her hand on my shoulder. Before I close my eyes each night, I say a prayer for my girls, in which I tell them not to be afraid of anything. Not even fire and for this I am somewhat of a hypocrite for if there is one thing I fear, it is fire. The word alone makes my hands burn and itch and my heart ache with grief. I've begged Dr. Warner not to cremate me after my death as I cannot stand the thought of drowning in flames.

It has been over a week since Alice disappeared. I have mixed feelings about what might have become of her. One day I picture her in a red convertible. She's wearing a long scarf that's blowing in the wind as she drives very fast along a winding countryside road, her hair and lips the same shade of brilliant red. Other days, I imagine her reunited with her brother in England, walking the rocky coast far away from her controlling father. But on occasion this ominous feeling takes over, and I feel something horrible has happened to my friend. Dr. Warner hounds me every day about her, and the secret gains power each time I lie to him. But I am not afraid; I will keep Alice's secret. Not only because I am her friend but because it's the one thing that has given me some kind of control over life.

Una Madigan
The Cape Perpetua Asylum for the Insane

"Where did you go, Alice?" I asked aloud not realizing I'd done so until my father groaned, and I was pulled from Una's story. Iquickly tucked her journal back into my bag and stood next to the bed.

"Dad? Can you hear me? Are you in pain?" *How could you believe that sterilizing a woman, any woman, was your right? Do you know what happened to Nix Madigan? Did you have something to do with her disappearance? What did you do to Mike to make him hate you so much?* These questions didn't materialize but nonetheless they were there making the air in the room heavy as if it was holding onto its breath. I wonder if my father felt it too, and this is why he began coughing. His throat sounded dry and his lips were cracked and peeling so I reached for one of the oral swabs on the table. I rub one across his lips and inside his mouth; the scent of mint catches in my nose. When I get up to throw the used swab in the garbage, I hear the sound of my father's voice.

"What was that? Dad? Did you say something?" He didn't respond. The way sound travels is odd. I instantly thought of my cello. The last time I played I could barely get my arms around it because my stomach was so big.

Instead I placed it on the floor before me and plucked one string at a time. Long after I'd touched a string, the memory of the sound still lingered in the air, waiting to be captured by something that could contain it. An ear, the wall, a floor. My heart.

Maybe because the air in the hospital room was thick and dry that it took a moment to reach me or maybe my mind needed more time to process what I'd heard my father say but had not deciphered, right away. Perhaps he was just hallucinating; the doctor said to expect this. Whatever the reason, my father's words had circled the room and found their way back to me like the lingering note of a cello. There was no mistake about what he'd said. The words echoed in my head: *Alice is dead.*

It occurred to me then that I had not remembered seeing the name Alice in the database at the attorney's office. I didn't know her last name and Alice was a pretty common name—certainly there must have been a few. If it was true what my father said then how did he know? And why was there no record of her death? The deceased patients had been clearly marked as such. Who was this Alice woman and what happened to her? Maybe Una Madigan knew. I was almost through with her journal. Maybe there was a revelation in the last few pages.

On the way home to shower and rest, I called Tracy at *Bridewell, Turner,* and *Associates* to see if I could come by in the morning.

That night, I had one goal and that was to finish Una's memoir. I made myself a large mug of Earl Grey tea because I needed the caffeine then sat down at my kitchen table with her journal. It would have made things a little easier if Una mentioned Alice's surname in her writing, but I wasn't even sure she knew it herself. The asylum would have been one place that sort of thing wouldn't have mattered.

Stigmata

I dreamed of Alice again. It was so real that I was almost fooled into thinking that she had returned. She stood at the end of the bed, watching over me but saying nothing until I sat up and called her name.

"Alice?"

"It's me honey. Just checking in on you to make sure you are alright."

There was something different about her, but I couldn't tell what it was until she turned toward the moonlight that glowed through the window and cast her shadow on the wall; a large ominous shadow that seemed to hover over her as if it would at any minute engulf her. She was dressed in a long silky white gown, her favorite for sleeping, and it appeared soiled and torn. I couldn't recall what she was wearing the last time I saw her but because she was now in this particular gown, I believed that she must have left during the night when everyone was asleep, myself included.

Alice moved toward me in a gliding movement that I recognized but refused to accept—a graceful, elongated stride as if her legs had somehow become unnecessary in the time she'd been gone. When she reached the side of my bed, she sat and I noticed the tear of blood dripping from her hairline. It strolled past the corner of her eye and down her face, and I was instantly reminded of my childhood in Ireland and of widow Crowe whose Virgin Mary statue had eyes that bled with the stigmata. I found this association rather strange because of another secret that Alice told me, one that I refuse to write on these pages. It's much too dangerous.

The drop of blood made its way to the edge of my friend's porcelain face. She made no attempt to wipe it as it dangled for a brief minute before falling off and disappearing into the air. I thought I heard it land. The sound was like a large rain drop on a window pane.

"Alice. You're bleeding. What happened?"

She didn't answer me. Instead she smiled and said, "I haven't forgotten about you, Una. Don't you forget about me." These words echoed in the room for what seemed like forever.

With open eyes, I sat up in bed but Alice was not there. I called for her anyway. It was still dark outside and though I lay back down, I could not sleep. On the wall before me, I stared at the shadow of an angel that the moon had cast upon the wall. I knew it was from the fountain they'd recently installed in front of the property. There were two angels but only one captured the light of the moon. I wondered if it was this image that provoked my nightmare about Alice. Being at the asylum has slowly started to poison my mind, creating illusions that I couldn't be sure existed.

In the morning, Adele arrived with my meds. Pinned to the

lapel of her nurse's jacket was the blue brooch Alice had given her. I'd rarely seen Adele that she wasn't wearing it. I often wondered if she wore it because it was sentimental or because she knew its true value. The sapphire brooch probably cost more than she made in a year.

"Morning, Sunshine," she called to me as she set her tray on Alice's empty bed. "How are we doing today?" she asked while handing me the little paper cup of pills. I'd long since stopped asking what they were and why I had to take them. "No Alice, yet, huh?"

I shook my head, still focused on my missing friend's bed.

"Well, honey, now don't you worry. They'll find her. I'm sure she is fine. God watches over his people. What have we got here?" she asked pointing to a dark amorphous spot on my bed near the place Alice had sat in my dream. "Looks like blood. Did you hurt yourself?"

"I'm not sure. I don't think so."

Adele checked my arms and legs and looked carefully over my face, holding my head in her fingers like a mother would do to clean a child's face. "Well, that's odd. I don't see anything. I'll see if I can find you some fresh sheets as soon as I'm done with my rounds, okay?"

I nodded, still unsettled by the thought that my dream of Alice might not have been a dream. If it wasn't a dream then... I couldn't bear to think about it.

The same dream continued for what seemed like weeks and at the same time, my heart flutter grew more intense. I repeatedly woke up on the floor, weak and disoriented. It became so extreme that I was moved to the infirmary for a while. It was getting harder and harder to keep up my writing but I felt I must.

When I was finally brought back to my room, my nightmares about Alice continued. Each time, she seemed to be bleeding even more. Her tears of blood were thicker and lingered longer on her face. Her shadow on the wall grew bigger, her body disappearing into it. Her words echoed throughout the night into the morning.

The last dream I ever had of her was on a night that Dr. Warner was having me monitored because of my erratic heartbeat. He had not said it, but I knew that he was worried about me. Peggy had been worried, too. It was in her eyes. It was her name I screamed when I awoke from my dream of Alice.

"Peggy! Peggy!"

The door flew opened and she ran in to me. "What is it, Una? What?"

"She's dead, Peggy. Alice is dead."

"No. Why do you think that?"

"I don't think it, I know it. I saw her. I mean, I've suspected it all along, I was just hoping that I was wrong. But, tonight when she came..."

"What Una?"

"Peggy, she wasn't wearing any shoes. They never wear shoes." I knew I was rambling. "Alice is dead. Something terrible happened to her. Please go get Dr. Warner."

"He's gone home for the evening, honey."

"Peggy, please. I must speak to him. Call him back."

"Can't we talk to him, tomorrow?"

"No. I might not be here tomorrow. Please, call him in. I have to tell him something very important." I felt the sweat beading on my face and neck.

"Okay, honey. I'll make the call. Hang on. I'll be right back."

It seemed like only minutes before Dr. Warner came into my room though I know that hours must have passed. Peggy was with him and she closed the door behind her. She was carrying a syringe and the small bottle that I knew would make me go to sleep.

"Dr. Warner. Alice is dead." I cried uncontrollably.

"Miss Madigan, we're going to give you something to make you relax." He motioned for Peggy. "We have to keep your heart rate down."

"No!" I screamed. "No. Don't you understand? Alice is dead. I know because I saw her, and..."

"And what? What is it that you want to tell me? Why did you call me out of bed for this nonsense?"

I tried to stifle my tears. "Alice wasn't wearing any shoes. She's gone. The dead never wear shoes. Somebody hurt her."

"What on earth are you talking about? You know I don't believe in this sort of nonsense. You just need some meds and a little rest. Peggy, help Miss Madigan go to sleep. Then I can also go to sleep."

"Wait. I have something else to tell you." I looked toward Peggy, hoping that I would not hurt her feelings. "In private."

"I have nothing to hide from Peggy. Tell me what you have to tell me."

"It's about your mother," I said hoarsely as I watched his face grow dim at first then redden with anger.

"That's enough, Miss Madigan. Peggy." He moved his finger to signal that she should go ahead with the syringe.

"She comes to me, your mother," I continued. "I know about her. How she died. Her wrists—"

"Shut up, Una. Shut up!" He held his hand up to keep Peggy from administering the medication. "Peggy, will you wait outside, please?"

Confused, she asked, "Are you sure?"

He nodded toward the door. "I'm sure."

"Well, okay but if you need me, I'll be right outside."

Dr. Warner waited for the door to close. "Who the hell do you think you are? How dare you bring up my mother. Who told you? Who? I demand you tell me who told you about her."

"No one. I already told you. She comes to me. I know you found her. I know what it did to you to see her like that. All that blood."

"Stop it. Please stop it. Why are you doing this?"

"Because it is the only way you will believe me about Alice. She really is dead. You have to find her. Someone has hurt her and she won't rest until she's found."

Dr. Warner sat on the edge of the bed with his head in his hand. "This is too much. We will talk in the morning." He stood and I could see that his eyes were wet. I never knew he was even capable of showing emotion. As he walked toward the door, he turned around to face me.

"My mother. What does she want?"

I swallowed hard, reaching for the cup of water Peggy had brought me earlier. I took a big drink of it. "She wants to tell you that she's sorry. She never had a chance to apologize." And then I told him what his mother had said. I didn't understand what she had meant by it but I assumed that Dr. Warner did. He repeated it and slowly walked out the door, leaving it open behind him as he strolled past Peggy who was still waiting in the hall. She looked in on me then pulled the door closed.

I didn't see Dr. Warner or Peggy any more that night. Exhausted, I managed to close my eyes only to wake from another dream, one in which my brother Finn, who had never came to me before though I begged him to do so, guided me toward the ocean. I turned around only once, fearful of doing so as I remembered what had happened to Orpheus, and waved to my beautiful twin girls who stood on the shore like morning and night. Nix leaned and whispered something in her sister's ear and Lux looked confused. I turned back to my brother, Finn, who had not aged, his color restored from the pale sickly hue and swollenness that had taken over his body just before he died. We walked on the water at first, and I couldn't tell at which point we'd become immersed in it, moving but now swimming toward the horizon effortlessly and without the use of our arms. Like a dolphin. Like a selkie. Along the way, we passed through the carcass of an old ship much like the one that brought us from Ireland and I knew that we were going home. We were on our way to the land of eternal youth, *Tir na Nog*, and I feared I was too old for it, but I could not help but thing that Hoyt waited for me there.

Above me, the swollen clouds turned the color of a bruise and the wind picked up. I heard my name in the waves, and this is what woke me.

It was nearly daylight when I retrieved my journal from the old suitcase to record the dream. The pinch in my chest became warm then cold then warm again. My last dream in this world was by far the best. Today is June 15th, 1960, and as I write this, I can hear the water calling for me.

Una Madigan
The Cape Perpetua Asylum for the Insane

There were no more entries after this, and I knew Una Madigan must have died not long afterward. Had she committed suicide? I couldn't be sure but it didn't sound like it. And where had her remains gone? More questions for my father whose illness had become his amulet. Three women that I knew of had vanished from the asylum. Una was dead, Alice may have been dead. What happened to the third? Where was Nix Madigan? Another question, one that had languished in the back of my mind throughout this entire ordeal involved much more emotion. Was my father a murderer? He was a bastard; that was for certain. But a murderer? Did he have something to do with Nix's or Alice's disappearance? Or for that matter, Una's death? I gathered the pages of the journal and secured them with string. Lux would be anxious to get it back. I could tell by the way she handed it to me the day I borrowed it. I climbed into bed and wasted no time falling asleep.

The next morning, I awoke to rain tapping on the windows. I peeked out the curtains to find remnants of the storm: a few branches in the yard and the stone birdbath filled with leaves. The weather station predicted storms all week, and I wondered if this had anything to do with the recent earthquakes the coast had been experiencing.

I was moving slower than usual, Ben's t-shirt stretched snugly across my cumbersome belly. When you're pregnant, everything takes longer. It was almost nine by the time I left the house. I'd managed to dawdle for over an hour. The line at Starbucks was too intimidating so I went into the convenience store on the corner to grab a coffee and a banana before I headed over to see Lux. She had called me regularly from the pay phone in the lobby of the Guardian to see if I had any news of her sister. Each time, she seemed more let down. I told her that I had not forgotten about her, but that I was preoccupied with my father who had been hospitalized; I just didn't bother to mention his name. In this way, I felt less guilty about keeping my true identity from her. How would she ever trust me again if she knew?

When I arrived at the Guardian, I didn't expect to find Lux in the lobby. She was in her night gown, her wet hair matted against her head and her shoes caked in mud. I approached the piano where she sat, playing a song I knew well. The words slipped involuntarily from my lips. *I'll be seeing you in all the old familiar places*...It was the very first song I'd ever played on the cello. I stood and watched over her shoulder, longing for the feel of my cello until she finished.

"I didn't know you played."

"I don't," she said, staring at the keys as if for the first time.

"Well, it sounds like you do."

"Oddly, I don't even remember sitting down here."

When she said this, I realized she was in that same fugue I'd found her in the morning she'd been inside the asylum. The day she fell. "You were at the asylum this morning, weren't you?" I asked delicately.

She nodded slowly. "I was sitting on the floor just outside my room. It was so cold. Colder than I ever remember. I must have been in one of my episodes or maybe I had just fallen asleep. The sound of my sister's voice surrounded me. She was humming a song our mother used to play on the piano. Then she leaned down and whispered in my ear. It woke me."

"What did she say?"

"She said, 'Rats live on no evil star.' It was just a dream. But I so rarely dream of her that I can't help but wonder what it means." She shivered, her damp gown sticking to her skin like wet tissue paper.

Rats live on no evil star was a palindrome that the poet Anne Sexton once read off the side of an old barn in Ireland. She made it into a poem about Adam and Eve. I was a huge fan of both Plath and Sexton while in college and had kept many of their books. My professor called them the Sob Sisters because of their morbid style. It was such an odd thing for Lux to say. She was an avid reader but this was so out of context that she must have been very confused. "Let's get you upstairs and into some dry clothes." I helped her up from the bench and it wasn't until we were both sitting with hot chocolate that she mentioned my huge stomach. I'm not even sure she noticed it before then.

"Are you having a baby?"

"I am." Though she told me she had long since given up on the idea of being a mother, I could tell by the way her eyes shone that she must have still thought about it at times. Thought about what it would feel like to give life and in return receive unconditional love. Maybe she was thinking about it when she reached for my stomach. Or maybe she was thinking that all women should have a choice. Without asking, she placed both her hands on my abdomen and leaned to press her ear on it. "I can bring him by any time you like," I told her. "You can hold him."

"I can?" She smiled, her right wrist tilting just enough to reveal the first few numbers carved into it. "Does that mean you are not still angry with me about your pen? I'm very sorry. It's just that, sometimes, I take things that don't belong to me. I don't mean to and I don't usually recall that I've done so."

"I know. I'm not angry." I reached for her right hand, gently turned it over and moved slightly behind her, focusing on the numbers. From left to right, I read them aloud: 80611. "Lux. Do you know how you got these numbers?" I asked as I ran my thumb gingerly over them. What they might mean?"

She sat quietly for a moment, and I could see her mind working, diligently.

"I was sick. In the infirmary. I'd lost time after my sister disappeared. A lot of time. A year. That's what they said. When I came to, I noticed my wrist was wrapped. I removed the gauze to find the numbers, bloody and swollen. I don't know where they came from. I can't remember. I've tried many times."

"Do you think you wrote them—carved them into your skin like that?" I pointed to her wrist.

"I thought so at one time but..." She looked down at the numbers then up at me. "I just don't know how it would have been possible."

"What do you mean?"

"Well, I'm right handed."

I recalled then what Peggy had mentioned about Lux once being able to write with either her left or right hand. "So, the numbers don't mean anything to you?"

She shook her head. "Not that I know of." She looked so full of sorrow, I reached to embrace her. I wanted to tell her so many things. To apologize for my father and what he had done to her and her family but I couldn't. She would think I had betrayed her. And hadn't I?

"Don't worry, Lux. We're going to figure this out. Together," I assured her. "Oh, I almost forgot. I have your mother's journal." Her face lit up when I handed it to her. "Thank you for letting me borrow it. I didn't really find any information that might help us locate Nix, but I got to know your mother a little better. I want to ask you something; it may be difficult to answer. Do you think she committed suicide?"

"No. I don't. She wouldn't have."

"What do you think happened to her?"

"I'm not sure but I think it may have had something to do with her heart. She had a defect that both Nix and I inherited from her. Maybe it consumed her like it will me, one day."

"You have a heart defect? I didn't know."

"Nix and I were both born with a hole in our heart. Quite appropriate for Irish folk, don't you think? Nix's healed but mine never has. I don't think I have much time left in this world. It's one of the reasons I'm so desperate to find Nix. I must apologize to her."

"Apologize for what you took from her?"

"Yes. I'm a thief whose repentance didn't come until later and by then it was too late. Nix was gone. I couldn't apologize to her. Not that she could forgive me even if I had the chance to ask her."

"And what was it that you stole from her? Do you want to talk about it?"

"Love. I took love from her. And something else. No. I can't."

Again, I thought of the Velveteen Rabbit; the pain of love that makes us all real.

"Besides," Lux continued. "I promised myself I would not speak of it until I could gain her forgiveness." She hung her head slightly and I could almost see the images of her past flashing through her mind, each one making her flinch a little as if she was being poked with a needle. She was full of guilt and grief.

"It's okay. Whenever you're ready I'm a good listener."

A knock at the door caught us both off guard. Lux got up and walked toward the door, while I examined the skeleton of a small bird resting on the window sill.

"It's my neighbor," Lux said over her shoulder.

I leaned to see a woman that remind me of Julia Child hand her a newspaper—an extra one, I'd heard her say with a faded English accent. Lux thanked her and closed the door. As she made her way across the small room, the building began to tremble ever so slightly but enough to cause her to lose her balance and fall. The newspaper pages scattered. "Lux! Are you alright?" I moved as quickly as a pregnant woman could to reach her, hoping that she had not been injured—especially now that I was aware of her heart condition.

"I'm okay. I just need to sit here a moment and get my bearings. Was that an earthquake? I've never experienced one before."

"The whole coast is on tsunami watch. Has been all week. Are you sure you're okay?"

"Yes. I'm fine. Just a little embarrassed." She reached to gather the loose pages from the newspaper, and I tried to help her stand as best I could without losing my own balance.

"It was nice of your neighbor to give you her extra paper. Does she do that often?"

Lux didn't answer. She was focused on something. The Local News section. And suddenly, I saw what she was looking at: an article titled, *Local Asylum Doctor Hospitalized*. Just beneath it, a photograph I immediately recognized. It was an old photo, taken when my father was healthy. This was easy to see even in black and white. He had stopped by the paper that afternoon to take Tom to lunch when one of our reporters snapped a picture of the two of them, standing just behind me as I sat at my desk. Shit. My stomach began to twist.

Lux looked back and forth from the photo to me several times before asking, "Is that you?" Her eyes were red with tears—anger or pain or both. I couldn't be sure. She began to read aloud. "From right to left: Tom Irwin, Dr. David Warner and daughter, Victoria Belmont." She stopped reading then repeated the words that had stung her. "Daughter, Victoria Belmont." Looking up at me, she asked, and I could not lie to her though I desperately wanted to. "Are you Dr. Warner's daughter? The Dr. Warner from the Cape Perpetual Asylum?"

"I am. But let me explain. I—"

"How could you? Get out."

"I'm sorry. I never meant to hurt you. I was only—"

She walked to the door and opened it, tears streaming down her face. "Leave. Now please."

I stood there until she screamed. "Please! Just leave!"

Long after she had slammed it in my face, I waited outside the door where I was sure I could hear her crying softly behind it. What had I done? I was the only friend she had and the thought of her being upset and alone filled me with horrible sadness. I wanted to run back inside and wrap my arms around her and tell her that I too believed my father had something to do with Nix's disappearance, but I knew there was no way she would believe me now. As I walked down the hall to the elevator, my own tears swelled in my eyes, and I wondered how I would ever be able to make things right again. There was really only one way and that was to find out what had happened to Nix. At that moment because I wanted so desperately to right what the universe had wronged, I was more determined than ever to find her sister.

Part Three

Sibling Rivalry

I sat in the car for a few minutes trying to compose myself before going inside the attorney's office. The clouds were growing darker by the minute, and I thought of what Una had said about the power of a secret. My secret was out. Would Lux ever be able to forgive me? Or would we both constantly be searching this world for a forgiveness that might never manifest? I felt the first few drops of rain dust my face just as I reached the building. It was a different kind of rain—not the mist I was used to on the coast but instead, large cold beads that clung desperately to my skin even with the warm wind that tried to loosen them. A storm was on its way.

The same young girl was at the front desk. She was on the phone and I was just about to take a seat to wait for her when Tracy came out and motioned for me to follow her.

"How've you been?" she asked glancing back at my bulging stomach as we walked in the direction of the room where the records were located.

"Good, I guess, considering."

"I didn't realize you were pregnant. My sister just found out that she's having a baby."

"Are you excited about becoming an aunt?"

"Well, I was until I found out that my ex-husband is the father of the child." She looked back at me once again. "My sister and I are not on speaking terms at the moment."

She didn't wait for me to comment on this, thankfully, and went on as if this little bit of information hadn't escaped from her mouth. "We finally got everything into the database so that should make it a little easier for you."

"I suppose you never discovered the missing files, did you?" Though I knew now what happened to the files, I thought I'd ask just in case one might have slipped through.

"No. Strangely, there are only a handful of patients whose last names start with M in the records that were brought here from storage. I've tried to look into to it but it's been quite a challenge. I guess since the facility is being torn down soon, not many are concerned about the records. In fact, you and one other person, the gentleman I mentioned previously, are the only two people to inquire about the missing or should I say, misplaced files. He was here yesterday morning, actually. But not for very long."

She opened the door for me but did not follow me into the room. "I've got everything set up for you. We've organized the documents two separate ways. Once in MedicWare, which shows the complete record and also in Excel, which is basically names, dates and significant comments. You can access both but they are large files so if the computer should log you off, just find me and I'll get you back in there. My office is at the end of the hall on the left hand side."

After I thanked her, I sat down at the computer still very curious about the other person who'd been here investigating the records. I felt a little guilty with not sharing with Tracy what I'd learned about the missing files, but I didn't know how to do so without involving Peggy and incriminating my father. I wondered if and when the time came, weather loyalty would prevail over morality. If my father had something to do with the disappearance of Nix or Alice for that matter, would I be able to turn him in, a dying elderly man? I wanted to think, yes, but I didn't know for sure how I would handle such a situation.

Tracy had minimized both programs for me at the bottom of the screen. I opened Excel because of its quick ability to sort terms alphabetically.

According to the document there were two hundred and seven women with the name, Alice, since the hospital began keeping efficient paper records in the early 1900s. Most of these women could be eliminated by the age they would have been in 1960 at the time of Una's death. In her writing, she had mentioned that Alice was only a few years older than her. I was looking for a woman between the ages of twenty-three and just to be safe, thirty. This narrowed down the search quite a bit but not without heartache. I came across several patients who'd been admitted at the age of four or five, dying a year or two later without anyone coming to claim them. I knew this because in the comments section, notes were written such as *Deceased* and/or *Not Claimed* or the letters NC that I recognized from before. These children were no doubt on the shelf in the room of forgotten souls at the hospital.

After recording seventeen names in my notebook, I minimized the Excel document and gathered my things. I walked down the hall and stopped at Tracy's office so I could thank her. I started to rap on her door, but I could hear her talking to someone, either on the phone or in person and I didn't want to interrupt so I thought I would send her an email instead.

On the way out as I passed by the receptionist, I mouthed the words *thank you* to her while she was ordering lunch for the office.

"Can you hold on for a moment?" she spoke into the receiver then turned to me. "I forgot to have you sign in this morning," she whispered. "Do you mind? It's our new policy. Tracy's new policy, really." She rolled her eyes and handed me a pen.

"No problem."

"Thank you," she said softly and returned to her call.

As I reached to sign, I realized the register was still turned to yesterday's page and that's when I saw his name wedged between two others. Because I'd been looking at names all morning, I leaned in closer to make certain I'd read it correctly. There was no mistake. *Michael Warner.*

My brother had been at the attorney's office. He was in town and had not even attempted to contact me. While trying to decide whether or not to be hurt about this, the realization came in a swift, sharp stab. Mike was the other person interested in the asylum's records. But why?

In Vitro

On the way to the hospital to check on my father, I called Joe to give him the results of my findings regarding the asylum patients with the name Alice. He sensed something was wrong right away, and I was curious if it was skill or because he had known me for so long that he was able to detect my worry and agitation. He already knew about Nix. Weeks ago I'd filled him in on all the details regarding her disappearance, and though I mentioned that my father may have known more than he could or would say— especially at the moment, I did not mention how suspicious of him I'd become. He may have been unethical but he was still my father.

I explained to Joe that I had not been entirely honest with Lux and that when she found out my father had been her doctor when she was institutionalized, she became enraged. Then I told him what had happened at the attorney's office afterward. I knew he was thinking the same thing that I was but just not saying it. Could my brother have had something to do with Nix's disappearance? He was too young to have known Alice but as I did the math in my head, his last year at the asylum was the year Nix had vanished. My intuition told me that whatever happened between Dad and him years ago must have had something to do with the Madigan twins. Or at least Nix.

Joe said he'd run the Alice names through and see what he could find and get back with me. He was quiet for a moment and this time, I knew what he was thinking so I asked if he wouldn't mind running a background check on my brother, Mike.

"And Joe," I added. "This is between you and me, right?"

"Of course it is," he answered genuinely then hung up but not without a brief hesitance that made me think he was going to say something else. Or maybe I wanted him to say something else. He was one of those friends you could go without talking to for years then pick up just where the conversation had ended like time hadn't passed at all. I had a few college friends I still kept in contact with occasionally and there was also Georgina, but when I really thought about it, Joe Larsen was my oldest and truest friend. Though I'd known him since we were just teens, what I believed really connected us was what we learned about life later: the unspoken grief of lost love and forgotten dreams.

The last thing I expected when I arrived at the hospital was to find my brother pacing around Dad's room. I wasn't even sure it was Mike until he turned toward me, and I met my own almond-shaped eyes, dark and deep. His thick, long lashes curled outward in an effort to reach his small round glasses, which he had not worn any of the other times I'd seen him. The black hair I remembered had in areas grayed into streaks of light, but I wasn't so sure if this was why he looked so uneasy.

"Victoria." It was almost a question. "I'm sorry I didn't get here sooner. Things have been difficult." He stared down at my stomach, and I imagined his mind trying to grasp how I'd become pregnant so quickly after my husband's death.

I reached to embrace him because I felt it was the proper thing to do. "It's okay. It's good to see you. How's your mother?"

He turned toward the window, his shoulders growing and sinking with the breath he'd caught with haste and released gradually. "She died last week. Complications of her heart surgery. It's been tough."

His expression was painful to watch. "She never forgave him, you know," he said as he looked over at our father whose labored breathing made the room feel like an air bubble lodged in a vein.

"You mean because of my mother? Because of me?" I asked delicately. I didn't know the whole story of how my parents had met, but I did know that Mike's mother took her son and left when Dad asked for a divorce. He'd met my mother, a young graduate student at a convention in Boston. She was just finishing her studies and had plans to return to London to teach. She never made it. Though she was twenty years his junior, they married and I was born months later. I kept a photograph of her next to my bed and sometimes, even still, I found myself studying it in an attempt to find similarities. Ironically, Michael had more in common with her physically than I did. It didn't take much for me to realize that it was because my mother with her olive skin, dark velvet hair, and black eyes looked like a younger version of Mike's mother. She had been replaced with a more youthful her. I could understand why she became embittered.

"Partly," Mike said. I was impressed with his honesty.

"Though I have my own reasons for not liking dear old Dad."

I didn't respond to this, but I cocked my head to let him know I was interested in hearing what he had to say. He quickly changed the subject.

"I didn't realize you were pregnant. Is...are you..." he was struggling.

"It's Ben's. I didn't find out until after..." It was my turn to struggle.

"I'm sorry. I'm a terrible brother for not keeping in better touch. I'd offer to buy you a drink but considering the circumstances, how about a cup of coffee. Decaf?"

I really did need coffee but I also needed answers. Why was Mike so interested in the records from the asylum? And, I hadn't thought about it until just then but how was he even able to gain access to them? I had to procure a written request. It was forged of course, but still. Mike hadn't been in the medical field for many years but he obviously had found a way. We were alike in that manner. Tenacious to a fault. Ben used to tell me how much he admired that about me even when it interfered with our relationship. "I don't do decaf. Make it regular and you're on," I said playfully.

We took our coffee to the indoor courtyard and sat at a table by the fountain, which was landscaped in flowers and plants. Outside, the cloudless sky was almost black. Drops of rain tapped percussively against the glass surrounding us.

"Looks like we're going to get that big storm they've been predicting," Mike mentioned as he sipped from the Styrofoam cup.

The steam from the hot coffee fogged the edges of his glasses. He removed them, held them up for quick inspection then set them on the table between us.

"You're welcome to stay with me while you're here. I have plenty of room. Or you can stay at Dad's though his nurse is still there at the moment." I didn't wait for a response before asking, "How long do you think you might be in town?"

"Not sure. I closed the bookstore indefinitely. I'm going to sell it I think. Travel for a while. Maybe. Lately, I've been thinking of visiting Ireland."

"That's an interesting choice," I noted, hoping he would get the hint that I knew a little about what was going on. That the Madigans were from Ireland, originally.

He looked at me, almost through me, our walnut-colored eyes mirror images. "Victoria, I'm not just here to pay my last respects. I mean, I did want to say goodbye to him, but I have another motivation for being here. In Cape Perpetua." He didn't wait for me to inquire. "It's complicated." His eyes though now focused on me were somewhere else, reflective of another place or time, and I suddenly felt a bond with him, as slight as it was and even though we were practically strangers. He was as lost as I was.

We talked a while longer about the baby and also about his mother's funeral. She had left him quite a bit of money. Funds he never knew existed. He told me how guilty he felt accepting them. "It's like a reward for losing," he said. "A trophy for being sad."

When we got back to the room, Dad was having one of his coughing fits that produced a dark greenish brown mucus that I often noticed on the sheets in the morning when I stopped by. It was always painful to see because I realized that he had probably been alone and nearly choked with no one around to help him.

Mike quickly made his way over to Dad and held up his head gently so he could cough and try and catch his breath. Dad never even realized he was there though, and I wondered if this is how their relationship had soured. Then my brother, who despised this man, took a tissue and wiped off the slimy black smudges from Dad's mouth. I watched, captivated by his compassion, wondering if it was possible that Mike could have once murdered a young girl. My intuition said, no; it wasn't possible, and yet still I was anxious to hear from Joe regarding the background check.

I wanted to stay with Dad a while longer so I gave Mike directions to the house and told him where to find the spare key. "Under the geranium." Ben used to say that if he was breaking into the place, it would have been the first place he looked. "Why?" I'd asked. "Because it's the closest plant to the door and people aren't that complicated."

By the time I left the hospital, the rain was coming down so heavy that even with an umbrella, I was soaked by the time I reached the car. My modest house sat on the outskirts of the city just off Hwy 101, not too far from the house in which I grew up but much less expansive.

I couldn't help but think of Lux as I passed through downtown. Most of the lights at the Guardian were out but I could see people moving about in the dimly-lit lobby like shadow figures behind a scrim. I wondered if Lux was one of them.

It was just about a mile after I passed the *Beacon* parking lot that I saw red blinking tail lights off the side of the road. Hazard lights. The sky seemed to have opened up even more if possible as I drove slowly by the empty vehicle trying to discern whether it was a Porsche or Karmann Ghia. I never was any good with cars. Ben used to find great humor in the fact that I couldn't tell a Mercedes from a Dodge. He would laugh until he noticed my embarrassment then he would tell me that what I had was a quality.

Looking in my rear view mirror, I could see the car was definitely vacant. I envisioned a little old couple stranded in the rain on the side of the road, trying to flag down help.

Much to my surprise about a half mile up the road, I spotted a man walking on the shoulder. His white t-shirt was soaked through to his skin; his snug jeans clung to his tan body. He was carrying a pair of running shoes, gripped in his fingers and dangling at his side. I'm not the type to pick up strangers but as I passed him, I caught a good glimpse of his face under the street light. It only took me a moment to realize that it was Jacob Moss from the *Beacon*. "Porsche. Definitely Porsche," I spoke aloud then pulled over to offer him a ride.

"It's Victoria. From the paper," I called through the fogged partially opened window. "Would you like a ride?"

He leaned and glanced into the car but only for a moment. It was raining so hard at that point he probably would have got in even if I had horns and a tail. "Thanks," he said a little out of breath. "I'm soaked. Sorry." He dropped his shoes on the floorboard then wiped his dripping face across his forearm; it did little good.

"I think I have a towel in the back seat." I reached an arm behind me to feel around for it. "Here. This should help."

"Thank you," he mumbled through the terrycloth. "You're the first person I've seen drive by. I guess the weatherman ran everyone off with the tsunami scare. I tried to call a friend but my phone's dead."

"I have mine if you want to use it."

"I think it might be too late now. Would you mind just dropping me off at the house? I'll call a tow truck tomorrow."

"No problem." The house I assumed he was talking about was really more of an estate. In fact, the fancy scrolled letters on the iron fence clearly stated it was *The Moss Estate*. It was an old Queen Anne mansion that was rumored to have once belonged to distant relatives of Grace Kelly.

We drove in silence for a few minutes; I fiddled with the stations on the radio to fill the void and turned it down only when he spoke.

"How have things been for you?" I assumed he was talking about Ben. I'd never spoken with him about my husband's death—in fact I'd never really spoken to him at all but I'm sure at one time, I was the talk of the paper once the news got around that I'd become a widow. Jacob casually glanced down at the bulge that before too long would require me to move the seat back to keep from bumping the steering wheel. It was starting to become humorous, these thoughts that brewed in people's minds.

Each time, I tried to guess what they were thinking. A lover on the side? In vitro?—the Latin word for, in or under glass. Lately, I felt a piece of glass divided me from the rest of the world; that I was being studied by all those trying to guess how a widow had become pregnant so soon after her husband's death.

"Okay, I guess. Difficult at times but I'm learning to accept it. "How about you? Are you ready to take on the world of journalism?"

"Not exactly, but I think it's the right thing to do." I could feel him looking at me, and I turned to make eye contact then focused back toward the road. "My father and I: We weren't close. Never seemed to see eye to eye on life. Don't get me wrong. He was a good man and he treated me well. My sister, however; she was a different story."

"I didn't know you had a sister, Jacob. At least I don't recall Tom Irwin ever mentioning it."

"Jake. Please. *Had* is the appropriate word. She died years ago. I still blame the old man for her death. And myself."

"I don't know what to say. I'm sorry." Thankfully, we had reached the ornate gate that surrounded the estate, and I rolled my window down to put in the code Jacob relayed to me. The rain seemed even heavier and colder, and by the time I finished pushing the numbers, the sleeve of my sweater was saturated. Jacob, smiling, passed me the towel I'd given him only moments before. He held onto it a little too long before letting go, forcing me to catch his dark blue eyes. Was he flirting with me or was he just being friendly?

My Volvo wagon wound its way along the curvaceous drive, littered with tall, thin pines that made me feel as if I was on a movie set.

I stopped directly in front of the house. The stained glass inside a wide wood door cast a rainbow through the porch light where prisms of color gathered.

"Do you have time to come inside?"

I glanced at my watch though I had no real intention of going inside. "It's late, my brother is visiting. He's waiting for me at home."

"I understand," he said genuinely. "Maybe another time." It wasn't really a question but more of a statement. Ben always said that the privileged had a way of making questions into statements. "Thank you for the ride." He reached for his shoes on the floorboard and I saw his expression change abruptly when instead of the shoes, he held in his fingers the locket I had hung over my rearview mirror days before. I had meant to ask Lux about it, but it obviously had slipped off the mirror and out of my mind. Jacob brought the locket close to his face as if trying to determine whether or not it was real, while it dangled gracefully in the colored light streaming from the porch. Before prying it open to examine the photo inside, he turned toward me and I could see his eyes were wet with tears.

"Where did you get this?" he asked, an accusation that was tinged with anger but most definitely a question.

"I'm not sure. It was left in my car. Why?"

"This locket belonged to my sister. She never took it off. It was supposed to have been buried with her."

"I don't understand," I responded, feeling just as confused as he looked.

"I gave Alice this locket before I went away to college in 1958. It was the last time I ever saw my sister. You see, my father, our father had her institutionalized while I was away. The Cape Perpetua Asylum. I never even knew. By the time I returned from England she was dead and buried," and with this he hung his head and wept like a child.

It occurred to me then that the reason the photo of the young man in the locket had looked so familiar was because it was a young Jacob Moss sans a tan and a doctorate in French Literature.

I turned the car off and sat with him until he gained his poise—not all of it but enough so I felt comfortable leaving him alone. I assured him that I didn't know exactly where the locket had come from but that I speculated that Lux, a woman who had once been a patient at the asylum might have dropped it since she was the last to ride in the car.

"She's the only one I can think of. I'll ask her tomorrow. First thing." I did not mention to Jacob what was really going through my mind. That his sister Alice may have been the woman under the fountain. And that she was pregnant when she died. If true, it was pure irony; the fountain had been a dedication by the Moss family and had unknowingly become her tombstone. As I drove back up the driveway, which seemed even longer and even more winding than on my way in, several different questions ran rampantly through my mind. If the locket belonged to Alice Moss and she was the woman under the fountain, how did Lux come into possession of it? Did she find the necklace somewhere inside the asylum the morning the body was discovered?

I only made it on the other side of the gate before reaching for my phone to call Joe. I was still in a bit of shock and didn't even say hello when he answered. I just cut right to the point.

"I think I might know the identity of our Jane Doe. I can't put all the details together yet, but I'm pretty certain it's Alice Moss."

"Moss? As in...Moss Paper? As in the *Twin Beacon*?"

"Precisely. The daughter of the late Randall Moss."

"I didn't know he had a daughter."

"Well from what I understand, not many people did and that's apparently the way he wanted it."

"How did you come to this conclusion?"

The rain slapped hard against the car in sheets so dense I could barely see the road. "I'm on my way home to meet my brother, right now. The weather is terrible, and my phone is breaking up. Can we meet tomorrow? I'll explain."

Ribbons of Light

It was nearly midnight by the time I pulled into the garage. My brother was asleep on the couch, and I felt bad for not being there to direct him to the guest room or make him something to eat. I didn't want to wake him so I got a blanket and put it nearby in case he got cold. Then I noticed his brown leather billfold on the end table. It was wrong on all levels, but I quietly picked it up, hoping he would not open his eyes and find me rifling through it. Inside, I found a couple of twenties and a five, a few credit cards, a photograph of his mother and surprisingly, one of me as a little girl. How long had he been carrying me around with him? I had no photos of him in my wallet or even at my house, and I suddenly felt an overwhelming sense of guilt. The Catholic kind. In the very back tucked behind his library card, I found another surprise: A small picture—an exact replica of Lux except for the long dark hair. It took only a second to realize that it was Nix. Paper-clipped behind the photo was a slip of paper. I carefully unfolded it, the creases worn so through that it was as delicate as lace.

What I found was undecipherable, written in some cryptic language I had never before seen. Though I saw no signature, certainly, it must have been a letter Nix had penned. Why else would it be attached to her photograph?

The only thing I could make out was the date, which looked to have been written with a different pen and in different handwriting. Perhaps my brother's? Across the top, it read *October 10, 1969.* This was just a few days before Nix had vanished. What kind of language had she used in the letter? In my one and only psychology class in college, I learned that, inexplicably, schizophrenics can sometimes speak other languages without ever learning that particular language. It was a bizarre speculation, one I didn't have time to digest properly because my brother stirred, and I quickly folded the letter, reattached it to the picture, and tucked it back in the wallet where I'd found it. Then I slipped around the corner into the hall and out of sight.

It was ridiculous to think I could sleep; my mind was too busy. I lay awake for over an hour thinking about the letter I'd found. What did it mean? Why was it written in that strange language? Other thoughts coursed through my brain as well. How could Alice be the woman under the fountain if she had been buried like Jacob had told me? Was she buried in Cape Perpetua? If so, she would have to have been in one of the two cemeteries within the city. I'd have to check records and try and locate her. This was the last thought I remember having before drifting off, waking what I thought was only moments later when I thought I heard the creak of my front door. It was a faint sound but one I had trained my ear to hear even in the middle of a deep sleep because I knew it meant that Ben was home. He'd try to be as quiet as possible in order to surprise me but by the time he reached our room, I'd be out of bed running to greet him. So, when

I heard the door, I automatically got out of bed, feeling the pain in my heart, once reality took hold that Ben would never be coming home again.

I rubbed my eyes to focus on the clock. It was not yet five, the dusky morning sky hanging low like a gray blanket saturated with the weight of water and ready to split open at any minute. The thought of it made my bladder feel as heavy as an anvil so I made my way toward the bathroom and it was then that I noticed Mike was no longer on the couch. It was him that I had heard leaving. Pulling the curtain aside just enough to peek out without being spotted, I saw him sitting in his car, the light on; he was fumbling for something in the glove box and eventually pulled out a set of keys and what looked like a map or diagram though I couldn't be sure. He held it up, turning it at different angles until he must have found what he was looking for. When he started the car, I ran for my sweater and shoes, grabbing my keys and purse on my way out the door, and tying my bladder in a mental knot. I was very anxious to know where my brother was going and more importantly, why he'd been so secretive about it.

Trailing him as best as I could without being noticed was only made more difficult by the lack of cars on the road so early in the morning. The fog helped some but when there wasn't a vehicle between my car and his, I was forced to make a fake turn every few streets then speed to catch back up to him. Thankfully his car wasn't going that fast due to the wet street.

I knew I shouldn't have been, but I was surprised when his car turned onto St. Dymphna, the one and only street that led to both the prison and the asylum. And I seriously doubted he was headed to the prison. Why would he be going to the asylum? What could he possibly need from that place after so many years had passed? I assumed whatever it was had to do with Nix. Or Dad. Did he think the missing files might still be there inside the asylum? Even if he did think there was a chance they would still be there, carelessly overlooked, why did he need them? What kind of information did he expect to get from them? None of it made any sense to me.

I drove slowly down Dymphna with my lights out and pulled behind a group of overgrown hydrangeas. It was limited camouflage, but it was the only choice I had. I half expected prison security to send someone to find out what was going on, but there were absolutely no cars on the road. I watched Mike get out of his car with a flashlight and head toward the front gates of the asylum, which were still sectioned off in yellow police tape and a *No Trespassing* sign that he blatantly ignored. We were more alike than I realized. He stopped momentarily in front of the empty space which once held the fountain angels then he quickly turned toward the doors that led inside. I squatted as best I could for a pregnant woman still in her nightgown, near the low hedges that graced the fence and prayed that the position would not activate my bladder. Mike searched his pants pocket, pulling out the small ring of keys I'd seen him take from his glovebox. I was surprised that he had kept them for so long and even more surprised when one of them opened the door.

Once he was out of slight, I moved as fast as I could to the door, catching it just before it closed. I used the penlight on my key chain to guide me down the hall in the direction I'd seen him walk. He made a sharp right at the end of the hall and I ran to catch up, holding my stomach along the way.

Peering around the corner, I watched Mike stop every few steps to study the paper in his hand. It took me only a minute to realize it was the map from his car, a diagram of the building. He tucked it back in his pocket and entered through a door on the left. When I inched a little closer I could see it was the Records Room, and I suspected once he realized the filing cabinets were empty, he'd be coming right back out. I couldn't see but I could hear the drawers opening and closing and then a grinding sound as if he was moving the metal cabinets away from the wall, most likely believing some of the records may have slipped out.

I had just made it back around the corner when the door creaked open, and I could hear the brush of his jeans. He was headed back my way, and there was only one door I had time to reach. I could see a mop or broom handle sticking out of it, keeping the door from closing all the way. I wedged myself quickly inside, hoping there was enough room for my stomach and waited for my brother to pass. He headed back beyond the front desk and to the left. I could see the light from his flashlight bouncing along the wall until it disappeared completely, and I was left in near darkness except for a sporadic florescent light that that blinked on and off every few minutes. It reminded me of something I once read about the ability of flashing lights to cause schizophrenia. As I tried to catch up I suddenly became aware of the birds flapping around frantically above me, some so close that I felt the air from their wings move my hair. Visions of Tippi Hendren flashed through my mind as I hurried to see where my brother had gone.

Off to the left there was some kind of community room, lined by windows, I imagined so the staff could keep an eye on things. There was an alcove with empty bookshelves and a couple of rickety card tables. A television, old and dusty with a huge crack in the glass, was still attached high on the wall.

As I crept carefully along, I noticed another room off to the side. Just past the piano I caught a flash of light—my brother's flashlight as it bounced down a narrow corridor, one in which I soon discovered ended abruptly at a heavy metal door that he had left slightly ajar. I could hear his footsteps, growing fainter with each step, and I waited until I could no longer hear them before I began my descent down the stairs after him. Mike had propped the metal door open with something. As I pushed on it and squeezed through, the odor of decaying earth was so pungent, I felt as if I had just entered the passageway to the *Cask of Amontillado.* After my eyes began to focus in the darkness, I stuck my hand out as a guide, and it went straight into what felt like a giant spider web.

"Aarggh!!" I screamed then covered my mouth, but it was too late.

"Who's there?" I heard Mike yell in the distance. I could see his flashlight bouncing toward me. "I know someone's there."

Shit. "It's me. Victoria." I said as I tried to brush the sticky strands from my hand and forearm.

"What the hell are you doing here?"

"I was just about to ask you the same thing. And *where* by the way are we?"

Before he could answer, there was a scraping sound followed by the smack of a door that rang out with permanence. Whatever Mike had wedged in there had slipped out.

"Well, right now we are both locked in the tunnel beneath the asylum," he stated bitterly while holding the flashlight up under our faces.

"You've got to be kidding me. Don't you have the key? You must have the key."

"I do. It's in the lock on the other side of the door."

"Oh my God." I thought of the article I'd found at the library. It stated that the tunnel had been permanently closed after a prisoner had been found dead on the tracks, the year the fountain had been erected. Though it had not occurred to me before, there must have been a connection between the prisoner's death and the skeletal remains, but I was too panicked at the moment to try and deduce it. "This tunnel has been closed for years. No one will know to come looking for us." I patted my sweater pockets for my cell phone, which I suddenly recalled seeing on the front seat of my car. "Shit. Shit!!! Why did you even come down here, Michael?"

"I had to."

"Why?"

"Because," he said with conviction. "I was in love—am in love with Nix Madigan. I can still see her eyes when I'm lying in bed at night. And sometimes they're there in the morning when I wake, watching me. I'll be sixty soon and not once have I ever felt with anyone what I felt with her. I came here because I thought the bones that were recently discovered might belong to her, and I wanted to find out what had happened to her so I could go on with my life. So that I could accept that I would not see her again, instead of constantly wondering."

I turned so that my face was not directly in the beam of his flashlight, but he must have already noted my expression.

"You know something, don't you? It can't be because the great Dr. Warner filled you in."

I shook my head. "No. He never speaks about the asylum. I know Nix's sister, Lux." It felt wrong to speak Lux's name as if I didn't have a right after I'd deceived her. "She contacted the paper months ago. I accidentally intercepted a letter that was meant for our editor."

Mike sighed. "Lux. There's a name I think of often. What did the letter say?"

"She was asking for help in finding her sister before it was too late; her health is declining and she thought by writing the paper, she might be able to get some assistance." I didn't want to mention to Mike that Lux suspected Dad might have had something to do with her sister's mysterious disappearance. Or that I had also been entertaining this idea.

"Nix vanished from this place in 1969, my last year here. I left angry one day and I never returned. Well, that's not entirely true. I came back to get her—to sneak her out and take her away so that we could be together but it was too late. She was gone. I quit the profession after that; wanted nothing to do with our father or the business. Literature is much easier to diagnose."

"I'd have to agree with you there."

Mike studied me in the warm light that outlined our faces but nothing else. "It's been difficult for me to be close to you, and I apologize for that but it hasn't been from bitterness toward you or your mother for that matter. And it wasn't jealousy that kept me away either. It was the man we share as a father. You see, he knew I cared for Nix. In his defense, she wasn't the first patient I'd been attracted to but the only one I'd ever loved. He knew this and yet he still felt it necessary to sterilize her, to torture her with shock therapy. I'd talked to him many times about it, and I felt we had come to an understanding—at least with Nix. I didn't realize until after her disappearance that he had scheduled her for another treatment behind my back. But it was too late. When I arrived, one of the nurses informed me that Nix had gone missing that afternoon and had not yet been found. I was sick to my stomach at the thought of it. I resigned that day and for days following I looked for her. All over. I checked other hospitals, the morgue. I stopped people on the streets to ask about her. The days turned into weeks and then months. My mother and I moved to Spokane where I continued searching the newspapers and checking with the police about missing people. The Cape Perpetua Police Department became so annoyed by me that they eventually stopped taking my calls, telling me that there was never a missing persons report filed on Nix Madigan. That bastard didn't even report her missing like he told me he had."

I didn't want to ask him but I made myself. "Do you think it's possible that she's still alive?"

He took a deep breath and let it out. "I think if she was, she would have tried to find me. She loved me; she was just upset."

"Upset?" Suddenly, I became very dizzy and nauseated. "I need to sit down somewhere. I don't feel very good right now. I'm cold. And I have to use the restroom."

"Hold this," he said as he handed me the flashlight then removed his jacket and wrapped it around me. "Over there," he pointed. "You can sit on that pile of bricks. I'm going to find a way out of here. I'm so sorry about all this, Victoria. I never meant for you to get involved."

I don't know why I felt the need to tell him, but I'm sure it was because in my heart I knew he had nothing to do with Nix's disappearance. "Michael, the woman they found here is not Nix. The fountain was erected in 1960 and whoever she was, she had to be placed there during that time. I assure you it's not Nix Madigan. Also, this woman was pregnant at the time of her death."

I could tell by the way he released his breath that he was both relieved and hurt. He must have once dreamed of having some type of life with Nix, a family, and our father had ruined it. At least now I knew what had ripped them apart. Love, the thing that was supposed to make us real.

"I'm going to get us out of here. I promise," he said genuinely.

"Here. Take the flashlight. I'll be fine." I reached in my pocket for the penlight and twisted it on. "I have this."

"I'll be back as soon as I can. I'm going to have a look around."

I sat there for what seemed like an hour, the echo of my brother's voice fading in and out in the dark as he called for help. Something ran across my foot and I screamed again but thankfully he didn't hear me. When I could no longer sit, I got up and walked over to the door and started to bang on it with the flat of my palm. "Hello. Is anyone there? Can somebody help us please?" It certainly must have been getting light out. I could see ribbons of it under the door. Mike eventually returned, defeated, and joined me. He had walked both ways up and down the tracks without finding another way out. We stood by the door, hoping we might hear the maintenance man. Mike began pounding on the door. My legs were numb and I was just about ready to collapse when I heard the key twist in the lock. We jumped when the door slowly opened, nudging us both out of the way.

"Everybody all right in here?" A large light hit our faces, and I put my hand up to try and filter it.

"Thank God," Mike said as he cast his own light on the face of our hero whose calm voice I'd already recognized.

"Joe. I'm so happy to see you." I reached to hug him and I felt my bladder weaken. "How'd you find us?"

"One of the correctional officers reported a couple of abandoned cars outside the asylum. When I saw one of them was yours, I figured you were in here somewhere. Is this your brother?" he asked protectively.

"It is. Joe Larsen, Mike Warner. I've got to find a restroom."

Mike chirped in. "On either side of the nurses' station. I can't imagine what kind of condition they're in, though. Do you want me to go with you?"

"Not necessary and at this point, I'd go in a mop bucket."

Joe handed me an extra flashlight. "Be careful. We'll be right behind you."

Obviously neither of them had ever followed a pregnant woman who had been holding her bladder for over an hour as I was out of sight before I ever heard their shoes on the stairs.

The first and closest restroom I found was before the nurses' desk just as Mike said but the door was locked so I kept on scurrying down the hall passed dilapidated furniture and paintings of devout saints hanging crookedly on the walls where the faded green paint had begun to peel off in curls. Vandals had already started tagging the place and when my light graced an image of St Clare of Assisi, I noticed she had a thick black mustache.

Once I found the restroom, my courage withered as I leaned on the door and shone the flashlight in front of me only to see the crepuscular eyes of a rat running across the floor and into a vent that had lost its cover. It was so dark I could barely make out the toilets; there were no stall doors. It was a risk but I had to do it. I fumbled for the light switch. A guardian angel must have been watching over me because when I flipped it, one fluorescent panel in the back of the room flickered on. Then off. Then on again. This building had serious electrical problems. The bathroom with its tiled floors and pedestal sinks reminded me of the bathroom of the Catholic girls' school I attended as teenager. There was a tiny window in the center of the wall near the back, and I could see the gray light of another wet morning as it slowly found its way into the room but not without great effort.

Desperation gave me enough courage to squat over the dirty toilet sans seat and pray for decent aim. I was never one to leave a toilet without flushing, but I couldn't reach my leg up high enough to kick the handle, and I wasn't about to touch it with my hand so I left but not without trying to recall which patron saint was in charge of dirty restrooms.

Upon leaving, I tried to turn the light off but even after I pushed on the switch, the bulb continued to flicker, and it was because of this malfunctioning light issue that I noticed the figure at the very end of the hall, shuffling along at an odd gait. If it was the janitor, I would have heard keys jingling. And it couldn't have been Mike or Joe. I snapped off the flashlight, hoping that whoever it was had not seen me. Relying on the dim light that had begun to furl in through the barred windows onto the cement floor, I eased down the hallway, my back against the wall, wondering *whom* or *what* I might encounter and *how* I would defend myself if necessary.

A Moth to a Flame

There are many speculations as to why moths seek light. Phototaxis is one. Insects instinctively gravitate either to or away from the light depending on their species. Moths are unique creatures for though they are nocturnal, they cannot—once they find light, keep from it even if it destroys them. This was my first and only thought when I realized I was following a small white moth down the darkened corridor of the asylum. It was foolish to think it might be leading me along as it fluttered and bounced against the walls in search of light like so many of the patients who once resided here, but I followed it anyway. It was the most logical explanation of why I was walking that particular path— the hall that led to places I didn't want to revisit.

The last thing I recalled from my earlier hours was climbing into bed with a book of short stories I found on one of the tables in the lobby of the Guardian. I don't remember anything after— arriving at the asylum or entering the building. I only know that my first realization of my surroundings came when I felt the moth's powdery wings brush my face. It was obvious that I'd lost time but that I had not fully regained it made me a little nervous. It wanted to come back, but I seemed to be caught in the area between my conscious and subconscious, teetering precariously on the blurry border that separated the two. Quietly, I started to count as I continued following the moth, but I only made it to five before the darkness took me again and my mind went blank.

When I came to, I realized I was in a strangely familiar place. The room I had shared so long with my sister had changed so much since I'd seen it last. A single iron bed, the only piece of noticeable furniture had been stripped of its stained mattress, which looked as though it had been gutted by a whaler, some of the stuffing lying next to me where I sat on the cold hard floor with my back planted firmly against the wall, desperate to recount the stolen moments that had led me there. Oddly, my index finger was blue. Thinking I must have somehow smashed it, I brought it to my face for a closer look and discovered it was dried blue paint. On the wall beside me, the word, MUVO, painted in blue. Looking around I saw on the floor near the mattress, an old set of tempera paints—the kind Nix used. The plastic containers were sealed shut with dried paint—except for the blue one, which was open. It was the smell of lilacs lingering in the room that reminded me that my sister had came to me again during my episode. My black outs were the only time I ever saw her and if I accepted that she was there only in spirit, I'd have to accept that she was no longer alive so I refused to look at her feet; I could not handle the pain if I discovered they were bare. She had not spoken to me this time. Instead she dipped my finger in the paint and guided my hand to write on the wall. I studied the word. What was *muvo*?

I focused on the pile of papers scattered in front of me, some still sticking out from the side of the mattress where my secret hiding place had once been. I must not have cleared it out entirely when I left the asylum. I could not help but begin to straighten the papers.

They say crazy people hear things others don't and maybe there is some truth to this for I heard the wings beating before I noticed the beautiful creature basking in the morning light on the sill of the window: the white moth I'd seen earlier in the hallway. It fluttered quickly up toward the glowing bulb that must have fallen from the fixture in the ceiling and now dangled by a single black wire. Had I switched on the light or was it already on and that's why the moth had brought me here? Or had we both been attracted to something, knowing without doubt that it had the power to destroy us?

I was reminded of what Thomas Carlyle had written: "What gained we, little moth? Thy ashes, Thy one brief parting pang may show: And withering thoughts for a soul that dashes, From deep to deep, are but a death more slow."

I reached my hand inside the rip in the mattress and with little effort removed a couple of folders, worn thin and discolored around the edges. Digging deeper, I discovered more. By the time the mattress was emptied, I had a small collection of these folders beside me. I didn't have any idea how they may have found their way inside the mattress, into my secret place, but I noticed immediately that the first folder had my mother's name written on it. The two behind it belonged to my sister and me. Curious, I flipped through the rest of the folders, all of which began with M;

people I did not know or at least did not remember knowing. Where did these folders come from? I didn't have much time to think about this question because I suddenly became aware that I was no longer alone in the room.

An Angel's Heart

At first I thought it was because she was still angry with me that she had that bizarre emptiness in her eyes. It was a look with which I'd become increasingly familiar; I knew she was both aware and unaware of my presence so I called to her again.

"Lux? Are you okay?"

"Victoria. What are you doing here?" I reached for her hand as she struggled to stand, almost falling myself as my foot slid on what looked like a set of paints.

That seemed to be the question of the day. "I was just about to ask the same of you. You had another episode, didn't you?"

She hung her head as if she should be shamed by this. "I think so. Or maybe I just fell asleep. I'm not sure."

"Are those yours?" I pointed to the container of paints, noticing only then that the blue had splattered over my shoe. The same blue I could see on the tip of Lux's finger. "Did you write that?"

"Partly. Nix helped. She was in my dream. She wanted me to write it. She guided me."

"What does it mean?"

"I don't know."

She squatted down and gathered the loose papers and folders

from the floor. I stooped to help her. Where did these come from?" I flipped through the files: Madigan, Una. Madigan, Lux. Madigan, Nix. Matthews, Athena. Mason, Lenora. Meyers, Thora, Michaels, Rhonda. Mills, Janet. And lastly, Moss, Alice. The missing M files. "Where did you get these, Lux?"

"They were in my special hiding place in the mattress. I don't remember how they got there." Her face contorted slightly and she reached for her ear, covering it with her palm. Was she in some sort of pain?

"Are you alright?" I asked but she didn't answer. Instead she took her free hand and covered her other ear. "Lux? What's wrong? Are you in pain?" I reached for her and she cried out, startling me so that I dropped the folders.

"Don't you hear it? Can't you hear it? It's so loud."

"Hear what? I don't hear anything. I'm sorry. What is it?"

She slumped against the wall and slid down it, her palms still pressed firmly to her ears. "The baby. It's crying. Somebody help her. Please!" she screamed rocking bath and forth, her eyes tightly closed. "The baby."

I knelt beside her, using part of the mattress for all the weight being put upon my bony knees. I placed my hands gently over hers. I didn't know what else to do. Did Lux have some strange six sense that let her know that we found a dead infant on these grounds or was she just hallucinating? I wanted to tell her that it was safe now, the baby; it was with its mother. Lux began to rock back and forth as I tried to comfort her. In the hallway, I could hear my name being called.

"In here," I yelled back, the sound of footsteps outside the room slowing as they became louder. Suddenly Joe was just behind me, my brother in tow.

"Are you alright?" he asked dropping to his knees on the hard floor.

"I'm fine. But something's wrong with Lux."

"Lux?" Mike asked. "What's she doing here?" He sounded discerning to the point of discomfort.

"I'm not exactly sure," I replied. "I don't know what to do for her. She hears a baby crying. It happens frequently. This is the worst I've ever seen her, though." Lux's cries echoed loudly in the hollow room. She continued rocking back and forth. Her eyes tightly closed. It was painful to watch, and I felt completely helpless.

"I don't remember her ever going through this before. Here, let me see if I can help," Mike said. Joe stood and I began to gather the files off the floor, reaching for the loose papers that had slipped out. Mike knelt beside Lux, trying his best to console her. He said her name very calmly several times before she stopped rocking and opened her eyes. The last tears ran slowly down her face. She stared intensely at him as if trying to find the place where he belonged in her memory.

"Michael."

"What in the hell are you people doing in here?" an irritated voice called from the threshold of the door. "You are all trespassing!"

We turned to see an undersized figure in a blue maintenance

uniform. He could have been my age though his height and diminutive characteristics made him appear much younger. I tucked the files under my arm inside my sweater, hoping they would not slip out.

"It's Martin, isn't it? Detective Larsen." Joe extended his hand. "Remember? We spoke the other day. I'm in charge of the investigation regarding the remains discovered on the hospital grounds."

"Oh yes. I remember." His brows grew together, emphasizing his dark and tiny but kind looking eyes. "How did you get in here? You can't be in here." He seemed very nervous.

"The door by the fountain was open. Perhaps you forgot to lock it last night?

The man scratched the top of his head where the light from the bulb bounced on the shiny skin between the long thin strands of hair, which he raked back with his fingers.

"The door was unlocked? Hmm. I thought for sure I checked it before I left. Anyway, this ward is closed. It's unsafe. You shouldn't be in here. I could get in serious trouble. And you could get hurt. I'm going to have to ask you to leave."

"No problem," Joe told him. "If I need to get back in here I will just bring a warrant with me next time. Sorry for the trouble."

"It's okay…it's just that I don't want to lose my job.

"I understand."

Behind us, Mike had already helped Lux to her feet. He'd managed to calm her but she looked pale and disoriented. I avoided eye contact with the maintenance man as I waddled passed him, pulling my upper arm as close to me as possible so that I would not lose hold of the files. At the last minute I glanced up and caught sight of his name tag. City of Cape Perpetua. Martin Burrows. Burrows. I knew that name. But from where?

Outside, the sky was blanketed in gray and a light rain had started again. Lux was oddly quiet as if all of her energy had been drained by what had happened to her inside. She kept looking over at Mike and apologizing. She had this longing in her eyes that I could swear was steeped in passion.

"I'm so sorry, Michael. I'm so sorry." I had read somewhere that people with OCD often feel the need to express regret. Lux was always apologizing for something.

"Will you walk Lux to my car?" I asked my brother. "I'll take her home. I just want to talk with Joe for a minute."

"Sure," Mike said. "After, I'm going to head to your house. Get some sleep if that's alright with you. This has been a very exhausting morning. We'll talk later, okay?"

Once he and Lux neared the car, I reached into my sweater and under my arm. "Look what I have," I touted, pulling out the folders.

"Are those medical records? Did you take them from the hospital? What were you doing in there at such an hour? I'd be forced to arrest anyone else."

I nodded, guiltily. "I'm sorry. I had to. I've been looking all over for these. They're the missing M files from the time my dad worked at the asylum."

"Where were they?"

"Lux had them. This whole time. They were tucked in her mattress."

"Where did she get them?"

"Remember I told you about her strange black out episodes where she can't recall time. I think she took them and doesn't remember doing so and that's why she constantly comes back here. To this place. Subconsciously she must know that the mystery of her sister's disappearance lies in those walls somewhere. Or maybe within these." I motioned toward the files: All three Madigan files and a bonus. I handed him the Alice Moss folder. Maybe there's something in here that will help identify your Jane Doe. I haven't even had a chance to tell you about the locket."

"Locket?"

"I discovered an old locket in the front seat of my car on the same day Lux had been at the asylum—the same day the remains were found. I didn't think anything of it. Hung it over my mirror and was going to ask her about it but it slipped off and I forgot about it. Well, last night, driving home in the rain, I saw Jacob Moss—you know Jacob, right?—my new boss at the paper. Anyway, his car had broken down on the side of the road, and I gave him a ride. When he got out he saw the locket on the floor. He picked it up and immediately became very emotional. Come to find out, he gave that locket to his sister, Alice, before he went away to school. His photo is still inside it. He never even knew she was at the asylum. His father never told him that he'd sent her away." As I said this, I realized Jacob Moss and I had fathers who were good at keeping secrets.

"So how did Lux get a hold of the locket?"

"I have no idea but I plan on asking her the first chance I get though I doubt she'll be able to tell me."

"Well, how did you and your brother end up here in the middle of the night?"

"Long story, short: I followed him and got us both locked into the tunnel."

"Do you know why he came here of all places?"

"I think he was looking for these." I tapped the folders with my palm. He told me he was in love with Lux's sister, Nix, and that he thought the bones under the fountain might belong to her. I don't think he's a killer Joe. I really don't."

"His background check came up clean but that doesn't mean anything. Jeffrey Dahmer's was spotless. In fact, come to think of it, so was Ted Bundy's."

"Great. That makes me feel better." I looked back toward the car and watched my brother gently pull the seatbelt across Lux. "I should get her home. She doesn't look too good. Let me know if you find anything in Alice's records."

On the way back to her apartment Lux remained quiet. I tried to explain to her how sorry I was that I'd misled her about my father; it wasn't my intention. The letter she'd been writing to the paper caught me totally off guard when I inadvertently intercepted it. She stared the entire time out the window like a zombie. It was as if she was incapable of registering anything I'd said until upon hearing that my father was dying, she turned toward me and said, "I'm sorry about your father," then continued staring out the window. She had told me during one of our first meetings that she no longer needed the meds she was prescribed upon her release from the asylum though she still received her prescriptions. I wondered now—seeing her like this, if she might need to start taking them again. But this was unfair. I remember also that she never had the episodes until she came to the asylum.

It wasn't until I had her upstairs and resting with a cup of hot chocolate that I sat next to her on the bed and brought up the locket.

"I don't remember any locket," she said, her eyes searching desperately for some kind of memory of it.

"Do you recall the morning you fell at the asylum? You'd been inside and collapsed as you ran out the door. The angels were being removed that day. Remember?"

"The angels. Yes, I remember." Her face contorted in pain.

"I know you told me that you liked to visit the angels. Do you think it's possible that you were by them that day and that maybe you found a heart-shaped locket there—near one of them?"

I could see her mind wandering behind her eyes. "The angels remind me of Nix and they're gone now. But," she started then crawled out from under the blanket I'd thrown over her. She reached under the bed and pulled out the suitcase tucked underneath it. After rifling through the old case, she held a painting up so that I could see it. "I have this. Nix painted it."

I took the paper from her, turning it around in every direction trying to decipher what Nix had painted and why Lux felt it was so important to show me at that moment. When it finally registered, I could see the painting was an abstract image of two angels with exaggerated wings and haunting faces. At their feet, a single flower blossomed. Or so I thought until I looked closer and saw that the flower was actually a heart and the stem, a winding chain. Was it crazy to think that Nix really knew there was someone buried under the fountain? And that this woman had warned her...what was it Lux had said? I thought for a moment then it came to me. Nix claimed that the woman beneath the angels had told her that one of the urns in the Cremains Room was empty. There were over 5,000 cans in that room or so I remembered reading in a photo story one of our photographers from the *Beacon* had submitted. The images of the cans lining the shelves flashed in my mind alerting me to the daunting task that lay before me. I'd have to sneak back in the asylum and try to find out which, if any of the cans were empty. How was I going to do that when I had no idea where the room was even located?

At the moment there were other empty things I needed to contend with—mainly my stomach. The baby had begun to kick over an hour ago, producing a hollow thud that reverberated across my stretched skin. We both needed food. On the way home, I got a sandwich from the deli and finished it in the car, my thoughts getting lost at every red light. How was I going to break into the asylum without being caught? Should I involve Joe? The last thing I wanted was to jeopardize his career.

It wasn't until seven thirty in the evening that I woke from my nap. By the way the covers were twisted off the bed, I'm not sure how much rest I really got. The house was silent, and I assumed my brother was still sleeping. I'd left him a note telling him to help himself to whatever, should he get up before me. I noticed that he had found the spare room on his own. He must have starting feeling a little more comfortable.

I sat at the kitchen table near the French doors that led to the patio and the back yard. At one time, in the days when Ben was still alive, I dreamed of having it landscaped with beautiful flowers and plants and shrubs that created labyrinths that wound mysteriously to the center and ended in some type of elaborate birdbath or fountain. Instead, it had become a large empty plot of grass, a metaphor for me, bare in some spots, overgrown in others. I'd let the blackberry bushes have control and they battled with the wild roses the Oregon Coast was known for.

I focused on the files in front of me wondering how Lux had managed to keep them hidden for so long, realizing of course that she was probably able to do so because they were a secret even she didn't know. I looked through the folders, while keeping an eye out for my brother, not sure that I wanted him to know that they were in my possession just yet. There was something very personal about this whole thing and selfishly I felt as if it belonged solely to me.

In Nix's file, I found pages and pages of psychiatric notes and documented therapy sessions, both mental and physical and ranging in dates from her initial arrival to her final days at the asylum. The titles of some of these documents made me both sick and angry: *The Family Tree Folder*, which was basically the same type of chart a canine would have in dog show, a *Single Trait Sheet* recording allergies, skin disorders, etc., an *Individual Analysis Card* that contained both physical and mental traits and characteristics, temperament, and personal appearance but also noted genetic behaviors. There was a study titled, *Questions on Heredity*, a questionnaire the patient filled out regarding his or her twin or sibling. This contained questions about height and health but also others about dreams and the patterns of the hand as if the survey were being conducted by a palm reader. It was sickening to think that these people's mental capacities had been based on the characteristics of blood relations. When I came across the *Supplemental Report on Mentality of Feebleminded Children,* the first thing that came to mind is how could *feebleminded* be an acceptable psychological term? Under the subtitle Mentality, Nix's file read:

Subject Nix Madigan seems to be suffering from schizophrenia and/or Dissociative Identity Disorder though not as apparent as many other cases. She is a mirror twin whose sibling has shown as of yet no aggressive signs of DID but possible OCD. Both girls seem intelligent though Nix seems to have difficulty with basic writing skills. She often day dreams and can be unresponsive in this state. Subject claims to have contact with people/spirits that are no longer alive. This disorder could be inherited as her mother, also a patient here, displayed some of the same feebleminded characteristics. Will prescribe electroconvulsive therapy coupled with Thorazine and analyze results. Subject exhibits signs of pyromania and self-inflicted cuts. Will investigate further.

The very last form in the file was authorization for Nix's sterilization. My hands trembled with anger as I read over it.

Lux's folder was full of the same type of doctor's notes— examinations from her first week at the asylum until her last. My father had retired while she was still there and so for a while she was treated by another doctor, who seemed to have just duplicated my father's diagnosis that Lux had OCD. He recorded that she fell into a deep depression after her sister disappeared, and that it was this that caused her spells of lost time. She began to hear the baby crying only after her sister was gone and so it was believed to be part of her depression; she had been kept on the Thorazine, her dosage increased when the cries of the infant became too much for her.

Lastly, I leafed through Una's papers, mainly out of respect as there was nothing I could do to help her now though I was curious what had happened to her. Had she been buried on the asylum grounds somewhere? Cremated, her ashes misplaced or tossed into the wind? How could have my father been so careless with human lives? Was it because he felt they were expendable? What I did notice was that Una's patient number like Nix's had been crossed out so thoroughly that the paper had become thin in that spot. I flipped back through her folder to double check. Still curious, I also looked in Lux's. Her number was there but it was faded and difficult to read. I had to hold it up to the light to try and make out the numbers.

I heard the water running in the bathroom; my brother was awake. Quickly, I scooped up the files and took them to my room, stuffing them securely into my laptop case—not exactly sure why I felt the need to continue to keep them from Mike. Maybe he would be able to explain things I didn't understand if I gave him the chance. Was I being protective because I wasn't sure of my father's involvement in either Alice's death or Nix's disappearance or did I still consider Mike a suspect? I wasn't sure.

Back in the kitchen, I brewed a pot of coffee and tried to finish a crossword I had started what seemed like a week before.

"That smells delicious," Mike said when he sat down at the table.

"Did you get some rest?"

"I think so. In and out. I can't stop thinking about Lux. Her condition must have worsened after I left. I should have stayed. Maybe I could have helped her."

I got up and grabbed two cups from the cupboard. "I'm not so sure that would have made a difference. Don't beat yourself up over it. You did what you had to do." I got the half and half from the fridge and set it on the table. "And Dad didn't make it any easier."

"I guess. It's just that..."

"I know. You feel responsible. But you're not. I assure you. I do have a question for you though. It may sound a little bizarre. Did Nix ever mention a woman *under the angels*. A woman with a baby?"

"Yes. On more than one occasion."

"So you were familiar with her...ability?" I didn't wait for an answer. "Did you believe her—about the dead?"

"Not at first. She said she could prove it to me if I gave her a key to the Cremains Room. So I did." He poured cream into his coffee then began looking for a spoon.

"Behind you. In the drawer by the sink. And did she ever give you proof?"

"She would spend hours in that room, but I never knew what she was looking for. She never told me. Maybe I should have asked more questions. I made mistakes at the asylum—many of them—but Nix made me a different person. She was very special. I don't think I'll ever get over her. I'm sure none of this is news to you. You know what it's like to lose someone you love. I'm sorry I wasn't there for you. I wanted to be. Dad made it very difficult."

I didn't know what to say to this. Thankfully I didn't have to say anything because we were interrupted by my cell phone. I took it into the living room, mouthing to Mike that I'd only be a minute. It was Joe calling to give me the news that Jane Doe had been identified. He said that they were able to get a positive ID from DNA and blood type thanks to the file I'd given him.

"You were right. The remains belong to Alice Moss. You sure you never worked homicide before?" he chided. "Now that we have the who; we just need the why and how. Any ideas Detective Belmont?"

"No. Her poor brother thinks she's buried. He's going to be devastated when he finds out.

"Well, let's keep this between you and me for right now. The last thing we need is a family member getting involved. It'll just slow down the investigation, and we'll never find out who killed her."

Just then there was a knock at the front door. I thanked Joe for calling then got up and peered furtively out the living room window. It was Jacob Moss. What bizarre timing. Shit. I'd forgotten to call him about the locket. How was I going to face him when I knew his sister was not only never given a proper burial but pregnant at the time of her death? He knocked again a little harder.

"Is everything okay?" Mike's voice called from the kitchen. "Do you want me to get the door?"

"I got it. Thanks."

"Alright. I'm going to jump in the shower if you don't mind."

"Oh sure. If you haven't already found them, the towels are in the hall closet," I called back then took a deep breath and opened the door. "Jacob. I was just getting ready to phone you." My eye began to twitch from the lie. "Come on in."

"Sorry to just drop by like this. I was just wondering if you had a chance to talk to the woman you mentioned yesterday. About my sister's locket. I brought a photograph of Alice. Maybe you could show it to her." He was still a wreck, his abysmal blue eyes so full with grief that I wanted to hug him. He stopped between sentences as if he needed that breath in the middle in order to propel him. He extended the picture to me.

"She's beautiful," I said as I took it from him, unsure of whether or not I was happy about being able to place a face with the woman who had lain under the fountain for years, undiscovered, her brother never even knowing that she'd been sent to an asylum. Or that he was an uncle. "Please. Have a seat. Would you like a cup of coffee? Glass of wine?"

"No. But thank you. I can only stay a minute." He sat on the edge of the couch.

I moved to the chair across from him. "The woman I mentioned has been under the weather. As soon as I can talk with her, I'll let you know." My eye felt like it was going to fall out from twitching. "I do know that she didn't know your sister personally but her mother might have."

"Her mother was also at the asylum?"

"Sadly, yes. She died there when she was very young, though. I was thinking that your sister might have given this woman the necklace and that she in turn left it for her daughter, the one I know." I realized that this was ludicrous to even say but he looked so desperate for answers. I wanted to try and mollify his pain.

"My sister would have never willingly taken off the locket. I know this much."

"This might be too personal of a question, and if it is please say so, but do you know why your father would have sent Alice to asylum?"

"Alice was fantastically wild. Funny and outspoken and frankly, she never put up with anybody's shit, excuse my language. She was also a big flirt and this often landed her in trouble. She had two abortions before she was even out of high school. My father and she never connected after my parents divorced. My mother went on to live another life without ever looking back. She remarried and had other children, never really taking into consideration how Alice and I needed her too. I took solace in books, but Alice, she took it much harder than I did, and I think this is why she was so frivolous with life and money. And herself. But my sister had a huge heart. She was a good person. An angel. And I feel like I, too, let her down. I should have never gone away to school." He hung his head.

"Jacob. I'm so sorry. You shouldn't blame yourself. How could you have known?" Though I was sitting across from him I could smell his cologne and feel the heat radiating from his body but also sense the immense darkness surrounding him. Strangely, it had somehow become a part of his handsome characteristics. I felt so guilty for not coming clean with what I knew about his sister— he deserved to know the truth, but I promised Joe I wouldn't so I bit my tongue and tried to keep my eye still.

"I should go." He stood and I followed him to the door. "Today is Alice's day and I promised her some flowers."

"Is she buried here in Cape Perpetua?"

"Yes. In the old cemetery behind St. Jerome's. I try and go every Wednesday. It's a tough location to reach; my father had her buried in the section for sinners so I have to scale the rusted fence. Hers is the only stone that faces the ocean. I bet he never even went to the funeral."

"Sinner? I didn't realize. Was she—did she?" I stumbled.

"She didn't kill herself. Her appendix burst but because she was at the asylum at the time of her death, she wasn't permitted to be buried in our family plot in the main section. At the time, it was the only cemetery in town and Father Donovan, the old crow that he was, believed the mentally ill were all afflicted with evil and shouldn't be buried on holy ground. They were all sinners in his eyes."

It took everything in my power to keep from expressing my feelings about Father Donovan and what I'd learned about him through Una's journal. What good would it do to condemn a dead man, anyway? Besides, I was pretty sure he had managed to condemn his own self and that the God he believed in would definitely not be fooled by simple geography. "How'd you know her appendix burst?" I asked.

"My father told me. Also, I have her death certificate."

Interesting, I thought to myself. My father forged a death certificate. "I'm sorry about Alice. I really am."

"You're sweet," he said and leaned in to kiss me on the cheek. I'd be lying if I said I hadn't been lonely or that it didn't excite me being that close to someone so handsome. So incredibly and unexpectedly, nice. Georgina would flip when I told her.

I watched him walk to his car, a white Mercedes that may or may not have been a rental. There was a huge bouquet of flowers like something given to a jockey who'd just won the Derby, taking up most of the back seat. I glanced down at the photograph of Alice I still held in my hand and for whatever strange reason, without any valid connection, it came to me. The name Burrows. I'd seen that same name in Una's journal. Clarence Burrows. He was the maintenance man Alice had flirted with in order to gain access to...where? I couldn't remember. Was he somehow related to the man who'd found us in the asylum?

I turned back toward the mantle where Ben stared at me from a photo I'd snapped while we were in San Francisco a few years back. *Don't worry*, I whispered to him. *There's no one in the world like you.* I rubbed my belly then went to finish my crossword, a puzzle in which the answers came much more easily.

Psychopomp

Early the next morning, I found myself at the gate of the asylum waiting for Martin to arrive so I could ask him about Clarence Burrows. Martin was obviously too young to have been working here during Alice's time, but it was too coincidental for him to carry the surname without being related in some way to the man previously caring for the grounds. This man, if he was even alive, would most certainly remember Alice. Just in case, I carried the photo of her with me.

When I'd asked my brother if he remembered Clarence Burrows, he said that he had, but he could tell me little about him other than that he was a quiet man who kept to himself most of the time. He retired a few years after Mike started working at the asylum. I'd also called Georgina but not just to brag about my encounter with Jacob. I asked her to see if she might be able to locate anyone by the name of Clarence Burrows that might live in the area. I was trying to avoid involving Martin especially after he had caught us trespassing but after an hour when I hadn't heard back from Georgina, I grew impatient and headed down to wait his arrival.

Mike said he would sit with Dad at the hospital, and I was grateful for this since the guilt of not spending time with him the last few days was really eating at me. I'd been in contact with his nurses and they all told me the same thing: that he had not regained his cognition and he could either live for another month or go at any given time. Pancreatic cancer was unpredictable in most cases. Sorry they couldn't be more positive.

By the time Martin arrived, it had stopped raining. He approached as I was shaking out my umbrella. I usually didn't carry one with me but with the erratic weather and the imminent threat of another storm brewing in the Pacific, I thought it would be best. I couldn't risk catching a cold or worse, pneumonia with the baby and all that was going on. I had experienced this type of weather my entire life and though I longed for sunshine each year, and made my own threats about moving, I knew I'd never be able to leave Cape Perpetua. For years, I'd listened to how one day, it might disappear, slide right off into the water because of shifting plates and global warming. Another Atlantis. But none of this frightened me. As eerie as people made it out to be, there was something special about it. I couldn't pinpoint exactly what it was, but I was connected to the city by what seemed like invisible ties that bound me to it; a presence that wanted to keep me here even as a child.

Whether he remembered me or not from the night before, Martin never let on. I told him I was doing a story on the closing of the asylum and trying to interview as many of the staff as I could locate to get their viewpoint on the decline of the facilities. He volunteered his grandfather Clarence's name without me having to put any effort into it, which saved me some time. I was actually shocked to learn he was still alive.

"Ninety-three this year," Martin bragged. "He's doing okay but..." He tapped his temple with his index finger. "Hasn't been so good up here since my grandmother passed if you know what I mean? I visit him twice a week. He's over at Whispering Pines. I have to warn you though; he doesn't talk much about this place. I always found that kind of odd since he spent most of his life here."

I thanked him and as I walked back toward my car, he called to me when he passed through the gate.

"Oh, I should also warn you that he's a big flirt."

I motioned to my stomach and told him that I didn't think that was going to be an issue and he smiled and disappeared into the building, his brown paper lunch bag swinging at his side.

Whispering Pines sat on the very edge of town near the water but not visibly so. I could hear the waves hitting the rocks but not see them. I'd only ever been here once before to visit a neighbor who'd broken a hip and needed specialized care for a few months.

The woman at the front desk directed me to Mr. Burrows' room.

"Are you a relative?" she asked."

"No. Actually, I know his grandson." Sort of.

"You mean, Martin?"

I nodded, hoping she wouldn't ask me any questions about him that I couldn't answer.

"He comes by often. A real sweetheart. Most of these folks in here don't even realize they have grandchildren because they're all too busy to visit."

I never got to meet my grandparents. My father's parents were gone before I was born and my mother's were terrified of flying, too elderly to even make her funeral. They died shortly after their only daughter was buried.

"Clarence just ate his breakfast," she continued. "So he should be in a pretty good mood. Down the hall. Left then right. His room is next to the water fountain. Enjoy your visit."

Being in a nursing home always made me a little uncomfortable. If you pass by the rooms and don't look in you feel like you are being insensitive. If you do look in and see something you wish you'd never seen then you suddenly feel like one of those people who can't pull their eyes away from a horrific car accident like the one that killed my mother. I tried to stay neutral as I walked down the hall but it was difficult especially when I heard a moan or a cry. One woman was swearing like a sailor, and I immediately thought of Peggy. The smell was also difficult to take—that indescribable but undeniable scent of decomposition that seemed to seep into the walls of these places. It's one of those smells that stays with you. Sure, you may forget about it but as soon as you come across it again, you know exactly what it is; the empirical foreshadowing of what we will all one day become.

I rapped lightly on the door even though it was more than half way open and when I didn't get an answer, I went on in. There was an elderly fellow in a yellow cardigan sitting in a wheelchair, which faced the window and looked out over a very well-maintained garden, resplendent with fall colors made even more brilliant by their wet leaves and petals. The old man's thinning silver hair reminded me of Christmas tinsel. He was the only one in the room though I could clearly see with the second bed that he must have a roommate. Or had one. I imagined lives were lived day-to-day in here.

"Mr. Burrows," I called softly then a little louder when he didn't answer. He jolted slightly and I realized I'd startled him. "Sorry to interrupt." He looked my way, adjusting his large square glasses to find out who had spoken but said nothing then returned to his garden view, paying particular attention to a bird hovering just outside the glass. "Martin said you might be able to help me."

With this, he turned only for a moment and smiled. "Martin is a good boy." He had an accent so slight I couldn't place it. English or Scottish perhaps.

"My name is Victoria Belmont. I'm a writer for the *Beacon*, Cape Perpetua's newspaper. I want to ask you a few questions. He continued staring out the window, and I thought he may have had a hearing problem. But then he spoke.

"That same sparrow lingers outside my window every day." With his long thin arm, he motioned to a rickety wooden chair next to the bureau and I sat. "I can't help but wonder if he's here to escort me over. My psychopomp. At my age you think about things like this. But, it's not the first time I've thought about dying."

"How do you know it's the same bird?"

"It only has one eye. Can you imagine what that does to his balance? If you think about it, he might make for a very unreliable guide. I could very well be doomed." He laughed, a deep throated chortle, one which made me believe he had accepted life because he had to and he would accept death the same way. Not because he had somehow understood the dynamics of either, but because he had resigned himself to both.

On the ride to the nursing home, I'd thought about what I was going to ask this man. Joe had already asked me not to inform anyone that we discovered the identity of the bones found at the asylum so I'd have to be somewhat creative.

"Mr. Burrows, I'm doing a story on Cape Perpetua's Asylum." He shifted uncomfortably in the wheelchair at my mention of this. I'm not sure if it was just my imagination but I also sensed a change in his demeanor but kept going anyway. "It's been in a state of decline for so long and now it's scheduled to be razed, and I'm trying to put together a piece about the Cremains Room, where the ashes of unclaimed patients were stored. You see, there's a group of people who want to ensure that these remains are properly cared for—you know, given an appropriate burial. The problem is that when going over the records, it appears that some of these people actually had relatives who had been looking for them even before their death and were never told that they had been cremated. It's caused a great deal of commotion as you might imagine. There are many cases but I'm really only here about one."

There were little beads of perspiration forming above his brows; he suddenly looked very ashen and distant. "Are you okay, Mr. Burrows?" I asked. "Do you want me to get someone?" He shook his head and I continued digging in my purse for the photograph of Alice.

"I was hoping that during your employment at the asylum that you might have remembered this woman." I held the picture in front of him. He studied it but did not take it from me. It was then that I noticed the thick milky opaqueness of his left eye, clouded over with what appeared to be a cataract. He had one eye like the bird.

"Sorry, I don't know her," he said quickly then turned to once again to watch the sparrow who had since perched on the sill directly in front of him.

"Will you take another look? Her brother has been looking for her for years. He's devastated. She would have been at the asylum in 1959."

"I told you, young lady. I've never seen her before." His breath labored and he began to cough. I'd clearly upset him.

"I'm sorry, Mr. Burrows. Would you like some water?"

He was coughing so much that he could not even answer me. Instead, he waved his hand at me. I wasn't sure if he was just refusing the water or if he wanted me to leave. I already knew from Una's journal that he had known Alice. He was lying but I wasn't sure why, so as I stood, I added one more thing to play on his sympathies if he had any.

"We have reasons to believe she was pregnant while at the asylum." I barely got these last words out before I heard the wheezing in his lungs and realized too late and only when he clutched at his chest, that he was asthmatic. I'd provoked an attack. After frantically scanning the room for his inhaler, which I didn't see, I ran for help.

I waited in the hall until the CNA had him back in bed and breathing normally though I could still hear him wheezing from where I stood by the water fountain. I apologized profusely to the young lady who seemed totally unaffected by what had happened.

"It's not your fault," she said. He's recovering from pneumonia so his lungs aren't at full capacity just yet. And his asthma complicates things further."

I stood there for a minute or so after she walked away. Mr. Burrows appeared to now be resting comfortably, his eyes closed, his breathing somewhat normal. I slipped quietly in the room to grab my bag, which I'd set on the floor next to the chair. The bird outside was gone. On my way back out, I'm not sure why I felt the need but at the last minute I turned to find Mr. Burrows' nacreous eye following me. He snapped it quickly shut.

Still visibly shaken by what had happened, I sat on a bench outside Whispering Pines, staring at the photo of Alice and trying to contemplate my next step. In the process of looking for Nix, I'd become sidetracked by Alice's death, and I couldn't decide whether the two events were related in some way other than by Nix's ability to communicate with a woman who had died years before she was ever at the asylum. If I found out how and why Alice died, would I then also find what had happened to Nix? And more importantly, would I find out that my father was connected to both? Did I want to know? This last thought was interrupted by the vibration of my phone, alerting me to messages. I'd forgotten I'd turned off the ringer when I arrived.

The first call was from Georgina telling me she'd located a Clarence Burrows at the Whispering Pines Nursing Home. She apologized that it took her so long but Tom Irwin had her making calls for him all afternoon.

The second message was from Joe, letting me know he had found some of Lux's papers mixed in with Alice's folder. He said it was for a procedure that he couldn't pronounce... 'bilateral something or other.' It hadn't occurred to me until just then that I had not seen her documentation for sterilization in her folder. It wasn't really news since I already knew she'd had the surgery. I'm sure very few escaped it. Alice managed to somehow. This made her pregnancy even more mysterious.

I called Joe to ask him if there was any record of a bilateral salpingectomy in Alice's medical documents.

"Oh, is that how you say it?" he laughed. "Let me grab the file." I waited for a minute—hearing the rustling of paper in the background. "I guess I should ask what the hell type of surgery this bilateral *slingtopy* is?"

"Salpingectomy. It's how they used to sterilize women. You know, to keep them from reproducing."

"Well, I don't need to search any longer then."

"Why?"

"Because, it clearly states on her entry paperwork that because of a botched abortion, Alice Moss wasn't able to have children. They would have had no need to give her the surgery."

I thought for a moment, recalling a conversation I'd had recently with a beauty queen who didn't believe in sterilization.

"Joe. Does it say who gave her initial examination?"

"Let's see." I could hear his big hands sifting carefully through the pages. "Uh...here it is. A nurse by the name of Peggy. Looks like, Gifford or Garrett."

I knew then how Alice had escaped being sterilized. Peggy had lied to protect her. She must have noticed the abortions listed on the entry documents and took matters into her own hands to spare her. I explained this to Joe and we both agreed that Peggy should be sainted.

"Now all we have to do is find out how she became pregnant," I said to Joe. "This might be the key to how and why she died." But, what I didn't know was whether or not this would help to find Nix. To make matters worse, Lux wasn't doing so well since the incident at the asylum. She'd taken to bed and barely sat up when I checked on her. I brought her food and juice and made her tea, but she did not have an appetite. When I made it back to the hospital to see how Mike was doing with Dad, I ran into the heart specialist I'd met in the cafeteria the first week my father had been admitted. I inquired about Lux.

"She says she has some type of hole in her heart," I explained to him. "Had it since birth, apparently."

"Sounds like ASD. Atrial Septal Defect," he clarified. "It's a congenital heart disease and usually hereditary. Depending on how serious it is, it might be repairable. But, not always. Her age is definitely a factor. I'd be happy to give you my opinion."

Chances of me getting Lux to see a doctor were pretty slim. I couldn't blame her though. I imagined her decision to avoid hospitals and doctors had something to do with my father. Dr. Redding, the doctor in charge of his care, was in the room when I showed up to relieve Mike.

Dad's color seemed to only be getting worse. The yellowish tinge to his skin had started to gray and in some areas mottle, a term that the doctor used when he told me that "It probably wouldn't be much longer. A few days maybe. A week at the most. I wish I had better news."

Mike looked tired so I sent him home to rest, assuring him I'd be home soon and that I'd call with any news if something changed. I sat with Dad until almost eleven, a time that practically guaranteed my brother would be asleep then made my way home or pretty close to it, pulling off the road about a block away into the driveway that belonged to Edith Simpson; she'd been staying with her son in California to spoil her new grandchild.

As quietly as possible I entered the side door that led to the garage and listened vigilantly for any sound that might indicate Mike was not in bed. When I heard nothing, I proceeded inside the house making a beeline for the guest bedroom door, which was thankfully not shut all the way. The room was silent. I slowly pushed on the door and stuck my head in just enough to see Mike on his side facing the window, an open book lying next to him on the bed. Seeing his wallet on the nightstand reminded me of the bizarre letter from Nix I'd found in it. What did it mean? Would I ever get enough courage to ask him? To let him know that I had been snooping was not something I looked forward to admitting.

Dangling precariously half off the brown billfold were the keys to Mike's car. I held my breath while I slipped them off the wallet then turned and walked quickly but quietly out the door, releasing my breath only after I'd made it to the garage again. There, I grabbed a flashlight off the wall and a flat-head screwdriver from the tool chest and stuck them both in my purse.

My brother's car, a light blue Honda Accord, didn't look like it would have an alarm, and I kept to this positive thought as I slid the key in the door. The overhead light came on instantaneously and I reached to turn it off.

In the glovebox, amidst insurance documents and a warranty for tires, I found a ring of keys, hoping, praying really that they were the same set Mike had used to get into the asylum. The map wasn't there. He probably had tucked it in his wallet but I wasn't going back for it. I'd have to find the Cremains Room on my own.

Mirror Images

The yellow police tape that had just a few days ago hung loosely around the iron gates had been saturated by the rain and now lay muddied on the ground. I didn't think about it before but the giant stone angels no longer laid where they'd fallen. They'd obviously been taken away and I couldn't think of where that might have been. The old angel graveyard? The recycled angels' depot? Where did fallen angels go? Alice? Lux and Nix? Lost angels who had not fallen from the sky but had definitely fallen from the grace of society. Ben believed that all homeless people were angels. He never passed by one without emptying his wallet. "You never know," he'd say. "You just never know. What if it's a test of humanity?"

I stepped over the tape and made my way to the door of the building. The adjacent part of the asylum that remained occupied, had in the last month been evacuated in preparation of the upcoming demolition. I would be the only person inside, and I wanted to not think about this as I pointed the flashlight near the knob and proceeded to try each of the keys on the ring. The fifth one worked and I bolted inside, closing the door reluctantly behind me as I became immersed in total darkness, my heart beating so hard and fast that it knocked against my rib cage and sounded like an old car. I felt like I was on one of those ghost hunter shows where investigators stay the night in old asylums to film the eerie happenings. The only interior light came from the florescent grid that was flickering behind the cage of the nurses' station. My flashlight bounced along lighting the way for me. The light created a narrow stream that let me only see a few feet in front of me as I eased along the corridor. I didn't have any idea which way I should go to find the Cremains Room so I would have to rely on my intuition. My father's thoughts came back to me regarding what he had said about women who relied on their intuition to guide them.

Since it was logical that the ashes would probably be stored in close proximity to the crematorium, my first goal was to find the morgue. Two thoughts totally terrified me. One was that morgues were almost always in the basement. The other was that my light seemed to be dimming. I couldn't remember when I'd last checked the batteries. I clapped it against my palm and that helped some, but I was still nervous as I passed the nurses' station, recognizing by one of the paintings on the wall that the restroom I used the other night was close by.

The hall at the end of the one I braved was a perpendicular dead end. If I went right, I would head toward the community area and if I veered left, I would head in the direction of Lux's room. My intuition told me to go left so I did. I walked for a while, passing by several rooms that gave me the creeps. I shone my light in a room that must have been used for water therapy. It contained long deep tubs that looked like coffins. Just down from there was an examination room still equipped with a rusted exam table. It had large wheels and belts with buckles that hung nearly to the floor, which was covered in what looked like a combination of crumbled plaster from the ceiling and medical books that had been destroyed by vermin and mold. Strangely enough, in all that mildew and decay, I swear I could still smell what I could only describe as the scent of fear loitering in the stale air.

I focused back on my path, passing on my left, the room that once belonged to Lux and Nix. I looked in only briefly, my light catching the word, MUVO, written on the wall. Lux had said her sister made her write it, but it was difficult for me to believe her, and I had no time for that right now. I had to focus.

Trying not to get further distracted, I crept on. Once I reached the end of that hallway, I had no choice but to turn left. It was especially dark, and I feared that any minute I was going to come face-to-face with someone or worse: something, but I took slow deep breaths and kept moving. I made a series of rights then a left, then another right, trying not to frighten myself with thoughts of not being able to find my way back.

I came upon a set of doors that had chains and a padlock wrapped snugly around the release bars. I pushed my face closer to the narrow glass panel on one of the doors and looked out onto what must have been the outside recreation area. There was one stray light from the perimeter that helped me identify the remnants of old tables and chairs and a few weathered picnic tables, some of their benches tilted sideways. For a second, I thought I saw a shadow move across the area just beyond the fence and I froze in fear before realizing it was just a raccoon. As I continued down the hall, I stepped in something sticky and my shoe began to adhere to the green and grey squared cement floor.

About half way down the hall, my light caught a small faded sign above one of the doors. *Morgue.* I shuddered and took a deep breath then proceeded to stand there for what seemed like forever in order to gain the courage to push on the bar that opened the door. It took a pretty good shove but it eventually gave in, and I found myself on a small landing where I saw the stairs that led to what I knew was the basement. In nearly every scary movie I'd seen, dead people were always kept in the basement.

I took each stair with caution, hoping my belly would not get in the way of proper positioning of my feet. The last thing I wanted to do was hold onto the handrail but when I nearly lost my balance, I grabbed for it—only it all but crumbled in my clutch. I could hear what I imagined were rat droppings crunching under my feet so I started humming to keep my ears occupied. It was only when I reached the bottom and the words, *in all those old familiar places,* grazed my lips did I realize what song it was that I'd subconsciously chosen to keep me company. It was the song Lux had been playing in the lobby. It was the song I first played on the cello. The song Hoyt had sung to Una in Heart's Cove. I felt the chills run up and down my arms.

At the bottom of the second set of stairs, I found a short hall with only one door at the end of it. I could tell by the frosted glass that it most likely led to the morgue and it took everything in my mind to psyche myself up to the fact that I would probably have to go inside there in order to get to the Cremains Room.

In front of the door, I reached for the knob, my hand hesitating but determined. It was almost a relief that I found it locked, but then I suddenly remembered that I had the keys. I must have tried seven or eight keys before hearing the click I recognized as success. Another deep breath and I opened the door. It creaked and I thought of Ben and our door at home and of his death. When I first learned of it, I tried to picture where his body had been taken. A makeshift morgue beneath a tent? An air-conditioned motel room piled with other unfortunate soldiers? And once I learned that his body had been blown into pieces, I even pictured an Igloo cooler being tossed about in a Hummer on the way back to wherever. I could still hear the wavering voice of the young soldier who'd been sent to my door. There were two of them but only one spoke. The messenger. He carried a folded flag and my eyes were saturated with tears before he said a word.

"Mrs. Belmont? Are you Victoria Belmont?" He knelt before me on one knee, extending the flag in front of him as if I were a princess about to accept a gift from a solicitor.

"No." I said. "No. I'm not her. No." But I was her.

"I'm sorry," he said when he stood. Then the soldiers both turned in synchronicity like marionettes and walked back to their vehicle without looking back to see that I had dropped into a pile on the floor.

I took in the smell of the morgue, a bitter medicinal scent that I was sure would be green or brown if it had a color. There were no windows for anyone to notice me sneaking around so I reached and hit the light switch. Several fluorescent lights flickered above me but only two remained on and I was okay with this. Two was better than none.

The room wasn't empty as I thought it might be. Silver tables with grooves and drains were scattered about, one still connected by a hose to a stainless double sink that reminded me of the kind used in restaurants by dishwashers. The cabinets, cupboards, and drawers appeared neat and orderly and there were no traces of rat poop or crumbling plaster on the floor. Oddly enough, the room was more preserved than all of the others I'd come across in the building and as morbidly ridiculous as it sounded, I couldn't help but wonder if formaldehyde had somehow seeped into the walls and floor and this is what helped conserve it.

Casually surveying the perimeter of the room, I saw what looked like a brick fireplace with a silver door. The crematorium. It reminded me of a giant pizza oven. I noticed a few other doors and once I tried them discovered only closets and storage facilities. But no ashes. I flipped the lights back off and pulled the door closed behind me. It's when I was making my way to the staircase that my light caught the door beneath the stairs. It was an old door, wooden with an iron knob. It wasn't a door I'd expect to find in a place like this. In fact, it looked like it belonged in an old Victorian orphanage. I tried the knob, which was loose but locked. Studying the keyhole, it only took a minute to realize that none of the keys on my brother's ring was going to fit. They were all modern keys. This lock required one of those old skeleton keys.

Expecting to find another closet full of brooms and mop buckets, I dug in my purse for the screwdriver. It was too difficult to hold both the flashlight and the screwdriver so I laid down the light and tried to jimmy the door. After what I imagined to be only about fifteen minutes but felt like thirty, I wiped the sweat from my brow and stood erect again, my back aching like I'd been kicked. One thing I did not like to accept was defeat. I slowly made my way up the stairs, comforting myself with the idea that it was just a broom closet and that I was wasting my valuable time trying to get inside. But, by the time I reached the top of the stairs, I knew I would not be able to leave there without getting into that room. I pictured the police trying to haul me away as I desperately pried at the keyhole, screaming like a crazy person that I had to get in there.

Standing in the hallway just outside the door that led downstairs to the morgue, I envisioned ways of picking the lock. I said it aloud this time: *I have to get in that room*. Perhaps if I found a hammer or something with some weight, I might be able to break the knob off. Would that even help me to open the door?

As I stood there contemplating my minimal options, I saw a light as quick and bright as a lightning strike, flash down by the doors that led to the outdoor area. I quickly snapped off my flashlight and backed against the wall. My heart was beating so fast it resonated against the wall like a drumbeat. I waited for a few minutes but when I heard nothing, I turned the flashlight back on and made my way down the hall. Just as I approached the doors, I saw her: my beautiful childhood friend, glowing like dust particles trapped in a silhouette of light. My intuition, the one my father had warned me against. She seemed to be waiting for me at the end of the hall but as I approached, she disappeared, and I would be lying if I had not at that moment questioned my own sanity. When I reached the end of the hall, however, I caught sight of her again briefly. Then she was gone. This happened again and again until I realized she was guiding me along. When she disappeared directly in front of the room that once belonged to Lux and her sister, I knew she wanted me to enter the room and that's what I did.

Instead of the musty damp odor I'd taken in before, I smelled only lilacs. So intensely that I became dizzied and had to brace myself on the threshold. And it was in that fragrant spell that I heard the words as clearly as if they were whispered into my ear. *Sometimes I take things that don't belong to me.* Lux had said this to me when I discovered she had my pen.

For reasons I can't explain, I knelt by the old mattress and wedged my hand inside it to the pocket that was once Lux's hiding place. Pieces of damp foam caked under my nails. Reaching as far back as I could, I groped around not sure of what I may be looking for until my fingers touched something hard and cold. It felt so much like a bone that I cringed. My apprehension turned to laughter when I pulled out a skeleton key. Lux must have taken it from her sister without remembering she'd done so. It had to be the key to the Cremains Room. I was sure of it. My excitement quickly diminished though when the flashlight, I'd held in my other hand, blinked a few times then went out completely. I engaged the button, pressing down as hard as I could, hoping for even a spark of light but got nothing. I was swallowed in blackness, not even able to see my hand in front of me. How would I ever find my way back to the basement?

Feeling my way into the hall, I turned in the direction I'd came from but then made a left when I should have gone right or vice versa and now though I couldn't see anything, my intuition told me that I was in an entirely different section of the asylum. I started to feel nauseated. My fear had come true. I was lost in the asylum. And I was scared. I leaned against the wall, my matronly emotions took over and I started to cry. Not just for me but for my child. Anything could happen to us at this point, and if I'd learned anything as of late, it was that real people are sometimes scarier than ghosts. I took a couple deep breaths then stood up, encouraging myself to be brave. My back must have grazed a light switch though I felt nothing and the hall suddenly became bathed in the yellow-green glow of fluorescent lighting. Each time a hallway intercepted another, a light would come on until I was once again standing just outside the door that led to the basement, without any idea of how I managed to get there.

Once I made it to the bottom floor, it was only a matter of minutes before I had the door to the Cremains Room open. The first thing I did was reach for the light switch. The room lit up in a jaundiced luminescence I would describe as sickly. Mistakenly, I had thought it would be a small room since it was seemingly crammed under the stairs. Instead, to my surprise, it was about the size of my garage. It smelled damp like a basement that had been flooded.

More dreadful than the photos I'd seen in the newspaper story, shelves and shelves of iodized cans, no bigger than the quart cans paint is sold in, lined the perimeter of the room. I was in such awe that I tripped over some sort of silver tray, sending it flying upward. When it hit the floor, it gave off a ringing sound so loud, I had to cover my ears, hoping that no one else had heard it. I propped it up against a wall so that I would not kick it again.

As I looked around at the cans, I understood that this was a much bigger project than I originally estimated. Potentially, I could be here for days, shaking the cans, looking for one that might be empty. And then what?

I started in the far left corner. Each can had been labeled in what looked like a piece of masking tape with a number written across it in either pen or pencil in no particular order. No names. Just numbers—some of them faded beyond legibility—probably much like they had when they were alive at the asylum. This made me feel like crying again, but it also gave me the strength to continue.

By the time I'd made it to the end of the first row, I was exhausted. I must have shaken over 100 cans, some of them fused together but none of them empty. When I got about half way through the second row, I turned and eyed the rickety old chair that was propped in the corner. When I turned back, a set of beady black eyes locked with mine and I screamed. "Jesus!" A rat the size of a squirrel jumped out between the cans, knocking three or four of them on the floor where he had landed. He scurried around the baseboard and disappeared. "Have you no respect for the dead," I scolded, my hand clutching my heart.

I bent to pick up the cans, feeling sick that one of the lids had become detached in the fall, its ashes spewed out onto the floor. When I went to scoop them up, appalled and a little unnerved at what I was about to do, I noticed tiny blue specs of glitter glistening under the light. What were they? The number on this particular can had faded so much that I could only decipher a five and a nine. I set the can aside and as I did so, I caught an unexpected reflection of one of the other cans in the shiny silver tray, I'd set against the wall. The numbers 11908 as distorted as they appeared were somehow familiar to me in a way that made me uneasy—the kind of feeling a person gets just before speaking in front of a large group of people. I picked up the can, turned it around and read the numbers written on the tape: 80611. It was only then that I understood. Reversed, in the reflection of the tray, they were the numbers on Lux's wrist. *Rats live on no evil star.* It all made sense now: her wrist, Nix's letter.

I used the screwdriver to pry off the lid. What I found inside was a combination of what looked and felt like sand with traces of silver in it. Strangely, it reeked of cigarettes. Was this what Nix had meant by empty? Did she mean, empty of human remains?

I tucked it and the can with the blue glitter into my bag and set the remaining ones back on the shelf, crossing myself afterwards then backing out of the room as if I had just performed some type of reverse hex. I closed the door behind me, making sure to lock it again.

As I climbed the stairs, I thanked St. Anthony, reciting the prayer that had become a mantra for me. Something lost had been found. Or more appropriately, someone. At least that's what my intuition told me. I prayed then that this same intuition would lead me safely out of the building, and though my friend did not reappear, I somehow was able to find my way back outside before the morning sun lit the sky.

Ashes to Ashes

The smell of bacon woke me the next morning. I was still in the clothes I wore for my covert operation and not entirely in bed— more on top of it, the covers haphazardly pulled over me. I had no idea what time I'd made it home but probably not more than an hour or so before daylight.

My brother's voice startled me. 'Victoria. Breakfast is just about ready." He'd made me breakfast? I'd stolen his keys and he'd made me breakfast. As I thought about this, I mentally retraced my steps from last night. Had I put both sets of his keys back? No. I'd put the asylum keys back in the glovebox but what had I done with his car keys?

"Victoria? You awake?" He tapped gently on the door. "I've got fresh juice."

'Yes. Sounds delicious. I'll be right there."

I quickly changed out of my clothes into my nightgown then grabbed my robe. It seemed odd and also a little ironical to be performing my morning routine in reverse, but I didn't want Mike to know that I'd snuck into the asylum using his keys.

He was busy scurrying around the kitchen. I grabbed my favorite mug and filled it with coffee. "It smells fantastic in here," I congratulated him. There was quite the spread on the kitchen table: scrambled eggs, fruit, and toast. He placed two pieces of bacon on my plate when I sat down. "You shouldn't have gone to all this trouble."

"Oh, it wasn't any trouble. Well, once I found my keys, anyway."

I sipped my juice half choking it down and he handed me a napkin.

"It's the strangest thing: I could have sworn I set them on the nightstand next to the bed last night but they weren't there. I looked all over for them. Finally found them on the floor next to the end table in the living room."

I swallowed a bit of toast. "Oh good." I recalled then that when I got home, his bedroom door was closed. He must have got up to use the restroom. I didn't want to take a chance on waking him so I set the keys on the end table next to the couch; they must have slid off onto the floor.

"That's what I get for having a couple of beers before going to bed, I guess." He shook his head and we both laughed. How long did you sit with Dad?" he asked.

"For a while. His doctor doesn't think he has much time, Mike."

"I know. I spoke with him about it. He's in quite a bit of pain. I don't like seeing that. We had our differences and there are things I will never forgive him for, but I don't want him to suffer. What I do want is for him to tell me what really happened to Nix. He owes me that much. Each day I sit with him, I ask him, you know. About her. Sometimes, I think he can hear me. Sometimes I see his eyes flicker, and I want to believe he is trying to speak; trying to do something good before he dies."

"Well, if it's any consolation to you, I've never been able to get much out of him when it comes to the asylum. He is a man of secrets. Maybe he wants to die with them." As we cleared the table and loaded the dishwasher, I asked Mike if he wouldn't mind sitting with Dad for awhile again today. "I have some rather important errands to run."

"I planned on it anyway," he told me. "You've done this way too long on your own. I'm not going to let you do it by yourself anymore."

"Thanks, Mike. I'm glad you're here." By the way, I'm sorry for reading your private love letters and stealing your keys, I wanted to say but didn't.

"Me too," he said.

I waited for Joe in the lobby of the Cape Perpetua Police Department.

"Sorry to keep you waiting. There's another tsunami warning and the phones are ringing off the hook. Everything from car accidents to lost pets." He walked me back to his office and closed the door. "You said on the phone it was urgent. Is your father..."

I interrupted. "No, nothing like that. Not yet anyway. It's just that I need another favor. I know you're busy and I wouldn't ask but it's important."

"Victoria, you know I'd do anything for you. Well, almost anything."

He had that look in his eyes again; that painfully sad

reflection that disappeared as quickly as it appeared. "Well, this is a delicate matter and I hate involving you, but I don't know how else to do it."

"You sound so serious. What it is?"

"Well, that's the thing. It is serious. Your job could be in jeopardy should anyone find out."

"Oh boy. What have you done? Does this have anything to do with Alice Moss?"

"I'm not sure. It may; I just don't know how." I dug in my purse for the remains I'd taken from the asylum. Somewhere in the last few months I'd become quite good at stealing.

"I'm afraid to ask. What in God's name are those?" he asked as I set them the cans on his desk.

"Not what. Who? They're ashes from the Cremains Room at the asylum."

"Oh dear Lord. And how is it that *you* have them?"

"Well, I'd rather not say." I smiled coyly.

"Victoria Belmont. That is a serious violation of the law. You could go to jail. Breaking and entering, possession of human remains…need I continue?"

"I know. That's why I need your help."

Joe began pacing behind his desk though clearly there wasn't enough room for a man his size. He ran his hand through the curls on top of his head, which only cleared the low ceiling by a foot then reached over and dropped the blinds on the window when he noticed an officer casually peering in.

"Please, Joe. Can you send these to the lab? For me?"

He stared into my eyes for a minute or two, sat back down in his chair and rubbed his hands over his face. Then he stood again. "Alright. On one condition: you either stop playing detective or join the force."

Laughing, I thanked him. "I'll need DNA if possible. And composition."

"Composition?"

"I don't think that both cans contain human remains."

He cocked his head and shot me a look that screamed: what in the hell are you talking about?

"Women's intuition. And I've been to the beach a few times."

He looked on even more confused but didn't ask. "Okay. I'm going to have to call in a few favors though. It could be a couple days."

"Tomorrow would be better."

"You're killing me, Torie. I'll see what I can do." I'd forgotten that he used to call me by that name in high school. He was the only other person besides my father or Ben I'd let call me that. Ben usually called me Vic or Victor when he was being funny. Joe had always been a good friend, and I wondered how and why destiny decided to separate us so long ago, but I quickly pushed this thought out of my mind. I didn't like thinking about it. About us. How and who we used to be. In no way did I feel shorted. There was no doubt in my mind that I was destined for Ben. We were meant to be together. But maybe there was more than one destiny—a sort of second chance for people like Lux and Mike. And me.

I walked around to embrace my big friend though with my short arms and big stomach it wasn't much of a hug. "You're a good man, Joe."

"Don't let that get out. I have a reputation to uphold around here." he said.

As I was pulling out of my parking space, Joe ran to catch up with me. He handed me a yellow envelope. "I almost forgot. Here are those papers from Lux's folder."

At the first red light, I briefly examined the medical documents that belonged to Lux while she was a patient at the asylum. I recognized the Sterilization Form immediately. It wasn't really any different from the others I'd seen. Morphine was listed and a few other drugs I had never heard of, and I made a mental note to research them the first chance I got. One in particular I jotted down on the notepad I kept in my purse.

I dreaded my next stop but it wasn't because I didn't want to see Lux. I had over the last five months become quite attached to her in a way I couldn't explain but one that I felt had more to do with just compassion and empathy. October was just a week away and this would be a very difficult time for her. She told me that she had not celebrated her birthday even once after Nix disappeared.

"Lux? It's Victoria," I said as I rapped on the door. She'd been home in bed for days and I became concerned when there was no answer. I turned the knob. The door was unlocked and I went inside. I could see immediately she wasn't there. The bed was made and her tea cup turned over on a towel by the sink. I called her name again just to make sure. Where could she have gone? After waiting in the apartment for her for twenty or so minutes, I left, hoping to either catch her in the lobby or maybe see her coming home from the corner store. It's not like she carried a cell phone so I had no other way of trying to find her. I'd stop by later and make sure she'd made it home. Still, I kept searching both sides of the street as I drove up Pollux towards the hospital.

When I reached my father's room, carrying two cups of coffee—one for Mike, I heard a woman's voice speaking to him behind the curtain that divided the room into two sections. Thinking it was one of his nurses, I waited respectively outside the room in case they were changing his catheter, which was too uncomfortable for me to watch. Since there was no sign of my brother, he must have felt the same way and went for a walk or to get a bite to eat. Growing impatient, I leaned my head in to see if I might be able to hear anything. What I heard made me drop the coffee on the floor. It splattered all over the wall and onto my pants. One of the nurses quickly brought a towel and began wiping up either because she was incredibly nice or maybe because she saw right away that I might have trouble bending down to clean it up myself.

"I'm sorry," I said. "Thank you," I called over my shoulder as I hurried into the room to find out if it really was Lux's voice I'd heard.

"If you could just tell me what happened to my sister Nix, I wouldn't bother you anymore. I know you're not well and I'm sorry. I'm very sorry. I'm not well either and that's why I wanted to come here. I need to know. We are both running out of time, Dr. Warner." She began to cry. "Please, I beg of you: if you know where my sister is or what might have happened to her, tell me before it's too late. For both of us."

"Lux? You shouldn't be here."

She stared at me like a child who'd was being scolded for reaching for the hot stove. "I know, Victoria. I'm sorry. I just had to." Her face was drawn and tired and she had dark circles under her eyes.

"Well, he hasn't spoken in days. Believe me, I've tried. How did you get here?"

"But he can hear me. I know it. I walked."

She looked so sad and desperate, and I couldn't imagine how much courage it must have taken her to step foot inside a hospital let alone speak to my father. She was the bravest woman I'd ever met. "Let's get you home, okay?"

"You're angry aren't you?"

"No. I'm not," I reassured her and I really wasn't.

On the way out of the hospital, I grabbed a cup of hot tea to warm her up a bit on the ride back to the Guardian. In the car, I tried to see if she might be willing to come back to the hospital and see the heart doctor I'd spoken to about her condition. She looked so pale still that I was really worried about her.

"I don't think so."

"But Lux, he might be able to help you. He's one of the best. Will you at least consider it?"

"I'll think about it."

"Okay. Good enough.

"I'm really tired," she confessed.

"I know." I parked the car and walked with her upstairs, trying not to let her see how I studied her face, remembering the photograph I'd found of Nix in my brother's wallet. The beautiful Madigan twins. Even in the strange hall lighting I found beauty and strength in those tiny lines that grew around Lux's eyes. I wondered if things had been different for her would she have married. Had children? Grandchildren? Thrown holiday parties and played cards on Sundays with the girls from her book club? Gone shopping with her sister? These were just normal every day moments that she would never experience because total strangers had decided her future. These decisions were based solely on her mother, a woman who'd continually been disadvantaged by the systems of the world. I made a promise to myself that no matter what happened with Lux and Nix and Alice, I would make certain people knew about Father Donovan. Dead or alive, a man like that should never be respected.

There were things I wanted Lux to know. Things like how sorry I was about how her family had suffered so greatly under my father's care. I wanted her to know how I truly despised eugenics and everything it stood for. I wanted to tell her how much I cared for her and how, no matter what happened, I would always be there for her. And maybe this is why at that minute I asked her if she would like to stay with me. In my house.

"It's nothing fancy, but you'd have your own room. And we could plant a garden. Flowers and vegetables and whatever you like."

I made her a sandwich then got her in bed and propped her feet up to try and alleviate some of the swelling. As she drifted off, I held her hand in mine and studied the numbers on her wrist. Read in a mirror they'd be a totally different set of numbers. Either she carved them into her own flesh knowing that she would not remember them or someone wanted her to know about the can in the Cremains Room. Was it Nix? How was that even possible? She'd been gone by then. What I did know was that since Nix talked about one of the cans being empty long before she disappeared, it couldn't very well belong to her. My intuition told me that the canisters or at least that particular cannister played a significant role in what had happened to Alice. And if one really did contain sand like I suspected, where were the ashes that were supposed to be inside?

Sapphires and Cigarettes

Mike caught some funky flu bug probably from spending so much time at the hospital so the next few days went by rather quickly with me wearing a path between him and Dad. When I came back one Wednesday evening from the hospital, there was a note taped to my door.

Just in the neighborhood and wanted to say, hello.

—Jake

I remembered that this was the day he visited the cemetery and placed flowers on a grave he thought belonged to his sister. I didn't know how much longer I'd be able to go without telling him what I knew. The guilt was eating me alive, but I also believed that this was a matter for the law to handle. Who was I to interfere just because I had a conscience? But when I really thought about it, it was this same conscience that forced me to interfere with things that I felt were immoral. It's one of the reasons I became a journalist.

After I checked on Mike, I put the kettle on for tea and called Joe.

"Hey you." He said. "I was just getting ready to call you. "I've got your results back. Once again, your intuition was right on target."

"Really?" I asked excitedly. "What did you find?"

"Well, the can with the blue sparkles definitely contains human remains—still waiting on the DNA results. Could be as soon as today. The interesting thing is the blue specs and this is very strange, are actually sapphire. Apparently, the heat from the crematorium is not intense enough to melt sapphires. They require a much higher temperature. It can break the stone down but not melt it entirely. That's why there are pieces of it mixed in with the ashes. My guess is that this person had a ring that was not removed before cremation."

"Sapphire though? In a mental hospital? Don't you find that odd? What about the other can?"

"Your intuition should be patented. The other can contained sand and cigarette ashes but no human remains. Any speculations as to why this might be, Detective Belmont?"

"Ha. Ha. I have no idea. No logical idea, anyway. Cigarette ashes? Really?"

"Well, obviously we know that it wasn't by accident that the can was filled with sand. Someone was trying to hide the fact that there was no bodily remains inside. But who would do this and why? I mean, there wasn't much of a monitoring system so why would they have gone to all the trouble?"

"Unless," I said, "the person who was supposed to be in that canister was missing."

"As in Alice Moss or Nix Madigan?"

"Precisely. But even so, why would there need to be such a cover-up? We are missing something significant here; I just don't know what it is. What about the can with the sapphire chips in it?"

"I should have those DNA results from the bone matter soon but even so it won't mean anything since we don't have a database to run it through. I mean, we don't have anything to compare the DNA to."

"Yeah, mental hospitals don't usually record patient's DNA, do they? I don't know, Joe, something tells me that those urns have something to do with Alice Moss, which by the way, you really need to let her brother know. He deserves to know the truth about his sister. He's a good guy and it's wrong to keep it from him." As I said this, something occurred to me—something so obvious that I could not believe I had not thought of it before. "Joe. If Alice's body was under the fountain and not buried then whose body is in the casket?"

"It's funny you should ask. I just sent the paperwork into the judge requesting exhumation of the grave.

"Well Jacob definitely needs to know now, and I think it should come from me first. I feel I owe him that much."

When I got off the phone, I started thinking of how I was going to tell Jacob about his sister. There was no nice way to try and explain how she and her unborn child may have both been murdered. It needed to be done in person so I called Jacob and left a message for him to call me as soon as possible so we could arrange a time to meet.

It occurred to me that I had yet to tell Mike that I'd asked Lux to move in. I would need him to help me clear out the back room for her since I really couldn't be lifting too much. When I peeked in on him to see if he needed something to eat, he was sleeping so I let him rest. I didn't know what his long-term plans were, but I would, of course, invite him to stay, though I suspected he would leave soon after Dad passed.

I drew a bath and sat in the tub for over an hour thinking about the blue sapphire chips sifting through the ashes like stars in a cloudy sky. Whose remains were in that can? And I was puzzled by how and why Lux's wrist was carved with the reverse numbers from the can that was filled with sand. Why was it so important that she know about that can? Unless whoever was in it had something to do with her.

The next morning, I waited for Joe in the parking lot of the police station. His white Toyota Land Cruiser had seen better days, the door showing a great deal of difficulty as he shut it and walked over to my car. I rolled down the window.

"I hope that's coffee you're bringing me," he said as he eyed the Styrofoam cup I'd tucked inside a plastic bag and was dangling out the window.

"No. Sorry. It's actually another favor, but I promise to bring you something special next time I come by."

"Let me guess. You want me to pull DNA off that cup?"

"They do it in the movies." I smiled as big as my lips would stretch.

"Yes, they do, but it's much harder in real life. Whose cup is it?"

"Lux's. She had tea on the way home from the hospital the

other day. And last night, I had one of my instincts that you are so fond of. Do you think the lab can pull her DNA off it?"

"Not sure, but they can try. Why, might I ask, do you need this?"

"It's just a hunch really but I was hoping we could compare it to the ashes I brought in."

"Can't hurt, I suppose." He took the cup and I started the car. "Did you get a chance to talk to Jacob?"

"No, but I'm headed to the *Beacon* right now. Hopefully, I'll run into him."

"Should get the disinter papers back today so we will probably be out there behind the church tomorrow morning digging up old bones and who knows what else? You're welcome to come."

"I'll be there with bells on."

Confidential

"Finally," Georgina called from across the room as I rifled through the stacks of mail on my desk. In a vintage floral dress that reminded me of a pair of curtains from the Seventies, she walked quickly over to greet me. "Oh wow. Who's ready to pop?"

"Thanks for noticing, Georgie," I said coyly, remembering how much she despised being called by this. "I actually have a month or so to go yet."

"Oh, it's true, then? Pregnant women *are* very sensitive. How are you?" She wrapped her arms around me.

"I'm okay. I miss you. I miss work. I feel like I've been gone forever."

She rolled her eyes. "Well, you're not missing much around here. There's a new copy clerk. Cute but way too young. Even for me. How's your father?"

"Not good. The doctor doesn't think it will be much longer."

"I'm sorry," she said. "I'm here if you need me."

"Thanks, Georgina. I appreciate that. Hey, have you seen Jacob, today?"

She raised her brows. "Why yes I have. He's wearing a blue shirt the same exact color as his eyes. If I wasn't in love before... He's in his office."

"I'll talk to you later, okay? We'll get together soon, I promise." I hugged her then went to talk to Jacob. His door was closed, but he waved me in through the glass window before I could even knock. His office was much smaller than I expected, furnished only minimally with a couple of modern looking chairs and two bookcases, one of which wasn't entirely full. I found this ironic for someone with his advanced education. He stood from behind his desk and quickly moved around it to greet me.

"Victoria. What a nice surprise."

"Sorry to drop in like this. I needed to pick up some things and also I wanted to see when would be a good time for us to talk. I need to tell you something. Not here, though." I suddenly recalled that the exhumation might be as soon as tomorrow. "And preferably before tomorrow, if possible."

"No problem." He walked back around to his desk and studied the open planner on it. "Let's see. I have a meeting I can't miss this afternoon. What about my house later tonight. After work? I'm a pretty decent cook. You might be pleasantly surprised."

"Oh, don't go to any trouble for me." What I really wanted to say was that he might not have an appetite when he heard what I had to tell him.

"It's no trouble."

"Okay. I'll see you around...seven?" He leaned over and wrote down some numbers on a yellow Post-it note then handed it to me. "The code. For the gate. The last storm knocked out the lines from the gate to the house. We're supposed to get another one tomorrow so I thought I'd just wait to have it repaired but in the meanwhile, I have no communication with the gate phone box."

I was just about to the elevator when I heard Georgina calling me. "I almost forgot," she said, running up to catch me. She handed me a white letter-sized envelope. This came for you a few days ago. Certified. I signed for it, meaning to bring it by your house but I forgot. Sorry. Hope it's not important."

I studied the tiny block print written in a determined angle across the envelope. It was addressed to me in care of the *Beacon*, and it looked like there had been a lot of effort put into each carefully planned letter. The word, CONFIDENTIAL, was printed in the same pressured print at the bottom. There was no return address.

"Who's it from?"

"I'm not sure." I thanked her then tucked the envelope under the rubber band with the rest of my mail. I needed to check on Lux to see if she had given any more thought to an appointment with the heart doctor then run by the hospital to see how my father was doing.

By the time I got home it was almost five. Mike was feeling better, up out of bed and watching some show about the decline of independent booksellers. I'd brought him a turkey sandwich from the deli next to the hospital and promised to cook something more substantial for him in the near future. After I spoke with him briefly about the possibility of Lux moving in, I jumped in the shower and tried to focus on finding something appropriate to wear over to Jacob's. It wasn't a date. I kept telling myself this but for some reason, I still felt guilty like I should be apologizing to Ben.

At 7:10, I waited on Jacob's porch in a loose black dress and red crotched sweater with dolman sleeves. Since I didn't want to arrive empty handed and bringing wine seemed so odd for a non date—after all I couldn't enjoy it anyway—I grabbed a basil plant from the grocery store. As far as I knew, basil did not in any way allude to romance, and I felt safe with this choice.

I heard my cell phone and quickly reached in my purse to silence it but not without first seeing Joe's name on the screen. I'd have to call him later. Just then the door opened and I caught the scent of something in the air behind Jacob who was wearing jeans and a fitted white t-shirt. He was barefoot, his tan manicured feet poking out from under the ragged hem of his jeans. There was a kitchen towel draped over his shoulder.

"Victoria. Come on in. Good to see you." He reached and kissed me on the cheek, and I nearly dropped the plant. I held it out toward him.

"For you."

He leaned and smelled it. "Ahh. Basil. Perfect. I'll use it in the sauce. We're having pasta. Homemade. It's the only way really."

"I'm impressed. Seems like a lot of work."

"It's not so bad. Can I take your sweater? Purse?"

I handed him my oversized bag. "Thank you." Taking in the gorgeous wainscoting and woodwork, the enormous wide staircase that was curved like a lock of shiny brown hair, and the stained glass window above the landing, I took a deep breath. "This place is absolutely beautiful."

"Built in 1887. They don't make them like this anymore. Let me get you something to drink, and I'll give you the tour. I have Perrier, ginger ale, coffee, tea?"

"Perrier's great, thanks."

"Make yourself comfortable. I'll be right back," he said then disappeared into the kitchen. I could hear the fridge open then the tink of ice in a glass, crackling as I imagined the sparkling water covering the cubes. This was interrupted by the sound of a cell phone. I busied myself looking at a group of photos in distinctive black frames on the wall; a young Jacob with his father and a photo of who I believed to be Alice standing next to a woman she resembled incredibly. Her mother? They both looked happy and I wondered if this image ever became haunting for Jacob. I moved along slowly, carefully studying the other photographs, listening to Jacob's mumbled voice in the other room. A few minutes passed and he came back through the threshold, his eyes empty and rimmed in red.

"That was Judge Nolan. He and my father were roommates in college and golf buddies until lately."

I wasn't sure where he might be going with this admission but then it hit me like a wet slap in the face. Shit. Nolan handled family matters.

"I know what it is you came here to tell me. Alice's remains were found at the asylum. Her grave is going to be exhumed tomorrow morning. Judge Nolan wanted me to know. Told me I could be there if I wanted."

"I'm so sorry, Jacob. I wanted to be the one to tell you. I thought somehow it might be easier but I know it's not."

"How long have you known?" He asked with impressive composure.

I turned my eyes downward. "A while. A few months. But, I couldn't tell you." He nodded and I knew that I had lost a respect I might never again regain. "I'm sorry. I truly am. I can't imagine what you must be going through right now."

"It's not your fault. How did she die? Do you know?"

There was no way I was going to lie to him about this though I desperately felt the urge for both our sakes. "Blunt trauma to the head." I don't know why I felt the need to say what I did after this. Maybe as a mother, I felt it was my duty. Or maybe I just couldn't bear to think about keeping anything else from him. "She was pregnant, Jacob." I felt both relieved and sickened at the sound of his scream, which echoed throughout the mansion and would probably always be there haunting it like Alice's smile in the photograph along the stairwell.

The Confession

When I got home, it was just after ten; Mike was already asleep and the house was quiet except for the wind that had started to purr against the windows in lieu of another storm that was scheduled to hit in the morning. I heard on the radio that the Oregon coast was once again under a tsunami watch and another possible evacuation.

I made myself a cheese sandwich—Jacob and I never got around to eating dinner. He was too upset so we sat and talked until I could barely hold my eyes open. He wanted to go to the exhumation even though I suggested that it might be very difficult for him. They wouldn't be opening the casket there, of course, but still. He insisted on going and I agreed to meet him there. Joe had left a message that the crew would be there at nine sharp so Jacob and I agreed to meet earlier and grab coffee.

After I all but inhaled my sandwich, I peeked in on Mike then took the mail I'd picked up from the *Beacon* out of my bag and sorted through it as I sat in my favorite spot at the kitchen table, sipping peppermint tea.

I'd forgotten about the mysterious letter I'd received—the one that Georgina signed for a few days before—until I came across it in the stack, the distinctive print catching my attention immediately. I set the other mail aside, eagerly opened the envelope and read.

Dear Ms. Belmont,

I must apologize for my behavior the other day. Your visit caught me off guard. I'm not used to seeing such a beautiful young woman in this place. If I made you uncomfortable in any way, please accept my apology. It was not my intention and as a man who has lived for a long time, I've come to understand that intent is what defines our true character.

It's not as if I have forgotten the time I worked at the asylum—particularly the day that Alice Moss died, but I had hoped in time that my mind would become feeble enough that the memory would cease to exist. However, in this hope lies the paradox of life for by forgetting that Alice died, I would need to forget she had lived and that would be impossible for me. I was in love with Alice. Unrequited love is never easy and yet there is something wondrous about the way it continues to give you hope for things otherwise unattainable. I married an amazing woman and we were blessed with an incredible son and grandson. Still there are days that my thoughts are pulled to Alice. You might find this immoral, but I think it is what has kept me around for so long. The elderly tend to ramble on and I'm tired so I should get to the point of this letter.

Douglas Fairbanks was serving time for armed robbery. He wasn't a horrible person intentionally but because life had stolen his mother from him at such a young age, he became embittered. He wanted revenge. Perhaps he felt vindicated by becoming a thief. At first, it was just typical teenager petty theft but as he grew into a young man, he started robbing banks until one day he was caught.

A tall muscular man, Douglas had a certain charm about him. It seemed to exude from his bronzed skin, frequently getting captured in his bright wide smile. Because of his good behavior at the Cape Perpetua Penitentiary, he was permitted to work the grounds, providing that he never attempted to leave them. He would occasionally escort prisoners to the asylum by way of the underground tracks that ran between the two institutions but mostly he was in charge of keeping the tunnel clear of debris so that the train could function properly. This is how he and Alice first met. You see, I would sneak Alice into the tunnel so that we could be alone. Had we ever been caught, I would have been terminated and Alice would have been punished.

No woman like Alice had ever paid much attention to me so when she batted her eyes or laughed at my jokes, it didn't take long for me to become enamored. God didn't give me much in the looks department but what He did give me was a vast knowledge of flowers and gardening and the ability to grow just about anything. Alice was impressed with this, and I was able to keep her attention until the day she saw Douglas Fairbanks. That was the day I lost her. I knew it the moment it happened. It was a strange feeling, as if my own shadow had walked out of my body and left an impression of where it once had been. I remember thinking that this was what death must feel like.

Love makes us do crazy things. I let Alice continue to see Douglas even though it broke my heart each time. There was an old abandoned railway car that had been pushed to the very end of the track. They met there on days that I was able to sneak Alice downstairs.

You would think that I might have left her down there and gone about my business to avoid the heartache I felt from hearing their laughter and the sound of their passion. But, as I've already said, love makes us do crazy things so I would stand nearby and listen to every sound, imagining it was me instead of him. It was during one of these times that I was caught just outside the old car. Douglas was furious. He had a temper like none I'd ever seen—a rage that flourished inside him and spread like fire. Alice had not told him that we'd been together and so he must have thought I was just some pervert listening in on their good time.

He never spoke to me or screamed at me. He just flew at me, pummeling me into the ground with his bare fist. Though I'd been in the Navy and could hold my own, I was no match for a man like Douglas whose arms were mounds of muscle and anger. The nerves of my eye were permanently damaged as you must have noticed during your visit.

We struggled with each other on the tracks, unknowingly working our way up the rail line. It wasn't until I saw the light of the oncoming train that I began to fear for my life. For both our lives. But then Alice was there, begging for him to stop. She ran up to him and tried to pull him off me but she wasn't strong enough. I can still hear her voice pleading with him to stop. "Please Doug. Don't hurt him! Stop it! I'll do anything! Stop it! You hear me? I said, stop it!"

I could feel the stale air from the approaching train tousling my hair. The tunnel wasn't lit very well so I knew the attendant if there was one, would not be able to see us until it was too late. I stood but Douglas pushed me back down. He began to strangle me with his bare hands as if I had been the reason his entire life had become what it had.

I started to lose consciousness but then Alice was there again. Brave and beautiful and full of determination. She jumped on his back and they both toppled over until he was on top of her. When I saw him raise his fist to her, I found the strength to stand and pull him off her. In all honesty, I don't think he knew at that point who he was hitting; so often the case with men who fly into uncontrollable fits of rage like Douglas.

When Alice was able to stand, she punched him square in the face. I've never seen a hook like that on a woman, and I still smile when I think of it. Douglas and I both flew backward from the force of it. I hit the wall and he tripped and fell on the tracks. The train was suddenly upon us. I tried to reach for him but didn't make it. Alice did the same from the other side but we were too late. Douglas was crushed by the first car. His body crunched beneath it like broken glass.

I pressed myself up as flat as I could against the tunnel wall; there was only a foot or so of room. When the train passed and came to a halt shortly afterward, I could see Douglas's mangled body twisted on the tracks. But what I saw on the other side was what destroyed me. Alice. She lay motionless, her head oozing blood from the wound the train had made. I knew in my heart she was gone; I screamed in pain at the thought of it.

I crossed the tracks, stepping quickly and carelessly over Douglas and kneeled by Alice's limp body. No heartbeat. No breath; her pale skin already growing cold. She was dead. I couldn't believe God could be so cruel. I pulled her behind a stack of cinder blocks into a small storage space so that no one would see her. To this day, I'm not sure why I did this. Was it to protect me or her? Either way, when the attendant approached in a panic, I explained that Douglas had attacked me for no reason. A fight ensued and that I had tried to reach for him when I saw the train. It was an accident. I never mentioned Alice. I couldn't.

Later, after the police had come and gone, I sat by Alice for hours, her beautiful face marred now with a wound that had reached into the bones of her skull. I begged God to forgive me. I couldn't lose my job, possibly go to jail. I had already lost Alice and that was enough.

I'd been informed a few weeks prior to that horrible evening that a fountain was being donated to the asylum. The area had already been cleared. That night, I dug a hole in the black dirt in the area where the fountain would sit. I placed Alice inside it. Then I took a short leave of absence. When I returned the tunnel had been permanently closed. I often thought about going to the police, but when I saw the angels in the fountain, guarding over Alice, I believed she was in good hands.

When you mentioned the other day that Alice was pregnant, I was flooded with grief at the thought that the child might have been mine. I guess I will never know.

My psychopomp is outside the window again, and it looks like he means business this time. I think he has been waiting for me to make my peace. Harriette, my late wife has gone on ahead of me and my son will soon receive a letter similar to this one. I hope he will one day find it in his heart to forgive me. My past has never affected the love I have for him, Harriette or Martin. If anything, it has only strengthened it.

I've instructed the staff to mail this letter once I'm gone. If you are reading it then they have served me well.

Thank you for seeing that my confession finds its way to the authorities. I've carried the burden of it for much too long. Also, if you wouldn't mind, please give my apologies to the Moss family. I never meant to hurt them with my silence. Grief often doesn't let us act as we should.

Clarence Burrows
September 26th, 2007

How Alice Moss had died was no longer a mystery. As sad as it was, I was relieved that my father had not been directly involved. Alice's death seemed almost not worthy of the tragic ending that befell her, Clarence and even Douglas. I remember finding the article mentioning the prisoner's death that day at the library when I first began my research. I had the key to Alice's death with me the entire time but just didn't know it. That's how life is sometimes. The answers to questions are often right in front of us and yet it's the process of searching for them that really gives them meaning in the end. Was what happened to Nix right there in front of me as well? I mean, I was happy that Alice could rest in peace now, but I wanted to help Lux so that one day, she might do the same.

I thought about poor Jacob and this time, I didn't ask Joe what the proper procedure was for letting him know. I simply picked up the phone and dialed his number, waking him on the third ring. After I told him about the letter from Clarence, I gave him the option of meeting me in person so he could read it himself. Instead, he had me read it to him over the phone. Was this so I wouldn't see him cry again or because the winds had downed another tree on Hwy 101 and we were separated not by a forty-seven-year old murder but by a hundred-year-old deciduous?

"I'm still planning on coming, tomorrow," he said once I finished reading the letter. He was referring to the exhumation.

"Are you sure that's a good idea, Jake?" It was the very first time I'd called him by that since he asked me months ago. It just slipped out.

He assured me he would be fine. I called Joe at home right after to tell him about the letter.

"This is one of those annoying cases. The kind with the ending that just really pisses me off. Anyone who could possibly take blame in this case is dead. Randall Moss? Dead. Douglas Fairbanks? Dead. Clarence Burrows? Dead."

"You left out one." He was silent either out of respect or

denial. "David Warner. My father."

"Alive but not well. And besides, he's your father."

"I know, but I still think he should share some of the responsibility."

"I second that motion," my brother said nonchalantly as he walked into the room. He was obviously feeling better and got up to get a drink of water. I wanted to fill him in on Clarence's confession so I said goodbye to Joe and told him I would see him in the morning for the exhumation. I was not looking forward to it but at the same time, I was anxious to discover who was buried in Alice's grave.

Atlantis

It was extremely warm for an October morning, but I wasn't fooled; a rain storm slept uneasily beyond the cloudless sky. The cool fall air had been replaced with a heat that radiated from the trees, which were on fire with rich, ocherous colors that brought about long, tall shadows and thoughts of pumpkin pie. I had to drive up Hwy 101 and meet Jake at the fallen tree, which still obstructed the road, prohibiting him from driving anywhere unless he headed north toward Astoria.

He was there waiting for me in a blue running suit and a pair of dark grey New Balance with a red stripe. I had not pegged him as a runner though it wasn't because of his stature.

"Thanks for picking me up," he said as he got in the car. He smelled like fresh pine. "Odd weather, today. Don't you think?"

"Extremely. Feels like summer. You know what they say about the calm before the storm."

On the way to Ruby's Diner, he talked a lot about Alice, telling me some funny stories about his sister. We both laughed but he got very serious when he thanked me for being so honest with him. "Thanks for coming through for me, Victoria," he'd said as we pulled up to the cemetery. We sat in the car, sipping our hot coffee and watching the sky shift into shades of violet and black while the windshield became speckled with rain drops.

"I've come prepared," I told him as I reached behind me and grabbed two umbrellas from the back seat.

"Not surprising," he said.

We made our way across the cemetery toward the back area, which was sectioned off from the rest of the cemetery by an old fence that must have been black once but had over the years iodized from the inclement weather. The patch of land seemed to dangle just at the edge of the earth, and I wondered if this was done with intention. The warm air had disappeared, replaced by a cold wind being pulled in from off the ocean. It started to really pour as we walked toward the small gate that in Father Donovan's eyes divided the good from the evil. I wondered if the wet ground would make it better or worse for exhuming a coffin.

"Do you have a key?" I asked when we reached gate.

Jake chuckled, his umbrella pulled down close over his head. "No. I don't. In fact I don't think anyone has a key. Probably by design. I suppose they do as I've always done. Climb over."

"What?" This was infuriating. Unacceptable. Not the climbing over. I'm sure even with my awkward stomach I'd be fine. It was upsetting that no one had been given a key. People were buried here, separated from the rest of the dead either from being poor or unsound or stillborn. Their loved ones couldn't even visit them respectfully after they had been quarantined in this corner for being bad examples of what humans were supposed to be in the eyes of the Church.

Jake helped with over the fence but not without some

difficulty—a few grunts and a pull in my favorite sweater. We were both soaked at that point. "I promise you, Father Donovan," I called toward the chapel. "By the end of the year, this fence will be gone. Even if I have to personally tear it down myself." Jake giggled at my anger, but I really meant it. I'd been raised Catholic, but suddenly I found myself questioning the values I'd been instilled with as a child.

My cell phone had been vibrating like crazy. I'd looked down to see Joe's number, but I knew if I told him we were already at the cemetery, he would worry so I didn't answer.

"Her—the grave is over there." Jake pointed to a marble statue of what looked like a girl facing the water. We walked over to it. I was a little nervous about how close the gravesite was to the edge of the earth. I ran my fingers over the smooth granite bird perched on the girl's shoulder. Her other arm was extended out as if she was reaching for something.

"I'm not sure why my father chose this particular statue. But, I guess it doesn't matter since she's not actually buried there. Do you think the coffin could be empty?"

"No. I don't think so. I'm sure they would have checked, right? Do you know why the grave is facing the water? Even the handmade crosses face the opposite direction."

"Not sure, but I've always wondered the same thing. I thought originally it might have something to do with the position of the sun. A friend of mine, now a professor of Sociology at Cambridge, wrote his dissertation on the many ways the dead are buried in different cultures. Pagans were the first, I believe, to bury the dead so that they would face the rising sun. Christians continued this because they wanted the dead to face God, their maker. Whoever is in that coffin, however, is facing the setting sun for whatever that might mean."

"But also the water." As soon as it slipped from my lips, I had an epiphany. Water for a girl who had always heard it calling her name. I was so trapped in thought that it took me a minute to realize the ground was shaking beneath me.

Jake looked over, concerned. We both stood paralyzed in uncertainty.

"Was that—"

"A tremor?" he finished. Yes, I believe so. We need to seek shelter. Now would be a good time to do that, I think."

But it was too late. He had barely finished speaking when the ground rumbled beneath us as if it hadn't eaten in years. I clutched the only thing I could reach: the grave marker of the little girl whose marble white eyes seemed to emanate an otherworldliness that belonged to those who had passed over. And maybe soon to us.

Jake grabbed hold of my arm and stretched his other arm out toward the rickety fence to stabilize us both. I was frozen in fear just steps away from plunging to my death on the rocks below in Hearts Cove like my umbrella had only seconds before. Joe and I had gone there as teenagers to make out like the rest of our peers. He had been my very first. We had taken precautions. He broke up with me soon after. These memories flashed before me like a virtual album of photographs along with a slew of others—the kind of flashbacks that generally happen to those who are facing immediate death.

The vibration of the earth suddenly pulled me to my knees. We had gone way past the tremor stage and though I'd never experienced an actual quake, I knew now that I was in the middle of one. I feared for my life but more the life of my child. The same child I questioned keeping only months before. Perspective changes everything.

Because I was dizzy, I closed my eyes but that seemed to only make things worse so I reopened them. Jake was trying to get me to loosen my grip on the statue, but I was afraid to let go. Then the earth broke apart beneath me, and I could feel the girl quickly sink into the ground as if she was being sucked out by a vacuum, I screamed louder than I ever had in my life but this didn't keep the ground from disappearing under me. Before I knew it, I was dangling in the air. I looked down only briefly at the rocks below at Hearts Cove. I shouldn't have. They appeared to me as sharp knives. The only thing keeping me from plunging to my death was Jacob's tight grip on my wrist and part of my sweater, but I could feel the sleeve slowly sliding off my arm.

"Oh my God. Help me, Jake. Please." I stared up at his face. It was overcome with fear and something I hoped was tenacity.

"I got you," he said calmly. "I got you." He let go of the fence and reached for my other hand, which was flailing behind me somewhere. "Look at me." But I couldn't. "Victoria, look at me. Don't look down. I'm not going to let you go." As he tried to assure me of this, I started to hyperventilate. "Give me your other hand."

I don't know why I asked, but it just came out. "Do you think you can look after Lux for me?"

"I won't be around to do so," he said between breaths. "You see: if you go. I go. And I'm not ready to go yet."

The ground seemed to have stopped moving, but I couldn't tell for sure since my eyes were focused on the rushing water beneath me, where I watched old wreaths of plastic flowers hit the waves and float away like a funeral procession. "I'm going to pass out."

"No. You're not." Jake's breath was labored. "You're going to be fine. Just breathe."

I'm not sure if I really did pass out or if I just closed my eyes for too long but when I opened them Jake had pulled me onto solid ground and into his stomach, his arms wrapped securely around me as he wedged himself against the old fence a few feet from the hole the earthquake had created. He was taking slow deep breaths as if he needed them to adjust to the idea that we were both still alive.

"Victoria!" I heard from across the cemetery. "Victoria, where are you?" It was Joe's voice and I raised my heavy arm, which took all of my strength.

"Thank God you're okay!" he said as he reached me, pulling me up out of Jake's firm grip and over the fence. "I was so worried about you." He eyed Jake in a manner I wasn't sure was jealousy or guilt for not being there to save me himself. "I've been trying to get a hold of you all morning. The DNA results are back. The ashes in the canister—the ones with the sapphires—are a perfect match to Lux's. As in an exact duplicate, which can only mean that—"

"That they belong to her twin, Nix."

"How'd you know?"

"I'm not sure. I just had a feeling."

The earth shifted again and both men grabbed onto me. "We should get out of here before the aftershocks start," Joe said. "I've already dismissed the exhumation team."

As we looked back in horrified amazement, we watched as the weathered coffin, which miraculously missed the rocks below, floated out toward the horizon and was swallowed by the surging waves. There was no sign of the marble girl. Either she busted into pieces on the rocks below or sunk into the water on impact. Maybe she would settle somewhere on the bottom of the ocean like the beginnings of some new Atlantis, where she would be discovered by the generations following who studied our culture in an effort to better understand us when we couldn't understand ourselves.

"Well. I guess we'll never know for sure who was in the coffin," Joe spoke austerely.

I said nothing, choosing instead to remain quiet about the epiphany I had earlier. If my instincts were correct about the coffin, I wanted to know how and why. The man who could answer these questions, unfortunately, wasn't speaking much these days, but I couldn't let that discourage me from inquiring. I wanted answers. Answers I knew he had.

I asked Joe if he wouldn't mind going by the Guardian to check on Lux. "She's on the second floor. Apartment two-thirty-seven. And Joe," I called as he opened his car door. "Will you take Jake home for me, too? I need to check on my brother then get to the hospital."

He looked over at me in a way that let me know that I was pushing it. "Actually all the houses along the coast have had a mandatory evacuation. He can't go home, right now, and I know for a fact that your brother is already at the hospital. When I called the house looking for you, he was just leaving."

"I actually need to go by the paper," Jake said. "I got a message that it's in pretty bad shape. Hopefully, no one was injured."

I looked over at Joe, again, asking him with my eyes.

"Alright," he said. "I'll drop you off on the way downtown."

It was the last thing he wanted to do. "Thanks, Joe. I owe you."

Unconsecrated Ground

The hospital was running on a generator since the quake knocked out power on several floors, my father's included. The staff was scurrying around, chaotically. I was surprised to learn from one of the nurses who darted by me in the hall just outside Dad's room that my father was having a moment of clarity. He hadn't been totally silent over the last few months but most of the time he mumbled words with no clear meaning. His doctor had already warned me that terminal patients often have lucid moments the closer they get to death.

"You mean, he actually asked for me?" I questioned the nurse.

"Yes. Broken and weak but understandable. He went right back to sleep afterward," she told me. "Your brother's sitting with him now."

Again, Mike had surprised me with his compassion. Part of me wondered if he was so kind to Dad because of me—a way to make up for lost time. I knew even before meeting Lux that time could never be found. What was lost, was gone forever, and the only thing we could do to amend this was to live completely in the moments we had.

As I neared the bed, I saw my father's foggy eyes open. He looked directly at me without ever noticing my pregnant stomach.

"Torie," he said. "My vic-tory." The sound of his gravelly voice brought tears to my eyes. I was happy to have him back if even for a short time.

"Dad." I took his hand. It was warm, the veins running through it, dark and swollen like blue ink.

"Hi Mike," I greeted my brother. "Thanks for being here."

"I had no choice, really. The entire Oregon coastline has been evacuated. Glad to see you made it through the quake. I was worried about you."

"It was interesting. I'll tell you about it later. How's he been?"

"In and out. Some clarity but mostly just rambling. He said your name a few times."

"Mike. I don't know how else to tell you this so I'll just say it. Joe—Detective Larsen ran DNA tests on some cremated remains *found...*" my eye started to twitch "at the asylum. When he compared it to Lux's DNA, he found that—" I took a deep breath. "One of the containers of ashes was a perfect match. A match that could only come from a twin. I'm sorry but the ashes belong to Nix."

He looked away but only for a second then turned toward our father. "Nix never ran away, did she?"

I answered. "No. I think in your heart, you already knew that though. Now, I need to ask Dad some questions. It could be difficult for you but this may be my last chance to find out how Nix died. I wanted to give you the opportunity to wait outside."

"Okay." He stood, hesitated a moment or two as if he didn't know how to process what I'd said then came to stand behind me.

He put his hand on my shoulder. "I'm going to stay."

I leaned down and called to my father, softly. "Dad?" When he didn't respond, I called to him again. "I need to ask you some questions about the asylum, okay?"

"The asylum? I don't like to talk about that place." He said this in a dry voice just above a whisper.

"I know you don't but this is really important. I need your help. Do you remember Nix Madigan?"

It took him a very long time to respond.

"Yes. She was a patient at the hospital." He started to nod off. I placed my hand gently on his chest.

"Dad. What happened to Nix? Do you remember?"

His face contorted in anguish. "She died."

I looked over my shoulder to check on Mike and squeezed his hand to let him know I was still there. "How did she die?"

"I'm so tired. Can we...can we talk tomorrow?"

No, Dad. We have to talk now. How did Nix die?"

"During electroconvulsive therapy," he finally let out. "The machine shorted out and she was electrocuted. It was a horrible accident." He swallowed hard. "I didn't know there was something wrong with the machine. It happened so quickly. She felt nothing."

He opened his eyes then closed them as if keeping them open took too much strength. "I couldn't tell you, Michael; I knew you loved her. I'd seen the two of you together, saw how you were, heard the rumors. I only wanted to protect you."

Behind me, Mike's face was streaked with tears. He had

bitten the blood from his bottom lip, and I'm sure the salty tears stung as they moved over the bite but he did nothing to wipe them away. I squeezed his hand again.

"I should have told you but what good would it have done for you to know when there was nothing you could do to save her? I told the staff that Nix had run off. It was wrong but it was the only way. I'm sorry, son. I'm sorry. All these years, I wanted to tell you the truth, to apologize to you, but I could never find the courage."

Dad was having such difficulty that I felt horrible forcing a confession from him, but I had no choice. If I didn't pursue this, the answers I needed, we needed, would die with him. "And then you had her cremated and put into the Cremains Room, scratching out the identifying numbers in her records in hopes that she wouldn't be discovered."

"I did." His face cringed in pain. "I'm so tired. Please."

"I know. I'm sorry. I'm tired too, but I need to ask you one more thing."

"No. No more questions. I can't."

"It's about Una Madigan. What happened to her? Why did you put her body into Alice Moss's grave?" This had been my epiphany while at the cemetery, and though I couldn't be totally certain, in my heart, I felt I knew it was the truth. "Why?"

He was as silent as I was relentless. "Why Dad?

His labored breath was pained and I questioned if what I was doing was ethical but I didn't stop. I had to know. "Dad? What happened to Una? Why was she buried in Alice's plot?"

"Una died in her sleep." His voice cracked. "She had a heart condition. Because she was afraid of fire, I promised her I would keep her from being cremated." This came out in a whisper and Mike and I both leaned in closer to hear him better.

"At first, I tried to bury her in the graveyard behind St. Jerome's but Father Donovan would not let Una be buried anywhere on church grounds. It was the only available graveyard at the time. According to him, she was evil. He believed that Una was responsible for the curse of twins that plagued Cape Perpetua. When Alice disappeared, it was my only chance. I forged a death certificate, using her name instead of Una's..."

With this, the man I thought was made of steel broke down. I leaned in close to him, caressing his forehead, his hair soft and greasy under my hand.

He started coughing and I reached to prop a pillow behind his head. I tried to offer him a sip of water but he refused.

"It's okay, Dad. Go on,"

"Father Donovan was okay with Alice being buried behind the church providing the grave be a part of the unconsecrated ground; patients from the asylum could not be interred on holy ground. Una always talked about the water so I buried her as close to it as possible beneath a stone of a little girl who looked out toward the ocean. Afterward, I scratched out any identifying numbers listed in Una's file then filled her canister with ashes from one of the coffee cans the staff used for cigarettes."

"My mother? How could you keep that from me," I heard a fragile voice behind me, knowing before I turned around that it belonged to Lux. She was standing next to Joe just inside the door. They were both soaking wet. In her hand she clenched the suitcase she stored under her bed. She wore a loose grey dress with a white rounded collar. I noticed immediately the blue sparkling brooch pinned above her breast near the collar. Tears streamed down her face, and I wondered how long she'd been standing there listening. She began to count quietly.

"Joe, what are you doing here?" I let go of Mike's hand and walked over toward him.

"The Guardian is in bad shape. The earthquake took out quite a bit of the second and third floors. They evacuated the building. I couldn't find Lux. Someone told me that they had seen her walking in the direction of the asylum and that's where I found her. She was sitting on the stairs; she didn't look right. She said there was something inside that she desperately needed. When I asked what, she couldn't tell me. I had to physically carry her to the car. There are only two shelters set up. One at the high school and one here. I didn't know what else to do."

I started to thank him but my attention was pulled again to Lux's brooch. A few of the stones were gone; the empty gold girdles as obvious as missing teeth in a smile. Could that have been the pin that Alice had given one of the nurses at the asylum? "Where did you get that pin, Lux?"

"It was a birthday gift I gave my sister years ago," she said in a voice laced in tears. "She promised to keep it forever but..." She looked over at my brother as if she had suddenly remembered something. "But she didn't. She couldn't. She was too upset." Once again, she glanced over at Mike who looked on in confusion as did Joe. I wanted to tell Lux that her sister had—in a way kept her promise since a portion of the stones had been found in with her ashes, but I thought I should wait for a more appropriate time when I could explain what had happened to Nix.

I was just about to wrap my arms around her when the room started to vibrate. The lights dimmed and the chair by the window shuddered across the floor in our direction. Screams bounced in the hallways, and I could hear glass shattering around me. Things flew out of cupboards and we all covered our heads. My father's I.V. began rolling toward me, beeping like some sort of bomb that had only minutes before detonation. Then suddenly the room was blanketed in darkness, accompanied by an eerie silence as if I'd been buried alive. I could hear voices, distant at first. Then nothing.

Aftershock

When I opened my eyes, I quickly closed them due to the bright light beaming through the window across the room. At least I hoped it was a window and that the light was not the one people speak of when they experience crossing over. There was a smell I recognized. A blend of pine scented cleaner and coffee that had been on the burner too long. Where was I? I tried a few more times to open my eyes but my lids were heavy and sticky. I could hear talking. Two women, whose voices I didn't recognize.

"You know, that drug made from those hippie flowers." She paused a minute then spoke quickly. "Angel trumpets. That's what they're called."

"You mean scopolamine?" The other woman laughed. "Oh gosh, they don't use that anymore. Haven't for years. They used to pair it with morphine to put women in a twilight sleep. No pain. No memories. Now they just give 'em a shot of Darvocet and send them on home."

I don't know how much time went by again before I managed to pry my eyes open. Mike was sitting in the chair next to the bed reading the newspaper. The light in the room was different. Cast in blue instead of orange. Had an entire day gone by?

"Hey," he said when he noticed my eyes were open. "How are you feeling?"

"Where are we?"

"In the maternity ward at the hospital. During the aftershock, yesterday, you fell and hit your head pretty hard. Knocked you out cold. They were worried you might go into labor so they moved you up here."

I touched the knot on the back of my head. "I feel like I've been run over by a truck. Yesterday? Oh God, I just remembered. Is Lux okay? She heard everything. And Dad is he—"

"They're both okay. Lux took a spill; she broke her arm. The doctor in ER wanted her to stay a few days. She's been moved to a room upstairs. The good thing is that the heart doctor you spoke to regarding her condition is going to have a look at her while she's there. And Dad's been sleeping. I don't even think he realized what was happening."

"And you. How are you?"

"You know. I'm doing well, surprisingly. It's the best I've felt in a long time. Acceptance is the first part of healing, I guess."

"I should go check on Dad. Will you find my clothes?"

"I'm not sure that's a good idea. You realize you're on bed rest until the baby is born, right?"

"What? No. I can't stay here like this. I have things to do. Who's going to look after Lux and—"

"Lux is fine. I just checked on her and she's sleeping. They actually sedated her because she kept finding her way to Dad's room. She's pretty upset about her sister. You have dark rings under your eyes. You should rest. We don't want that baby coming out before it's due. By the way, have you even decided on a name?"

"Not yet but I hope it will come to me when the time is right."

"I'm sure it will."

Just then a nurse came in the room. "Sorry to interrupt," she said. "I'm going to pull this curtain closed. You've got a roommate coming in. She won't be here long. Her water broke in the hall and she's ready to bust." She had a very distinctive voice, and I suddenly recalled the conversation I'd heard earlier that morning. More importantly, I recalled a particular word.

"Excuse me," I said as she yanked to loosen the curtain. "Were you talking about some drug derived from flowers this morning?"

"I'm sorry," she hesitated, looking puzzled. "Oh." She laughed again. "Yes. You heard us? I do apologize. We have a pediatric nurse in training who questioned whether scopolamine was still in use."

There was that word again. Where had I heard it? "What is scopa..."

"Scopolamine." She spelled it out for me—"Either an O or an A. It's been so long I can't remember."

I was positive then that I'd seen or heard that word somewhere before.

"It's something that when mixed with morphine created a sort of euphoria for delivering mothers. They felt nothing and remembered even less. Some mothers couldn't even recall that they were pregnant. Imagine that? It's no longer used because it caused black outs and even permanent amnesia in some women."

I heard a gurney being wheeled in and the groans of a woman I'd probably soon be emulating. The nurse finished pulling the blue divider curtain between the two beds and started comforting the woman next to me.

"What's wrong?" Mike asked.

"I don't know. It's probably nothing. Overactive imagination."

"Well, it's funny that you mention that because right now, I'm imagining a cheeseburger, fries and a shake. You want me to sneak you in something?"

"No, but thanks."

"Be back soon, then. Oh…" He reached in his jacket pocket and pulled out my phone charger. "You might need this. Your cell phone is in your purse in the drawer. Call me if you change your mind."

Mike and I had grown closer over the last few months. It was as if we'd never been estranged and yet, I still had a feeling that he was keeping something from me. I could see it in his eyes at times, the guilt. He wanted to tell me but couldn't for some reason.

After he left, I dug for my cell phone and plugged it in. There were fifteen messages, most of them were from Georgina, but I was too distracted to listen to them. What the nurse had said continued to bother me but I didn't know why. It was right in front of my nose, I just couldn't see it. I pulled my note pad from my purse to record the word the nurse had spelled out for me. I flipped through the small spiral notebook looking for an empty page. Then I saw it. The same word I was about to write. Scopolamine. I suddenly remembered where I'd first seen it. It was the word that was written in Lux's sterilization paperwork, which if I remembered correctly also noted morphine. Two things that hadn't been in any of the other sterilization forms. I recalled the nurse's words regarding scopolamine: 'When mixed with morphine, it creates a euphoric state where there is no pain and often no memory of ever giving birth.'

When they brought dinner, I had no appetite so I pushed the tray aside. I must have dozed off again afterward. My brother was there when I woke. It was dark outside.

"You were mumbling," he said.

"What did I say?"

"Ovum. Isn't that Latin?"

"Yes. For *egg,* I think. I was dreaming. She whispered in my ear."

"Who whispered in your ear?"

"I don't know. Mike, can I see the letter in your wallet?"

"The letter? What?"

"The one from Nix."

"Oh my God. You seriously went through my wallet? Unbelievable."

"I'm sorry. I meant to tell you. It was a while ago. Can I just see the letter? Please? It's important."

He grumbled as he stood and pulled the wallet from the back pocket of his corduroys. "Here. You want the photograph, too?"

I ignored his sarcasm and tried to see if the letter, written backward as I had already figured out, had anything in it that might further develop what was forming in my mind. "Did Nix suffer from dyslexia?"

"No. Not really. Mirror twins often see things backwards and this is how they write them, too. Nix wrote this way. She used to say that she was the twin trapped behind the mirror."

Ovum. Muvo. The word Lux had painted on the wall at the asylum. She'd told me that Nix had guided her, and I never really believed her because I didn't understand. Lux had not been pulled back to the asylum just because of her missing sister. "Oh my God." I handed Mike the letter then dropped my feet over the side, one hand pinching the back of my gown to keep it together. I felt dizzy and I wasn't sure if this was because I'd not been out of bed all day or if because I understood now why Lux was so haunted by the cries of an infant.

"What's wrong? Where are you going?" Mike called. I didn't answer. Instead I walked down the hall to the elevator that would take me to my father's room. Mike trailed behind me.

"You're not supposed to get out of bed, Victoria. That's what bed rest means. You could lose the baby," he called.

Chewing on the nail of my index finger, I ignored him. "Where are you going? What's going on?" he pleaded as he caught the elevator door and followed me inside.

It dinged open and I rushed out without saying a word. I could feel him on the back of my heels.

"You're barefoot, you know. Do you know what kind of germs

are on a hospital floor?"

He was right, but I couldn't think about that now. I had one thing on my mind as I marched straight into my father's room and up to his bed.

"Dad." I touched him gently. "Dad. I need you to wake up now." His skin was the color of ash. It broke my heart to think that this might be the last time we ever spoke, and I was angrier at him then I'd ever been. I should have known that he would never just divulge his secrets. Not all of them, anyway. I pushed the control so that the back of the bed came forward in hopes that it might wake him. He opened his eyes slightly; little yellow slits that looked like they belonged more to a reptile then a human being, and I hated myself for thinking how appropriate it was that they appeared this way.

"Torie," he whispered then smiled. "I've missed you so much."

He wasn't going to make this easy. "Dad. Listen to me. Lux was pregnant wasn't she? You waited until after she had the baby to sterilize her, didn't you?"

Mike started coughing which sounded more like he was choking. "I'm okay," he said between coughs. He nodded and I turned my attention back to my father whose smile had faded. He looked past me toward the window. "Victoria. My victory."

I wondered again why he referred to me as this but I didn't ask. "Dad. We're talking about Lux Madigan. Her baby. She did have a baby didn't she?" Again, Mike started choking. He reached for the plastic pitcher of water on the table next to the bed. "What is wrong with you?" I mouthed to him. He shook his head then

336

poured some water into a cup and drank it down very quickly.

"Una," my father said. I interrupted him. There was no time to waste.

"No, Dad. Lux. We're talking about Lux."

He started again. "It was Una who changed my mind."

"He's obviously confused," Mike whispered across the bed.

"I'm not confused," Dad stated austerely. "My mother's suicide is what prompted me to attend medical school."

Mike and I looked at each other, confused. We both shrugged. Our grandmother had committed suicide? I remembered very few photos of her around the house growing up. Two at the most. But what did this have to do with Una?

"By becoming a psychiatrist," Dad continued, "I wanted to prove that we are all individuals and not always the apples that fall from the genealogical tree. But somewhere along the line I became part of the people who believed that we were what our parents were. Inside I fought bitterly against this idea." He started hacking. "I mean if what the Eugenics Board said was true, then I too would be unsound. Like my mother. Being constantly surrounded by these gene studies, I gradually began to accept it. Now I realize it was out of fear that I did so. But, Una...she changed my mind. She said that my mother had came to her with a message: nurture can win over nature." He repeated it then continued. "I struggled with this for a long time. Could a child who came from an unstable set of parents have a normal life should that child be raised by another set of sound parents? Could nurture really triumph over nature?" He began to cough, trying desperately to catch his breath.

"Dad. I don't understand what this has to do with Lux's baby? Lux gave birth to a child, didn't she?"

He weakly raised his hand, pointing toward the water pitcher. Mike poured some in a cup and put the straw to his dry, cracked lips. He sipped and swallowed but not without great difficulty.

"You see, Victoria. There was only one real way to prove this theory. And," he started hacking up dark green phlegm. I reached for some tissue. "And I did prove it. You are my proof. My victory."

"What are you talking about?" My patience was thinning and it showed in my heightened voice. "Lux had a child. What happened to that child? You have to tell me." I was crying now, angry and confused, my tears heavy and warm. I felt suddenly weak in my legs. The room started to spin. My father was a murderer. He killed Lux's baby, and this is why she'd heard it crying. She wasn't schizophrenic. She suffered from a repressed memory of her child. The poor woman.

"Dad!" I screamed, feeling a sharp pinch in my lower stomach. "How could you? What did you do with the baby? What—did—you—do with Lux's child, you bastard?"

His eyes widened as he stared blankly up at the ceiling and spoke with such clarity it sounded like he had become possessed by the spirit of a healthy man, one who wasn't yellow and old and remorseful.

"There were two," he said. "Two babies, connected at the side. Conjoined twins. Little girls, one of which died within hours. Her ashes, I released to the wind, for the freedom in my heart I knew she deserved."

"And the other? What did you do with the other child? Answer me this minute," I pleaded.

He looked my way, a tight painful smile unfurled from his dry lips. "I brought her home with me. You are that child. My victory." His last words as he placed his hand over mine: "I'm sorry. Forgive me."

"Oh my God!" I screamed. "Dad? Dad?" He was silent. I was completely numb even to my tears. I only knew they were there because of the salt that stung my lips. I was Lux Madigan's daughter; the one she could not forget; the one whose cries had haunted her for thirty-eight years. I'd felt so close to her not only because we'd both lost our other halves but because she was my mother, the woman who had given me life and longed for me without ever knowing why.

The emptiness I'd felt my entire life suddenly made sense. I'd been silently searching for my lost half so that I could become whole. I placed my hand over the scar that had once joined me to my twin sister. It seemed more pronounced than it ever had as if there was a trench being dug beneath my skin, a subcutaneous path toward my heart.

Looking over at Mike, I thought he might faint. Dad's final words had drained the color from his face, but it was immediately brought back by the sound of Lux's painful banshee-like cry. She had slipped inside the room, once again; the bulky cast on her arm silhouetted against the eerie green glow of the hallway lighting. Her shrill scream pierced the air, then lingered until I felt my feet grow wet and warm. My embryonic sac had ruptured, shattered in the same way I pictured an opera singer breaking glass with a high-pitched note. The baby pushed outward, defiantly prying my pelvic bones apart so I felt as if any minute they would break, snap like chopsticks. Out of nowhere I envisioned a ship crashing into rocks, the wood splintering into toothpicks. The pain became so intense, I couldn't breathe. I gripped the rail of the bed but couldn't hold on to it. Mike ran towards me in slow motion and only then did I realize my knees had buckled.

The Beauty of Pain

The light on my face was warm and bright but my body felt cold and numb as if the two were, in no way, connected. There were sounds around me that I couldn't distinguish right away until I realized people were talking.

"Push, Victoria. You have to push," a strange voice demanded.

The words registered in my mind but really didn't mean anything. Push what? Was I dreaming? The pain hit me suddenly, an intensity I imagined accompanied those being eviscerated. I tried to scream but nothing came out—not even air as if I was underwater where no breath could reach me. Then I gasped out like I'd somehow reached the surface, recognizing then that I was in labor.

"She's back," I heard a woman say.

Another voice. "He's crowning. Wait. We have a problem. The nuchal cord's around the neck. Victoria, don't push. Do you hear me? Don't push."

But by then I felt I had to push: it was no longer my choice.

"Heart rate's dropping. We're losing him. What's that smell?"

"Victoria, this is Dr. Tash. We need you to stop pushing. The baby's in danger. Do you understand what I'm saying?"

During my last ultrasound, I'd been told that it was quite common for the nuchal cord to be wrapped loosely around the fetus's neck. This thought flashed in my mind only for a second, devoured quickly by the immense pain that shot through my body. I cried out.

"Clamps. We're going to have to cut. Victoria, listen. We have to cut the cord. After we do this, we're going to need you to push again in order to get your baby out as quickly as possible so he can breathe. Do you hear me?"

I had heard him, but I was so weak, I couldn't respond. My eyelids felt as if they were made of lead; I struggled to keep them open as I drifted between the past and the present. Me as a child; me as an adult. The swing behind the house I grew up in; the Indian Maiden; the church where Ben and I were married; our honeymoon in Paris; his funeral. The abortion that tore Joe and I apart; the baby I was delivering now.

"Victoria. Stay with us. Her heart rate is dropping, Dr. Tash. What is that? Am I the only one who smells flowers?"

"Nurse Moore, epinephrine. Now. Twenty cc's. We're losing him."

Other voices called out but I couldn't understand them. I didn't want to understand them. They faded in and out until the room suddenly became silent. The silence made me question whether I'd lost my hearing or if because the pain was so intense there was no room for anything else—not even sound. Then I saw her, a radiant light brighter than the light hovering above me, brighter than any light I've ever seen. It only took a minute to recognize my old friend, the glow that guided me since childhood. My first thought was of my twin sister. Had she been my intuition, my guide all those years—even when I pushed her away?

The amorphous figure slid incongruously between the hospital staff, surrounding the surgery table. They were totally unaware of her presence—other than the surgical nurse who had caught the euphoric scent of lilacs she brought with her. I began to relax, closing my eyes for what seemed like an eternity. When I opened them, I could see that the light had settled into the shape of a woman who is outlined in a hazy cobalt glow as if she was alive with electricity. She is holding my baby and my heart aches at the thought that she is going to take him with her even though I can still feel him motionless between my thighs like a rock. I'm not sure how long she was there before she turned and glided toward the door, the scent of lilacs trailing behind her in close proximity like a past that refuses to be forgotten. On the other side of the door, she used her blood-covered finger and wrote from right to left on the glass window. Backwards—on the other side of the glass. When she'd finished, she turned and faded, the scent of flowers left lingering in her wake, drifting under the door until I was overwhelmed by their aroma. My weighted eyes try desperately to read the word she'd written on the window, but I became distracted by the movement between my legs.

The silence that had taken over the room moments before broke like crystal with the sound of a crying baby. My baby. His cry immediately becomes an ineffaceable part of me, more indelible than blood. It is only then that I understood exactly how Lux must have felt when I was taken from her so long ago. She'd lived all those years believing that I was real without ever knowing I truly existed. Each time she was pulled back to the asylum was because I had lived in her heart and her blood, not just her mind. Maybe in this way, time could be found, brought back for just that minute.

With my beautiful boy pressed against my chest, it came to me like I knew it would. Though I would never know whether or not he really existed, he had been real to Una, my grandmother, and this is why I chose the name, Hoyt for her great grandson. Benjamin Hoyt Belmont. It was a name that would signify for me what it had for her; a way to understand that it is the combination of beauty and pain that gives life meaning. Without one, the universe is only half of what it should be.

Later, when I asked one of the nurses about the writing on the window of the door she had no idea what I was talking about. She replied compassionately. "You need some rest, honey," and I was left to consider that my pain had in some way ignited my imagination.

The Birthday Gift

In the weeks that followed Hoyt's birth, life continued to change. I wondered when it would level out where every day didn't contain some surprise, a secret from the past that in some way or another shaped the present. I learned from Mike the details of what had happened between him and Lux years ago, and though I thought nothing could shock me anymore, I was wrong. It would take time for me—for both of us to accept that he was my biological father. After all, I was just beginning to accept him as a brother. Regardless, I respected his courage for telling me. When I spoke to Lux about the incident, she said it was one of two things she wished she could have forgotten. When I asked her what the other thing was, she looked at me with furrowed brows and said, "I don't know." And as strange as it was, I believed she really didn't know. I understood how a person could push something so far out of their mind that the memory almost ceased to exist. Almost.

I never mentioned to anyone what had happened during Hoyt's delivery. I wasn't sure the woman I'd seen had anything to do with the fact that Hoyt and I had both survived. In my state, I wasn't even sure she had been there at all. Each time the memory flashed in my mind, I remembered some other detail, but it was the glass blue eyes that made me think of Nix. I found it ironic that I'd been searching for her for most of the year and she'd been there with me the whole time, trying to fill the emptiness I felt at being only half of something, while at the same time, leading me to discover my true identity in that half. Had I inherited the gift that belonged to my grandmother and aunt or had Nix been just as desperate to find her sister as Lux was to find her? I wasn't sure. Was it Nix who had carved the numbers into her sister's wrist or had Lux, in one of her fugues carved them herself after she somehow discovered the truth in the medical records? After all, Peggy had mentioned that at one time Lux was ambidextrous though after her sterilization, she'd forgotten. What I wanted to believe was that we'd both been helped by someone—or something other than our intuition.

The one thing that continued to nag at me was my memory of what was written on the glass in the delivery room. Thinking about this while at the kitchen table reading the paper, I came across an article a coworker of mine had written about the recent earthquake's devastation. Apparently, and much to my amusement, the sinner's graveyard had succumbed to the water below, taking that damn fence and all its ignorance with it. For some reason, then, it suddenly came to me: the word Nix had written across the glass. I got up and used the dry erase board on the fridge to write it out. I-g-n-o-s-c-e-r-e. Ignoscere. I had no idea what it meant even when the word was reversed. I was still trying to figure it out when Lux came in and read over my shoulder.

"*Ignoscere*. In Latin, it means, to forgive. I didn't know you knew Latin."

"I don't." With slight hesitance, I explained to her what had happened to me during delivery—what had been happening to me since I was a child; she looked a little scared. This fearful look was soon replaced by a smile, and I think this was because she must have realized that my inheritance would not be under the same scrutiny as hers. What had been given to me was mine to keep.

"You have the sight," she finally said. "The Madigan gift."

"Do you think Nix's message was meant for you or me?" I asked carefully.

"Not sure. One thing is for certain. She never was any good with conjugation." She looked at me with serious eyes, but I could see a smile begin to form beneath her lips. We started laughing and this couldn't stop even with the tears. It was the first time I'd ever heard my mother's laugh and saw just how many of her back teeth were missing. What she had endured, I would not let the world forget.

She'd continued to surprise me by attending Dr. Warner's or I guess I should say my grandfather's funeral a few days after Hoyt's birth. I even caught her crying, which ruined my own plan for trying my best not to. The truth was that neither of us had any harsh feelings toward the man. I'm not sure why but maybe because we both had a deeper understanding of what it meant to exist. Real people have flaws and the world is made of light and dark and good and bad and beauty and pain. It's our job to try and find the balance between these things.

It occurred to me one morning as I walked along the shore that the universe might be trying to do the same thing; that the curse of twins in Cape Perpetua was not from an ill-fated ship or from a woman suspected of fraternizing with the devil. It was retaliation against the idea that a certain group of people believed that they should somehow control free will. The Eugenics Board was the true curse, and I was going to take on a personal crusade to educate the world about it. It could have been my imagination but as I walked up the hill to head back home that day, I heard the name Una in the waves. When I turned and looked out across the endless water, I could see through the fog, the jagged silhouette of the Indian Maiden whose sadness had immortalized her in stone.

In his will, the man I once knew as a father divided his estate up evenly between his two children. He had no idea that Mike was my biological father, and I wondered if he still would have considered me a victory if he had known. After all, he had stolen his own son's baby and since I had his genes as well as the Madigans, my success in life could not be attributed entirely to nurture. Nature had a little to do with it. She always does. Knowing this would have certainly destroyed him since his strength was ingrained in his determination, not his heart. But if there is one thing I was grateful for is that he was able to apologize before he died. It was up to us whether or not we would ever accept it.

In a bizarre twist, he had requested cremation. Mike kept the ashes with him at his apartment, an old turn-of-the-century building he discovered while walking downtown one day. It was one of very few buildings that had not been damaged by the quake, and I suppose he found some type of comfort in its fortification. I wasn't sure that he and Lux would ever be friends, but I felt that what they had lost would forever bind them in a way that no one could or would ever completely understand. Grief has a way of doing that sometimes.

The afternoon of October thirteenth, I'd baked Lux a birthday cake. Chocolate with butter cream frosting. She hadn't had one since 1969 on the last birthday that she and Nix had together, and I felt it was time for a celebration. She'd been adjusting to the house more each day but when Hoyt cried out in the middle of the night, I'd find that she often reached the crib before I did even though it was in my room. I worried about her still. Her heart defect could not be repaired; the doctor had warned me that our time could be limited to a few short months or she could go on living for years. But wasn't that how life was for everyone?

"Her heart is in charge," the doctor had said, but this was something I already knew. We Madigans have always been led by our hearts, even as in my case, when taught not to.

Lux's OCD characteristics seemed to be less obvious as each day passed. I'd still come upon her counting at times. I told her that when she felt the urge, she should rock the baby and this seemed to help.

At the small celebration I'd arranged for her, Joe showed up with flowers but they were for me and not Lux. A week before he had stopped by with an unexpected gift for both of us. He had risked his job by taking Nix's ashes from the lab but he must have felt it was the right thing to do. He said the investigation might go on for years, and he saw no reason to keep Lux from her sister any longer.

I'd only invited a few people to the party. Mike, of course. Joe. Georgina. And Janice. I went back and forth with whether or not I should invite Jake when Joe would also be there but when I let Georgina in, Jake was with her and from the smile on her face had been since the night before. They both smelled of clove cigarettes. He seemed a little uncomfortable about it and for a minute, I was too. But then Joe, obviously sensing my discomfort, was beside me like he'd always been, his hand on my shoulder just enough to let me know he was there. At the hospital, I'd asked him to be Hoyt's godfather not only because I knew he'd be the best godfather in the world, but also because I knew he would have made a fine father as well if I would have given him the chance. In some way, I guess I had taken his choice, and in this way I was no better than the Eugenics Board.

Just after Joe lit the candles on the cake and Lux blew them out, a crew of men showed up at the door with a special delivery. Jake, from where he was standing, raised his wine glass slightly and nodded to let me know that what I suspected was true. It wasn't difficult to guess that he was responsible. Who else had that kind of money? Lux's face lit up when though the curtains she spotted the angels strapped on the back of the flat-bed trailer in front of the house. The pair had been completely restored, and I couldn't think of a better place for them than in the back yard to serve as a memorial for Una and Nix and one day for Lux. I asked her if she wanted to place Nix's ashes under the angels but she told me that when the time came, I was to mix her ashes in with her sister's and set them both free, sapphires and all. She said that she had always wanted a gravestone because it was proof that she had once existed, but somewhere between when we first met and now, she found other proof.

I didn't know what was going to happen with Joe and I. It was too soon to tell, and I knew he was waiting on me to decide but with this must have come a little apprehension based on the last decision I made for both of us. A decision I'd come to regret. The abortion was the reason Joe broke up with me in high school. I'd pushed the horrific memory of it so far out of my mind that I was certain it no longer existed, but it refused to be forgotten. I would never go that route again. But I understood that without a choice, there could be no *for* or *against*. People continually took advantage of their ability to choose, and this might never change, but in the future, I would give special care to any and all of my choices.

Guiltily, I knew I would not let the word, *widow*, become a permanent title for me. It was okay for now, but one day, when the time was right, I'd make it a piece of my past. I would not become immortalized by grief. I would not become stone. I glanced over at Ben's photograph on the mantle, regretful that I'd never told him about the abortion. I would probably never tell anyone else either. There are those secrets that demand discovery and others like mine that render the keeper powerless.

Obscure Things

It was the flame of the candles that brought it back to me. Or maybe it was the wish. Of course, I'd never really forgotten; I'd just blocked it out of my mind hoping it too would disappear, so that I could go on. It's what she would have wanted, my sister. Maybe she really had forgiven me. Or maybe she had no way to forgive me and she wanted me to forgive myself.

I sat outside where the angels had been placed near the tangle of rose vines. They were empty of roses, but like Lincoln, I've always felt that it was thorns that had the roses and not the other way around.

The guests from my party were still lingering inside. I could hear their laughter spilling out into the back yard as I flicked the lighter I'd snatched off the table. The young dark-haired girl had placed it there after lighting the candles on the cake. Holding the lighter, I stared at the flame trying desperately to find comfort in it as my sister had, but the only thing I felt as I ran my finger through the blue glow was guilt.

The guilt of what I'd done. *Obscuris vera involvens.* Virgil. The truth can be enveloped by obscure things.

That day at the asylum when Michael brought the cake out to us, to Nix, I made a wish. A birthday wish. The only candle on the cake was already out so I never once thought my wish would be honored. I closed my eyes and wished my sister would just disappear so that I could have Michael to myself. I thought I loved him, but how was I to know that jealousy, who so often masks herself as love, does not give you a choice. The pain of that wish devours me now as the events of that day cover me like icy water so that I can barely breathe.

People were filtering back inside the asylum for quiet time. I lingered behind purposely so that I could talk to Dr. Warner. I didn't want Nix to go through a shock therapy session. I wouldn't have wished that on my worst enemy. Had I known that's what the doctor was planning, I would have never told him that Nix had stolen the blue brooch. I only wanted more time alone with Michael. I knew he would come looking for his camera—the Pentax I swiped from the table, so after Peggy came for Nix, I put on the long black wig and waited for him. But Nix must have escaped from Dr. Warner and then she found us. Michael and me. I never meant for that to happen. I loved my sister, and as I sat there looking to the angels for guidance, I could not think of one single thing I could do to make it right except to remember. It was the only way that I'd be able to forget or move on from what I'd done. Forgiveness comes with remembering. I knew that now. Memories have a way of healing. When people say forgive and forget what they really must mean is sometimes you have to remember in order to forget. Forgetting doesn't mean expunging entirely; it means accepting enough so that you can face yourself in the mirror.

That afternoon, after she'd caught us, I'd picked up the brooch Nix had dropped in the hallway and when Michael ran off looking for her, I tucked it in my hiding place in the mattress. Even when I left that place and took the brooch with me, I pushed what I had done so far from my memory, it became what it originally was, a brooch I stole from one of the nurses. And now, it was a reminder of what I'd really done. I not only took the brooch, I also stole my sister's life. Not directly, of course—I was logical enough to grasp this, but in a way that would always make me culpable. It was my fault Nix was dead, and I wanted, as I sat there staring into the stone faces of the seraphim, to wish it had been me that died that day when the machine malfunctioned, but I couldn't. Not because I was afraid but because if it had been me, I would have never known my daughter and grandson.

With the angels watching, I unpinned the brooch from my sweater and held it in my palm while the brilliant sun sparked against each of the blue stones. Though I did not recall my pregnancy or delivering Victoria, I somehow remembered my daughter's cry, and I feel it was because of this that my weak heart—the one that was perpetually damaged, had kept on beating. The heart is the strongest muscle in the body. Hole or no hole.

"Are you enjoying your angels?" Jacob asked as he joined me outside. He carried a gold-colored drink that resembled amber beneath the light of the sun.

"I am. They are a very nice gift. I'm not sure who to thank."

Though I said this, I could tell from the first moment I'd met him that he was quite fond of my daughter, and it was because of this that I'd received the angels as a gift. I wondered how long he could keep his secret.

He smiled. "They're special to me, too."

"I know. Victoria told me about your sister, Alice. My mother thought she was very special. I'm terribly sorry about what happened to her."

"What happened to *them*," he corrected. "And you."

"Me, too," I replied softly.

He sat next to me on the iron bench and leaned over so that his arms dangled off his knees. He sipped from his amber liquid. The ice cubes clinked pleasantly against the glass, and I thought only momentarily about the way a tooth sounded when it hit the floor after a shock treatment.

"They really are amazing," Jacob said looking up at the angels. I actually came out here to thank them for watching over Alice all those years."

I didn't mention to him that Nix had also watched over his sister in a way that even I couldn't completely understand. It no longer bothered me that I did not have the gift that my mother, sister and daughter shared. I realized that my episodes of lost time, brought Nix to me only because I imagined she was there. She was really only there because I wanted her to be—not just because I loved her and missed her but because I needed her to help me remember things that I could not—things that I did not want to remember. It was much less painful for her to lead me to the truth than for me to uncover it myself.

Now that I had what I needed from my memory, I wondered if I would still lose time? If not, then I knew I would not see my sister again and this saddened me. In the end, I didn't need to see the dead in order to know what it felt like to be haunted; I didn't need any gift to confirm that I was and always would be a Madigan. "I think it's going to rain," I said confidently.

"Really? But it's beautiful out here. We're supposed to have sunshine all week."

I stood. "I should head back inside. Please take as much time as you need out here. I can attest to the fact that these girls are good therapy. And they're pretty good about keeping secrets, too. I mean, should you have any."

I started to walk away but turned at the last minute just after the wind whispered my ear. "Here." I said as I handed him the sapphire brooch. It may have been missing stones but this is what made it real. I thought of the secret I buried so deep inside me for so long that it couldn't become real. I wouldn't let it become real, and because of this, I couldn't become real. "It belonged to your sister. I'm sure she would want you to have it," I told him. "It's not completely faultless, but you seem like a man who might appreciate this."

He smiled and thanked me, and I walked toward the house. I'd not yet reached the door when through the rays of the sun, I felt the rain on my face: small magical drops that evaporated in the warm breeze almost as soon as they touched my skin. Transience: it was difficult to accept at times but incapable of detracting from beauty.

In thirty-eight long years, I'd not made a wish. But birthdays are meant to celebrate life, and this year I'd surprised myself by wishing for the forgiveness it would take to enjoy the rest of time in Cape Perpetua, the city of twins and secrets and memories that refused to be forgotten. My wish wasn't for forgiveness from my sister, or Michael, or even my daughter. No, what I wished for when I blew out those candles was to be able to forgive myself. It's a difficult task to take on, one that involves a great deal of intent. I would choose to forgive myself. I'd come to realize that the choices people make in life can have an everlasting effect, but they aren't any more haunting than the choices they don't make.

I looked toward the angels one last time as I recalled Hugo's words from the end of another thief's story. "Without a doubt, in the gloom some mighty angel was standing, with outstretched wings, awaiting the soul." Jean Valjean did not die because destiny had wronged him. He died because he lost his angel. He chose to die because of this. It was a simple choice—one as effortless as day fading to night.

I let these thoughts embrace me for a few moments before heading inside to return the lighter I'd borrowed and steal another piece of cake.

Oregon Sterilization Form
Order for Sexual Sterilization

The State Hospital at_____

In re: _____No._____

This order for sexual sterilization upon the petition of _____and on the evidence introduced at the hearing of this matter, the Genetics Board finds that the said inmate is:

Insane ☐ Idiotic ☐ Imbecile ☐ Feebleminded ☐ Epileptic ☐ Blind ☐ Other ☐

And by the laws of heredity is the potential parent of socially inadequate offspring(s) likewise afflicted; that said, inmate may be sexually sterilized without detriment to his/her general health and the welfare of the inmate and of society will be promoted by such sterilization.

Therefore, on this date of _____ and appearing that all proper parties have been duly served with notice of the proceedings, it is ordered by Superintendent- _____ that a vasectomy/bilateral salpingectomy be performed on aforementioned subject on the day of _____

Signed and Validated

_____

In complete cooperation with the Eugenics Board of Oregon.

ABOUT THE AUTHOR

Cora Lockhart has lived all over the United States, but folklore always manages to lure her back to the south in the same way that a moth is relentlessly drawn to the light. Currently, she resides in the Atlanta area but dreams of moving to a decadent old Victorian Airstream on the edge of a bottomless lake with her kind, endearing and incredibly poetic mate, Seamus.
Please visit her website at:
www.coralockhart.com

Made in the USA
Charleston, SC
21 May 2012